Fighting for the Future

Cyberpunk and Solarpunk Tales

Edited by Phoebe Wagner

Android Press

Published by Android Press
Eugene, Oregon
www.android-press.com

ISBN 978-1958121313 (paperback)
ISBN: 978-1958121320 (epub)

Contents

Editor's Note   V

Introduction   IX
Andrew Sage

I. Cyberpunk Tales   1

Nano-Vibration   2
Brent Lambert

Property of PAUSE Ltd.   19
Ai Jiang

The Galaxy's Cube   31
Jeremy Szal

Do Anarchists Dream of Collective Sheep?   49
Izzy Wasserstein

Tomorrow Is Another Day   66
Louis Evans

II. Transitionary Tales   89

The Promise   90
Rona Fernandez

Root Cause   111
Lauren C. Teffeau

Broken Threads   136
Kevin Wabaunsee

The Robot Whisperer   154
Holly Schofield

III. Solarpunk Tales   165

The Strength of the Willow   166
Commando Jugendstil and Tales from the EV Studio

Solarpunks   177
J.D. Harlock

Materiality   186
Cory Doctorow

The Scent of Green   202
Ana Sun

Cloud 9   222
Christopher R. Muscato

The Holiness of Light   231
Cynthia Zhang

Author Biographies   248

Editor's Note

S ince its inception, solarpunk and cyberpunk have been in
conversation together. Cyberpunk's intense dedication and
love of technology in an environmental wasteland is reimagined
in solarpunk's right-tool-for-the-right-job usage of technology
in a damaged but healing, living world. Cyberpunk's individu-
alism is balanced with solarpunk's communalism. Even cyberpunk's neon is juxtaposed with solarpunk's solar panels.

This ancestry always felt like the right fit to me since my earliest
attraction to solarpunk. With this network in mind, I hoped to
jumpstart the next -punk subgenre. While some people argue
that -punk gets slapped on any word too quickly, solarpunk felt
like the next utterance of a conversation we never finished having
with cyberpunk.

When I set out to co-edit *Sunvault: Stories of Solarpunk and
Eco-Speculation* (2017), the goal was to create a general anthology
of fiction, poetry, and art so those interested in solarpunk could
have a starting point. The goal when co-editing *Almanac for the
Anthropocene: A Compendium of Solarpunk Futures* (2022) was
similar: the first general nonfiction collection of solarpunk in
hopes of jumping the genre from idea to action. In this collection, I set out to satisfy my desire to see the cyberpunk roots of
solarpunk flourish and restart the conversation I've always felt
whispering between these genres.

Indeed, the cyberpunk stories are reaching for the future that the solarpunk stories are wrestling with. Similar themes emerge, such as the beginnings and consequences of revolutionary action in "Nano-Vibration" by Brent Lambert, "Do Anarchists Dream of Collective Sheep?" by Izzy Wasserstein, and "Tomorrow Is Another Day" by Louis Evans. In the second half of the book, those revolutions may have been successful, but people—both human and nonhuman—must recover from the destruction wrought by capitalism, social injustice, and environmental degradation, which creates plenty of problems, such as in "The Scent of Green" by Ana Sun and "The Holiness of Light" by Cynthia Zhang.

In the middle of this spectrum, these stories imagine *how* communities shift, rebuild, destroy oppressive systems, and reimagine what it means to be in community with the rest of the living world, such as in "Broken Threads" by Kevin Wabaunsee, "The Robot Whisperer" by Holly Schofield, and "The Strength of the Willow" by Commando Jugendstil and Tales from the EV Studio. Importantly, though, these stories do not shy away from critique, even of desirable societies as often found in solarpunk stories, such as in "Root Cause" by Lauren C. Teffeau, "The Promise" by Rona Fernandez, and "Solarpunks" by J. D. Harlock. Among these stories, the authors consider how technology has been used to hurt people and the living world, but also how technology can be used to build communities and expand our notions of personhood, such as in "Property of PAUSE Ltd." by Ai Jiang, "The Galaxy's Cube" by Jeremy Szal, "Materiality" by Cory Doctorow, and "Cloud 9" by Christopher R. Muscato.

While I leave it to Andrew Sage to explain the history and deeper connections between cyberpunk and solarpunk, I will say the reason this anthology matters is because neither vision of the future is certain. These stories show we have the tools to revolt and organize against a cyberpunk future, but let's not forget those lessons in our hopes to achieve a solarpunk reality.

How to read this book:

Putting together an anthology never goes as expected. I'm always blown away by the submissions, and the writers end up changing my vision for the book. Initially, I imagined this anthology would have section breaks separating the cyberpunk, transitional, and solarpunk stories, but as I worked on organizing the book, I realized that was impossible. Of course, it wouldn't be—couldn't be—that delineated. The stories had their own sense of flow with no clear breaks, though there certainly is a sense of change from beginning to end.

As the editor, my recommendation would be to start at the beginning and read to the end. While many anthologies don't function in such a linear way, reading cover to cover will demonstrate the greatest sense of change as imagined by these amazing writers. If you are more interested in the cyberpunk stories, then I'd read from "Nano-Vibration" by Brent Lambert to "The Promise" by Rona Fernandez. If you are more interested in the transitional stories, I'd start with "Root Cause" by Lauren C. Teffeau and read through "The Strength of the Willow" by Commando Jugendstil and Tales from the EV Studio.

If you are all about the solarpunk stories, then I'd start with Kevin Wabaunsee's "Broken Threads" and read through the final story, "The Holiness of Light" by Cynthia Zhang. As you can see, there is overlap, and only a handful of stories clearly fit into their specific genre—but that is what makes this anthology important. We are currently living through tipping points, moments of great change, so we must imagine how to shape these moments and the futures they create.

Regardless, read this book in the way that works for you. I hope it inspires you to make your own stories and better your community!

Hope through action,
Phoebe Wagner, 2022

Introduction

Andrew Sage

When it comes to popular visions of the future, the dialectic of utopia and dystopia has thoroughly captivated our collective imaginations. These genres of speculative science fiction have introduced us to vibrant new worlds that nonetheless echo our own. The concept of utopia arose first, deriving from Greek meaning both "good place" and "no place." Fittingly, utopia is perceived as a picturesque society of inaccessible perfection. Dystopia followed shortly in response, from the Greek for "bad place." Dystopian worlds are terribly grim sites of totalitarian injustice and suffering. Utopia and dystopia have been compared, contrasted, and combined to explore what we desire and what we fear in our societies. The many manifestations of this dichotomy present us with an opportunity as a human community to observe our circumstances and determine our trajectory.

The utopic visions of solarpunk and dystopic horrors of cyberpunk have arisen to present and explore these possibilities. Cyberpunk societies are dominated by violence on all levels, much like our own, from the most interpersonal to the most impersonal and systemic, due to the corrupt heights of capitalism and unregulated technology. Conversely, solarpunk staunchly rejects the seeming inevitability of capitalist dystopia, even through the compounding consequences of climate crisis. Instead, solarpunk worlds explore the alternative possibilities of true social justice, tempered technological development, and sustainability through ecological harmony, presenting the real possibility of fantasy made manifest through bold anarchic praxis and flourishing communities.

Solarpunk and cyberpunk, as distinct yet interrelated manifestations of the subversive punk ethos, inevitably confront the destructive violence of capitalism, the tenuous interplay of technology and nature, and the complex relationship between the individual and their society.

The global rise of industrial capitalism has left an indisputable scar on the face of our planet. Worse yet, it seems as if humanity has resigned itself to the destructive tendencies of this political and economic system as inevitable, with no real, viable alternatives. Yet the continental proportions of capitalism's devastation can no longer be ignored. The climate crisis is climbing to its peak, with no end in sight.

Cyberpunk stories take this brutality to its extreme but natural conclusion. These worlds are high-tech and low-life. Faceless, totalitarian, multinational mega conglomerates dominate the people of this troubled future, even assuming the role of governments due to their monopoly over political, economic, and even military power. Societal decay is reflected in the nihilistic depiction of human connections, often transactional or coercive. Our protagonists typically struggle to navigate this calloused world or seek to rebel against it, reflecting the inhumane nature of capitalism's logic. Yet cyberpunk protagonists are typically unable to transform or even escape the reach of the system. The dystopic messaging is clear: imagine a boot stamping on a human face—forever.

Solarpunk stories, on the other hand, typically critique capitalism indirectly, portraying a world attempting to heal from the wounds it has left on its people and its landscape. The genre optimistically argues that it is not too late to reverse our course and work to repair the harms caused by capitalism through ecological restoration, ethical technological integration, and diverse, egalitarian human collaboration. But we must reject capitalism to achieve this better world. We must, in fact, reject all systems of domination in order to establish a free and equitable society. Solarpunk works, though not necessarily utopian, explore this alternative to the pessimistic view of cyberpunk dystopias. Characters in these worlds demonstrate what it would look like if we fought back against the alienating status quo and built something new. Solarpunk embodies the crucial recognition that utopia is the never-ending process of making a better world.

The harms of industrialisation under capitalism have exposed the volatile relationship between technology and nature. How can we justify our use of technology if the consequences have been as dire as the Great Pacific Garbage Patch, irreversible oil spills, the acidification and eutrophication of our oceans, the toxic runoff of rare earth mineral mining sites, the deforestation of our old growth forests, the loss of our topsoil, the unmitigated release of greenhouse gases, and the Holocene extinction? Depictions of nature are practically absent in most cyberpunk fiction. Instead, these sterile, man-made worlds are filled with sprawling, dense, and all-consuming urban hell. Concrete, glass, neon, and steel cover buildings and streets, with nary a tree or shrub to be found. Even food takes on an increasingly artificial composition. Nature has been stifled and forgotten or obscured by the smog of metropolis. On the other hand, technological innovations are as advanced as one can imagine. Advanced prosthetics, holographics, cryogenics, nanotechnologies, artificial intelligences, digitised consciousnesses, and more dominate the day-to-day lives of cyberpunk urbanites. How these technologies have become so widespread on a planet with limited resources or how these technologies even work may not be clear, but what is clear in cyberpunk settings is that human technological advancement excludes and exists beyond the natural world.

Solarpunk, on the other hand, is concerned with the development and application of technology in human societies, as well as how such technologies impact our environments. Although some fanciful interpretations of solarpunk have embraced fictional high-tech solutions, most practical understandings of solarpunk embrace low-tech ways of living sustainably with permaculture principles, DIY ethics, right to repair, modular and multipurpose tools and components, the abolition of planned obsolescence, vernacular material use, decentralised infrastructure, urban walkability, and the broad application of biophilic design. There have been critics of solarpunk's emphasis on solar panels, which currently require the use of rare earth minerals mined in exploitative conditions, but the wielding of solar energy need not be limited to conventional solar panels. Solarpunk fiction also embraces practices of ecological restoration, such as rewilding and soil regeneration. Ultimately, solarpunk seeks to find and maintain a balance between technology use and natural sustainability.

Several different bodies of philosophical thought have confronted the relationship between the individual and their society. Society does not exist independently of the individual and the individual cannot exist without society. We've evolved as social animals, almost like cells in a larger social body. In a cyberpunk society, this body is deeply ill. Its cells are alienated from each other, attacking and maligning its misfits, malcontents, and marginalised. Corporations have commodified every dimension of social and personal life, while hyperindividualism has total-ly eroded any conception of community, leaving a permeat-ing sense of desolation and despair. Cyberpunk protagonists, though nonconformist and self-expressive, are just as isolated as the rest of their society is from their humanity. Solarpunk societies, on the other hand, demonstrate a social body in the process of recovery. Individuals are embedded in social networks that exist to uplift each piece, and not just the sum of its parts. Individuals in solarpunk fiction have been unshackled from the restraints of capitalist relations to life and labour, allowing them to exercise, and so develop, their abilities to the fullest. The free association of all the people in community involves them in the process of thinking, planning, coordinating, and implementing the decisions that affect them in their society, rather than being alienated from power as in a cyberpunk world. The health, cre-ativity, and talent of the whole social organism is able to blossom and flourish, unrestrained.

The tension between solarpunk and cyberpunk is reflective of ongoing tensions in the real world that have yet to be resolved. The tension between hope and nihilism. Should we invest our time and energy into fighting to survive and thrive when it could all be for nought? Should we even try when failure seems not only possible but likely? How do we overcome centuries of de-struction, centuries of authoritarianism, centuries of propagan-da? Can we avert total apocalypse? We face a fork in the road. Unless we act now, our choice will be made for us. The stories presented in this anthology explore just a sliver of our many possibilities.

Utopia or dystopia?

You decide.

Nano-Vibration

Brent Lambert

Quazin threw his head back after sniffing the line and rolled his shoulders. The last part had nothing to do with getting the drug into his system, but it was a ritual he followed nonetheless. He looked at Dru and gave her a big smile.

This was her third time partying with him and the rest of the crew. Quazin wasn't sure if she was a good fit just yet, but sometimes it took a while. She was sweet and there seemed to be a spark of adventure lying beneath the surface.

"You want me to get a line ready for you?" Quazin asked. He usually did one first to make the newbies ease up. Yadis did it for him all those years ago.

Dru thought about it for a moment and shrugged. "Yeah sure, why not. It's been a long fucking week at work anyway."

Quazin smiled and unscrewed the small vial he carried with him most days. He tapped a small rock out from it and onto the counter. With one of his old metro cards, he broke the rock up into another line for him and one for her.

She did it and shook her whole body afterwards. "Whew! That one was good."

Quazin smirked. "Only the best."

Yadis was looking through his phone for the next song to play. His neighbors were chill enough to tolerate their weekend gatherings of loud conversations and even louder music. The two-bedroom apartment sounded close to an actual rave. The next song Yadis played had a bassline that Quazin was all too familiar with. He gave his friend a flat expression.

"What?! The song's good. I never told you to sleep with him." Yadis spoke with charm, even if his voice was nasally. He took a puff off his vape and started dancing.

Yadis was the one who took Quazin in and introduced him to the rave scene in Viejo Sun. He knew where to find all the underground parties, the ones that shrugged off the easy money of corporate sponsorship. The places where the unwanted, the discarded, and the broken could still congregate freely to party without judgment. Yadis had plenty of money; one look at the fingernail-sized diamond hanging from his earring made that clear, but he found his home amongst the nocturnal freaks. You wouldn't ever catch him on a yacht schmoozing with some grimy, slick-haired corporate exec and his too young partner.

By appearances, Quazin and Yadis did not look the type to be friends, especially close ones. But that was just how the rave scene worked. It brought together people that the world would otherwise say had no chance at unity. Quazin was a tall and wide guy who looked more likely to be a tough miner on the Moon than someone you couldn't get to stop dancing. Yadis was rail thin and never looked bad in an outfit. He walked through the world like everyone needed to catch up to him. Yet somehow, their friendship worked.

"You slept with a DJ?" Dru asks, mock shock in her tone.

Quazin groaned. "A few times. We're not a thing anymore."

"Which has nothing to do with his music still being jacked as shit," Ahala said, the last member of the crew.

Quazin couldn't argue with that. The music was good.

Ahala's personality was a bit like an angry porcupine's, but buried under that was a sweetheart with intense loyalty to the people she cared about. It's why she took so long to warm up to people. You couldn't just attach that kind of friendship to anyone. She wasn't out-and-out rude to Dru, but she definitely avoided making eye contact with her. Quazin figured as long as Ahala still offered her drugs here and there then they were good. It took them hanging out four times before she remembered Quazin's name. That's just how she was; you weren't important to her until you were.

Of course that didn't do much to chip away the last bits of skepticism Dru had about the scene. Music, drugs, parties in abandoned places and a defiant attitude against society's expectations was alluring but could be a lot to take in. Not everyone was built for it as a lifestyle.

"So is he the DJ tonight? The one you had a thing with?" Dru asked, the teasing intensifying in her tone.

Quazin smiled. The brief love affair hadn't ended that badly. "One of them. He'll put on a good set."

"As long as the party doesn't get copped," Ahala said. She broke in half a blue pill shaped like Mickey Mouse. "I'm really going to hate it if I waste a roll."

Dru frowned. "How likely is that to happen?"

"They did a good job keeping the party off all the corporate networks," Yadis said while cutting an eye at Ahala. "We'll be fine. I'm more worried about it raining. These shoes aren't cheap."

Nothing about Yadis was cheap. He wasn't the kind of obscenely wealthy that automatically required a face punch, but he never worried about how his bills were getting paid. He was generous with what he had, but never sought praise or acknowledgement for it. If there was anything that made Quazin decide Yadis would be his friend forever, it was that.

"Not like you can't get another pair custom made tomorrow," Ahala said.

Yadis ignored the comment and walked to a golden chest in the center of his living room. He entered in a number sequence and the chest hissed open, letting out a burst of cool air. Quazin knew what was in it. Dru didn't. He looked to see her reaction. This would tell him a lot.

Yadis reached into the chest and pulled out a thick, white python with three red eyes. He sat the reptilian around his slender shoulders and said, "Now the outfit is complete."

Dru's eyes widened. "Is that–

"A gene-mod of a Peruvian edition arctic python? Absolutely girl," Yadis said, giving an exaggerated twirl. "Neuron bonded. Doesn't need to eat or sleep. Just keep my girl cold and she's ready to go. Had to suck a lot of dicks to get this one."

Ahala laughed. "Doubt it."

"And you're taking it to a...rave?" Dru sounded completely befuddled and it just showed another element of her ignorance. Being extreme was just another accepted part of the scene.

It was why the corporations hated them so much. Their movement didn't fit into neat packages. It couldn't be sanitized. It took in all the people that the corporations wanted desperately to mark as undesirable. Undesirables living life, being free, and most of all, having fun, went against the corporate packaging. They pushed conformity as the key to a happy life and conformity could only be found in economic obedience to their product lines. Quazin had once towed that corporate line. He hated that version of himself now and saw a bit of it in Dru's question.

Yadis gave a patient smile. "There's no better place for extravagance than a rave."

They grabbed some solarboards off the street outside of Yadis' house to head to the party location. The neighborhood was littered with them. It's a nuisance to navigate the street when walking, but for most people here they've become the primary form of getting around. Leave them on the ground to charge up during the day, pulling on the sun's power, and take off with them at night. Dru wasn't as comfortable riding one as the rest of them. She hadn't been born and raised in the city.

"I swear these things get shittier to ride every year," Ahala said as she ripped around a corner.

"The corporations. Cost savings and shit," Quazin replied.

"Or maybe the two of you are getting worse at driving," Yadis called from the head of the pack. He knew how to ride a solarboard as effortlessly as he put together an expensive ass outfit. Quazin felt a lot of ease at that. The way Yadis moved through the world made what they did successful and not hobbled by a lack of resources. He could only wonder how Dru might handle the truth behind all their partying?

In time. They needed to make sure she could be trusted.

"You don't think a bunch of solarboards piled up in the warehouse zone isn't going to raise an eyebrow?" Dru asked. She was keeping up better this time. To her credit, she never asked them to slow down. More than anything else so far, that had earned her some respect from Ahala.

"Truth is, the corps know most of these parties to some degree," Yadis said.

They really couldn't escape from the corporate gaze. No one could. Society had foolishly let greed and slavery mask itself as progress. Quazin hated how much they were all tethered to these behemoths that they hated. But that wasn't going to keep them from fighting.

A few more minutes of riding and they were in the warehouse zone. It's late, empty and feels like they're the only people that exist for miles. But then Quazin heard the faintest hint of music and smiled. Ahala parked her solarboard against a busted hydrant and winked at him. "This is about to be fun."

"You're with me. What other choice is there?" Yadis said, tenderly stroking his gene-mod snake.

"How packed do you think it's going to be?" Dru asked, sounding a good bit more out of breath than the rest of them.

"Packed enough to find a decent hook-up," Ahala said as she clamped a blinking, purple choker around her neck. She pressed a few more buttons on it and three over-sized, floating purple skulls appeared around her head.

Holo-avatars. The latest trend to buck against corporations and their need to filter those they controlled into tight, little aesthetic groups. People just didn't work that way. Holo-avatars were a proclamation of that. Anyone thinking they could contain Ahala was a fool anyway. She'd been bucking against targeted advertisements her whole life.

"I don't think anyone here is going to be that desperate." Yadis burst into laughter.

Ahala caught the implication of his insult. "Fuck you."

"Oh, the line for that is around the corner and up the street."

They moved into the warehouses arranged neatly like a cubic forest of metal and stored greed. Quazin wondered how many people could be helped by the resources being stored here. The corporations kept their power through controlled scarcity. Make people think something was rare and that you were the only one capable of providing it—they'd do whatever it took to believe your lies.

"Which warehouse is the party?" Dru asked, looking up for any sign of neon lights flashing through windows.

Quazin felt Ahala elbow him. "You asshole! You didn't tell her?"

"Wanted her to be surprised."

Ahala tapped her foot against a manhole. "When we said this party was underground, we meant just that."

Yadis grinned. "Welcome to the rave!"

"The sewers? I mean sure this storm drain isn't as dirty as I expected–but the sewers?"

Quazin felt the smallest bit of exasperation creeping in. Dru's incredulousness had dragged on a bit longer than he hoped. "It's going to be great. Sable knows how to get locations."

Sable was the real reason they were coming to the party tonight. The music and the raves were necessary as spiritual resistance, but there was tangible resistance happening alongside it. That was what they waited to see if Dru could be trusted. And why they had been having a separate conversation the entire time.

<Sable, you have the data packs ready?>

<Who the fuck you think I am, here?>

<Don't get all pissy.> Ahala's neural voice cut in. <Tonight's package is too big to fuck up.>

She wasn't wrong. Tonight could be the boon a hundred cells needed to really ramp up sabotage and blackmail operations. It wouldn't crumble the corporations, but it might set them on the path to strangling each other. Quazin would pay money to see some of these boardrooms once tonight's package got out in the world.

<Just have the music going.> Quazin said. <We're almost there.>

"I can hear it! Hell yea! I'm ready to rage," Dru said, pumping a fist into the air to the rhythm thomping ahead.

Yadis snapped his fingers. "Oontz oontz music incoming, loves."

The storm drain was finally coming to an end when Quazin spotted a familiar face crouched down at the exit. He looked disheveled, as always, but was wrapped in a brand new blanket. At least the ravers were taking care of him. He didn't look at any of them and just kept rocking back and forth. Quazin knew the signs of withdrawal all too well.

Yadis approached first and knelt down in front of him. "Hey Han. You all right, love?"

Han looked up with blue-stained eyes and trembling lips. "Been hard to find it lately. That's all."

"I've heard." Yadis took Han's dirt-encrusted hands in his. "Just a little bit, okay? To take the edge off."

Han could barely nod. "Sure, sure. Always looking out."

Quazin felt a swell of pity and an intense desire to change the circumstances that led Han to become the broken man in front of them now. Drugs, like all immaterial things, were just tools. They could render good or evil. Heartbreak or joy. It just all depended on the hands they fell in.

Yadis pulled a small vial out of one of his jacket pockets. It held a blue powder. Just enough to have fun, but not enough to end up assigned with community service at a corporate "corrective camp." Quazin had lost a few friends to those. You never came back.

Yadis dipped the nano-ket into the vial and pulled out a small bump. He pressed it against one of Han's nostrils and waited for him to inhale. Han's rocking stopped and his breathing slowed. He closed his eyes and let out a deep, satisfied sigh.

"Thanks. Thanks, man." Han covered his face with his hands and let out a brief, feral sob. "I thought I was going to fall apart."

Yadis reached out and clasped his shoulder. "You won't. Not as long as we look out for each other."

Quazin nodded. "Damn right."

They left Han behind, and silence in the group lingered as the music's volume grew louder. Dru finally broke it. "Is it really a good idea to help an addict out like that? He's never going to get better that way."

"As opposed to leaving him a withdrawn, shivering mess on the verge of harming himself? Do you have any idea how much a rehab center costs?" Yadis asked, annoyance clearly carved into every word.

"And that's if the rehab center doesn't just turn him over to a private prison for some chalked up offense," Ahala added, no less annoyed but much colder in her delivery. She gave Dru a look that could freeze wildfires.

Dru didn't back down. "You don't cure addiction by feeding it."

"What I did back there was triage." Yadis' snake hissed as it picked up on his anger. "I'd love to take every Han in the world to somewhere they'd be seen as people worthy of love. But even you with all your faux concern don't see him as that. He's a problem to be solved. Not a brother. Not a friend. Not someone you help however you're able."

"You put the same drugs up your nose too, sis." Ahala looked her up and down. "Be thankful you only need the high to have fun."

Dru looked to Quazin for support. He couldn't give it. What Yadis did wasn't a perfect solution, but it was perfect compassion. The tools for real, substantial healing had been taken from people who wanted a world without productivity and profit as a foundation. So, like Yadis said, you had to triage the wound as best you could.

It's why they fought—to take the tools back.

Dru, realizing she was outnumbered, mumbled, "There's got to be a better way than that."

Quazin wanted to offer some sympathetic word, but it would have been more embarrassing for Dru than helpful. And also...his pill was finally starting to kick in. He could feel the tingle in his fingertips and the rush of his blood all indicating an incoming moment of peaking.

It was time to dance. It was time to get to work.

Quazin felt a thrill at how many people were packed into the tunnel. Sable's parties had maybe half this many people on a regular weekend. The high turnout both excited and made him more cautious. You never judged if someone was a regular or not. The point of the music was to unite. But regulars were reliable. You knew where they stood...

"Whoa!" Dru said with a wide grin—looked like her pill was kicking in, too. "Didn't know this many people could navigate a sewer."

Ahala and Yadis didn't respond. They just made their way into the sea of bodies. Quazin winced, but a quick look at Dru and she was already dancing. She was still new enough to the drug that other emotions couldn't work past the euphoria. She hadn't even noticed the snub.

<She fucked up. But c'mon, she ain't corporate.>

Quazin never spoke up in opposition to Yadis or Ahala and doing so now made his stomach churn. But he believed Dru had the potential to be one of them. He'd done his research on her; it would have been a mistake not to. She had a secret blog, he hadn't told the others, and on it she railed against every aspect of corporate life. She was already fighting and he knew he could show her a way that held impact. Dru knew what it would take to get rid of the rot. He wanted her to show some sign of it, though. Before she managed to completely turn off Yadis and Ahala.

<She's here for the party, not the culture. You'll see it eventually.> Ahala didn't sound like she was going to be swayed.

<We're here for a mission. Let's have fun and worry about our tag-along later.>

Tag-along. Not a good sign. Quazin believed the situation could be salvaged. They just needed to get through tonight. The high of drugs and victory would change everything.

It was just Quazin's luck that they walked into the thick of the party right when Black Camel was playing his set. As much as he would have liked to deny it, the man's music was good. It had been part of the reason why he was attracted to him in the first place. All of the graffiti in the sewer had been adorned with tiny, blinking black camel heads. He remembered when Sable had just started these parties and didn't want things to be too flashy because of his paranoia. Well-earned paranoia because this scene was one the corporations hated. It could be controlled or distilled into something profitable. Anything Sable earned past his operating costs went to the cause.

<Sorry we're late.> Quazin pulled a small plastic bag out of one of his pockets and shook it discreetly. Blue powder waited for him expectantly inside it. Being brazen about doing drugs was never a good idea. You kept it quick and quiet because you never knew if someone was undercover. <But we brought what we need.>

<Good. Then let's get this shit started.>

Quazin licked his pinky, dipped it into the tiny bag, grabbed enough of the powder and put it on his tongue. The rush of the drug would take a bit, but the information it contained hit him almost immediately. This was the crux of their resistance. Drugs were how they spread rebellion. Nanites containing information harmful to the corporations and their allies were bonded to the illegal substances. Everyone wrote off people like him, Yadis and Ahala as frivolous partiers too high to actually do anything of value to society. It was that stereotype they preyed on and that gave them a fighting chance.

They took it a step further. The information inside the nanites could only be accessed by vibrational patterns. Patterns found in the very music they danced to. Years ago, a group of ravers and DJs had developed the transmission method. It was a perfect cloak because no one really thought a group of "addicted partiers" could be the lynchpin to just about every wrench thrown in the corporations' plans for the last decade. Quazin was proud and happy to be part of it.

Still didn't mean he was thrilled about his former hookup being the DJ tonight. Quazin tried to avoid making eye contact with Black Camel through the crowd, but his intensity in trying to avoid it seemed to only make it happen faster. They locked eyes and Quazin wanted to melt into the man's arms all over again. It didn't help that the combo of the pill and the blue powder was enough to make even a brush of wind feel erotic. Maybe he could give him another chance...

Naw, that was just the drugs talking. And besides, there were plenty of other hot guys here. Black Camel had one job tonight and it happened right when the beat dropped.

Quazin felt a quiver run through his body as the nanites pulled away from the drugs and transmitted the information through the vibrational patterns and right into Black Camel's DJ deck. Once this party was over, Black Camel would pull the information and pass it right along to the people on the front lines of the fight against the corporations. And he would go on to live and party another day.

The nanites gave them as close to perfect plausible deniability as they could muster. Paper and electronic trails had found several of them locked up in the years before the nanite deployment. Quazin knew Ahala had lost a couple of friends she wouldn't talk about. The nanites gave them an alibi that the corps were hard pressed to find cracks in.

All drugs were eventually metabolized by the body. Biology became an ally in hiding their metaphorical fingerprints. And transferring the illegally obtained information through the music meant the people involved in their networks could go weeks or months without actually being seen in close proximity. It was hard to create the narrative of a rebel network if you never saw the rebels together.

All right, that was the first salvo of information delivered. Quazin danced and moved through the crowd until he found Yadis and leaned into his ear. "Delivery successful."

"And your man did it with style." Yadis grinned, swaying to Black Camel's music. He reached into his jacket and pulled out the bag holding more blue powder. "We still got more to deliver."

Quazin dipped his finger in it and took another hit. He felt bad for not telling Dru what they were doing, but it was just too risky. And he wasn't sure if she was ready yet or if she could ever be ready. Some people hated what the corporations were doing but would never muster up the courage to actually fight them. You could hate a thing and never spend a moment understanding how dangerous it was to you. He was starting to think Dru fell into that category.

Another hard beat dropped and more information was exchanged. Black Camel was keeping the house music dirty and full of bass tonight. Quazin's favorite kind. He would rather it be coming from another DJ, but rebellion meant taking your help where you could find it.

Ahala was completely lost in the music, the pill taking her to the point Quazin hoped to soon be at; where every rhythm, beat, and drop felt like pleasure running across your skin and in your ears. Just about everyone at the party was in that state, Black Camel taking his set to another level. Quazin couldn't pretend he wasn't impressed by it. When he first met Black Camel, the man was conversant about two things; the history of music and the history of how corporations found their way into every part of our lives. The combination had pretty much guaranteed he was going to sleep with him. He didn't regret the sex, just all the moments after.

Black Camel's set was drawing to a close when Quazin spotted Dru talking to someone he didn't recognize. Nothing about that really felt out of the ordinary until Dru pointed his way. That would have made him tense up if not for the drugs keeping him euphoric. He was experienced enough with his drugs to not let that feeling stunt his thinking. He had reason to be suspicious.

The guy was short, had a scar over his nose and walked too fast towards him. Quazin keeps his expression neutral even as his fingers tingled. "Yo."

"You gotta anything on you man? Your friend told me to ask you."

"Nope. Sorry."

"C'mon, man. Just a hit. I'll pay you."

Oh, so this guy was a complete idiot then. Telling a stranger you would pay them for drugs at a rave was basically asking them to walk into a drug dealing charge. Quazin took a step back and started swaying his shoulders to the music, wanting to create the illusion of carefree. "Sorry. Nothing for you man."

"What was that about?" Dru asked as the man walked away.

Quazin regretted not filling her in on what they were really doing here. "You don't ever tell strangers where you get your drugs, I don't care how good the music is making you feel. And you don't ever take anything from them either. Did you?"

It was a newbie mistake and in other circumstances it could be forgiven, but maybe Ahala and Yadis were right. Dru might not be cut out for this. His words were harsher in tone than he liked, especially when the pill was still working through his system. But this was serious. "Did you take any drugs from someone?"

Dru shrugged and rolled her eyes. "Yeah, I took a couple of bumps from the guy. You make it sound like I signed an Organ Loan Agreement or something."

Quazin caught the green tinge in her eyes then. His throat seized, and he knew two things very quickly; corporate spies were amongst them and he wasn't going to be able to save Dru.

<We got corps here!>

A commotion broke through the crowd, with many folks making a run for it. The DJ set came to a halt and everyone behind decks was getting ready for a fight. Quazin didn't blame anyone running. Being charged with direct defiance of the corporations was a charge that not only saw you disappear, but your friends and loved ones, too. The corporations liked to play at benevolent tyranny, but they knew when to make their messages loud and clear.

Fluorescent blue sunglasses suddenly appeared on the faces of about a dozen people in the crowd; the corporate spies no longer bothering to hide. Quazin wanted to jump into the fray, but Dru collapsed into his arms. He held her close and laid her gently on the ground.

"I'm so sorry I didn't tell you what this was all about earlier." But no matter how sorry he was, Quazin knew she would pay the price for his unwillingness to divulge. The drug working its way through her was going to wreak havoc on her nervous system. She'd never be able to walk more than a mile without writhing pain, her fingertips would always feel like they were being sliced apart. A cold breeze would leave her bedridden for a week. A normal life was gone for her. There was nothing he could do for her. Still plenty he could do for everyone else.

<Are we fighting?> Quazin asked, ready for the answer to be yes.

<No. Information is transferred. We get out of here and find out how we got compromised.>

<They poisoned Dru. Doubt she's the only one.> Right as Quazin said it, other people in the crowd started to drop. The corps had come here with a lethal objective and contaminated drugs were one of their easiest delivery systems.

<I'm sorry, Q. Shouldn't have been mean to her.> Ahala said, giving the most infinitesimal consolation the moment could ask for. Quazin didn't blame her though. None of them had ever really been good at putting emotions on the table. The music and the drugs had always made those things easier.

But it was what they had. That and the fight. So they ran, leaving behind too many people just looking for a good time. He had thrust Dru into a war she wasn't ready for. He fought back tears wondering when he first decided that he was.

Property of PAUSE Ltd.

Ai Jiang

At 6:50 a.m., the alarm within our PAUSE delivery trucks blared in a synchronized screeching, waking the employees and their families. Ten minutes until the work day started. I pressed a button so our seats reclined upwards. Next to me in the passenger's seat, my daughter raised two small fists, rubbing her eyes.

The truck was supposed to fully charge overnight and re-stocked with the day's orders, but I double checked just to be sure. Truck ignitions turned on one by one as each prepared to leave PAUSE Ltd.'s parking lot. I prepared to follow, kissing my daughter on the top of her head as she passed me a toothpaste pill and wet wipe.

"Good morning, Mama," she said, smiling.

"Good morning, my Shimei," I replied.

At the same moment, the daily digital reminder popped up on the truck's windshield: "Good morning, PAUSE drivers, we hope you have a smooth delivery day, and remember, you are a part of PAUSE as much as PAUSE is a part of you."

I recalled the ink drying on the thick contract I signed two years ago, making both my daughter and me the property of

PAUSE Ltd. But at least we got to live in what little comfort we could get. This was much more preferable than the neighbourhood we used to live in and safer.

"First delivery: Peony Village," a monotoned robotic female's voice came from the truck's all-surround speakers.

Peony Village was one of the high classed neighbourhoods we often made deliveries to—and it was also Shimei's favourite because of the name alone.

Colourful strobe lights and booming pop music attacked my senses, causing me to cringe as I approached my customer's house. Cars littered the streets. Cans and bottles of alcoholic drinks were discarded on the lawn of the mansion, but nobody was in sight. Behind the floor to ceiling window next to the front door, my customer—I assumed—stood with a strange smile stretched across their stubbled face. They couldn't have been any older than mid-twenties. I wondered if this house was theirs or their parents.'

I peeked through the glass divider between the storage area where Shimei and I sat. There was five thousand dollars' worth of seafood that was frozen in time within the oversized PAUSE delivery cube for large orders in the back of the truck. The steam and condensation in the cube stalled in the air, contained within its walls—a lovely portrait waiting to be set in motion again. The customer disappeared as I hopped out of the car and began unloading their food after turning off the PAUSE function on the cube. The steam resumed, wafting upwards, fogging up the glass.

I grabbed a few take-out containers at a time and loaded them onto the conveyor belt of the delivery slot set to auto-receive by the mansion's entrance. The containers retained the same heat as though they were fresh off the stove, burning my fingertips. But I smiled through the pain, knowing it might earn me a higher rating, a bigger tip. Then maybe Shimei and I could leave PAUSE, if that were even possible. I barely had enough to pay for her birthday cake last week when she turned four. Four. She would remember spending a large part of her childhood in the van. That wasn't what I wanted, but I had few other options.

I smiled at Shimei as she pressed her face against the window before she blew on the glass, fogging it up, her fingers tracing a heart.

By the time I finished loading the rest of the takeout onto the belt, several faces watched me from the window. One boy in the back sneered, baring his teeth. Probably drunk. I hoped Shimei had found something else to fix her eyes on.

When I returned to my car I noticed my customer waving, their phone clutched in their free hand. A smile made its way onto way my face. Fake. Necessary. For the rating, for the rating for—

I looked down at the car's notification system as it pulled open the PAUSE app:

Reason for refund: *The food was cold when it arrived.*

It was a blatant lie. I had delivered the food still steaming hot and in *perfect* condition to the customer. It was a known fact that the PAUSE function activated as soon as the cube was shut. I should have guessed my customer's smile was far from good-natured. Was he cheap or spiteful? I couldn't tell. But it didn't matter. I had just lost my delivery fee and potential tip for the order. And my four-star rating dipped to 3.8 because the ratings of upper-class customers like this boy weighed more than the others in the app's algorithm.

My smile wavered, but I kept my composure, waving at the boy and his friends before leaving. And for Shimei, I had to be strong.

"I'll be right back," I said to Shimei, who played with the small stuffed calico cat I purchased on sale for her last week.

I rounded the back of the truck, breathing cold air with short, shuddering breaths. Tears fell onto my hands as I dipped forward. I wiped my eyes a moment later, allowing only a few silent tears to escape. There was no time for self-pity. I still had other deliveries to make, and arriving late was not an option—though some malicious customers often tried to stall some of us so our pay would be deducted.

"Mama?" Shimei's head poked out from her window.

I dried my hands against my pants and peeked around the truck, smiling. "I'm coming, darling."

When I restarted the truck, the last delivery request popped up on the windshield. My heart quickened to a suffocating rate at the sight. It was an order from our previous neighbourhood. My hands tightened against the steering wheel as I was reminded of my sister's death and the high percentage of violence and "accidents" compared to the safety of places like Peony Village. Though PAUSE called the deliveries "requests," we didn't have the option to decline them.

"Are we going home now?" Shimei asked.

"Not yet, not yet. But soon."

And hopefully, we would soon have a real home. It saddened me to hear Shimei call PAUSE Ltd.'s parking lot our home. I reached a hand over, wiping the chocolate pudding from the corner of Shimei's mouth. At least they offered three meals a day. It was already more than I could ever ask for.

When we arrived in front of the house in our old neighbourhood, only two streets down from where we used to live, the truck's navigation system beeped.

"Face-to-face delivery requested," the system announced, the same words flashing on the windshield.

How odd. All my other customers preferred contactless delivery. PAUSE had grown at such a rapid pace since most thought it was a hassle, supposedly, to leave the house.

The light above the front door lit up in a neon orange glow. I glanced over at my daughter.

"Keep your head down," I said, motioning with my hand.

"Why?" Shimei asked. She was too young to remember what it was like to live here before we moved into the truck.

"For me?" I asked.

She frowned but nodded, ducking her head.

"Now stay still until I come back, okay?"

Shimei nodded again.

I made sure the locks were activated before I headed to the back of the truck to retrieve the last full delivery cube. Two containers of pasta, stacked on top of one another, without the lid, sat in the middle between the cube's transparent walls.

I stared at the steam, stalled in time, that rose from the top container. Those who hadn't heard of PAUSE would think the pasta was fake: it looked like a portrait, a three-dimensional model.

The front door opened, revealing an elderly woman with a cane. I exited the car and grabbed the cube before making my way up the pathway towards her. There was lavender and tulips sitting by the doorway, making the house seem much livelier compared to its neighbours with lawns littered with sparse grass, untrimmed, and untamed weeds reaching my knees. Some had trees with branches hacked off and leaves barely budding, though it was well into spring.

"Good evening," the old woman said in a soothing voice. Pearls around her neck glinted in the light.

For a moment I wanted to both laugh and cry, because she made it sound as though the sun hadn't yet gone down, that there were no shadows darting through the streets, and that there were no gunshots ringing in our ears every few minutes, making me flinch, making me think of my sister, think of Shimei waiting in the truck though I knew it was bulletproof. Behind the woman drifted calming jazz music, notes mixed with static, as though it came from a machine far in the past—a record player not from this time. An antique collector, perhaps. The record skipped a beat, and at the same time, a shot rang behind me. I couldn't understand why a woman who seemed quite well off would move to a neighbourhood like this.

"Good evening," I croaked. I cleared my throat and tried again.

I lifted the cube and prepared to triple tap its wall for release.

Another shot rang out, closer to this street this time, followed by a scream. I whipped around.

The woman and I shared a look. I flinched. She didn't. A stray lock of white hair hung down the side of her face, making her seem younger than her actual age, which may have been seventy at least.

"The ambulances don't come to this part of the neighbourhood anymore. None of them have enough to pay for the hospital bills, and they don't have insurance."

I nodded. It was something everyone in this neighbourhood knew, but I noticed the way she spoke about the people here as separate from her.

She looked past me to see someone running down the street and waved for me to come inside. I wanted to refuse, but I knew it was against PAUSE policy to deny the customer of requests directly related to their order. If the woman reported me, I'd lose the job.

I looked one more time at the truck, heart hammering in my chest, the cube damp from my clammy palms. Shimei wasn't visible through the van's windows, and I hoped she would keep herself hidden until I returned.

I followed the woman inside, closing the door behind me, the lock clicking automatically.

The woman disappeared around the corner. "In here."

I entered the kitchen, where there were candles and the smell of burning wax, something I hadn't seen, nor smelled, in a long time. Their flames cast the room in comforting warmth. I turned both dials on the cube, deactivating the PAUSE function. The top of the cube opened, flipping back along with the other three walls.

I looked around, listening. There was no one else in the house, but there was the faint crackle of a fireplace. An awkward silence had me holding my breath.

"Why don't you stay for dinner?" the old woman said with her hands clasped in front of her. She met my eyes with a steady gaze, reminding me of my mother. I held back a cough, the back of my throat drying.

"My daughter's—" I cut myself off when the woman looked as though she understood, but a certain sadness and disappointment shone behind the understanding. She had ordered two pasta servings just for this reason. What if it weren't me who made the delivery?

I smiled, still nervous as my thoughts flitted back to Shimei, but I replied, "Maybe for a bit."

The old woman looked up, returning the smile.

I noticed multiple takeout containers stacked near the fridge—some half full, most sat untouched—before taking a seat at the dining table. The woman followed my gaze.

"Ah," she said, "I always order extra for my daughter... in case she ever visits. We were close when she was younger..."

I had the urge to prod the woman further, ask her what happened, why it all changed. I thought of my own daughter, and how I would feel if she ever abandoned me. And perhaps she might when she aged, blaming me for forcing her to spend so much of her life in a small van.

"I should probably throw these, shouldn't I?" She laughed to herself, shielding her face—abashed. Then she looked up. I flinched at the sudden movement. "Do you think she might come back? Maybe when her father retires from the company?" Her eyes were wide, hopeful.

Sympathy welled and spilled from my lips. "I think she would."

We ate without another word for the rest of the meal—her with a small grin, me with my thoughts still on my waiting daughter: the silence of two mothers thinking of their daughters.

When I finished, the woman followed me to the door.

"Thank you," I said, bowing my head. Though our conversation was brief, it was nice to speak to someone who seemed to understand

I winced as another shot sounded outside, my anxiety rising with the bile in my throat.

When I returned to the driver's side, before opening the door, I noticed Shimei was nowhere in sight. In the space between the seats and the back storage of the trunk, the glass screen was lowered. Shallow, quick breaths escaped my nose. Another shot. I scrambled into the truck and into the back.

A shadow rested in the middle of the largest cube.

Shimei.

"How..." the doctor began when they opened the back of the car.

"I don't know," I ground out.

"No one has ever—"

"I know."

They whisked Shimei to the emergency sector of the hospital and left me sitting on the ground next to the car, still staring at the empty PAUSE cube Shimei had been in.

Another delivery notification pinged my phone. I raised it and was about to chuck it across the parking lot when I noticed when it said:

Tip: $300.

Note: *For staying. For being the first person I've spoken to in a long while.*

The tears returned when I noticed the name attached to the tip. Surely it wasn't a coincidence. She had the same name as the wife of PAUSE Ltd.'s CEO. I clicked to return the woman's money. I hated myself staying at her house for dinner. If I had gotten to the truck just a few moments earlier...

I thought of my mother, wishing I could call her and tell her what happened, but knowing I couldn't. I still visited her grave once a month.

After the sun had risen again, the doctor exited the emergency unit and trudged toward me with a haggard face, clipboard gripped in their hands. I knew what had happened even before they opened their mouth.

"My daughter," I said.

The doctor looked grim and nodded.

I swallowed, but the spit lodged in the middle of my throat.

We paused. I willed the doctor not to say the next words, but of course, eventually they did.

"The child... won't wake."

I didn't know why I drove to the old woman's house the following week after Shimei's funeral. Maybe it was because I knew it wasn't her fault. She'd lost a daughter to a decision that might not have been hers, or at least not hers alone.

When the woman opened the door, I fell to my knees, and she cradled my head like she had known me her whole life.

A year after the incident, my daughter sat in the middle of a museum, displayed bare for all to see—at least she felt bare even though she was still clothed in her penguin nightgown with the small tail in the back. She loved that part of it best and would run across the halls in a waddle, always looking behind her to see her tail flap.

I fought against it, the exhibition of her actual body, but my words didn't matter. They didn't care.

"This is for science," they'd said.

Why couldn't they just make a replica? I asked, mentally, not knowing the words left my mouth.

"It's not as authentic."

They tried to make themselves sound sympathetic, but all I heard was impatience as they explained to me that everything placed in the cubes became property of PAUSE Ltd. I wanted to spit in their faces.

Shimei's small body was still curled into a fetal position, eyes squeezed shut, one hand over one ear, the other holding out two fingers a centimeter from the cube's wall. And I couldn't help but imagine her as a newborn, cradled in my arms at the hospital, a small hand reaching for my face.

I pressed my palm against the glass, praying my daughter would feel the warmth of my fingertips, my touch. She was stalled, a statue, unreal—but I knew she was real.

"Excuse me."

I turned to see the security guard strolling toward me with a stun baton in their right hand, held up in front of them like an unspoken threat.

"No touching the displays," they said, jerking their chin toward my hand.

I blinked.

"But this is my daughter." My words hung in the air.

There was a brief silence, and it seemed as though the entire room paused, as though we too were within the cube with Shimei. No one moved. No one spoke. The security guard and I stood staring at one another, with everyone else in the museum gawking at our interaction, breaths held—unmoving.

The Galaxy's Cube

Jeremy Szal

I t was another sweltering night in New Bangkok, and Jharkrat wasn't selling anything.

The crowds were always here. They strode under lanterns and weaved through sluggish traffic, broad streets slick with blood-warm rain. Rusty frying pans hissed with fury as chefs cooked bubbling pastries in oil, spinning carousels draped with rice noodles. Curlicues of smoke coiled upwards from make-shift shrines. People shouted and bargained, exchanging burlap sacks of spice and seed to tourists, probably from Earth. Canoes sliced across the canal, battering away flotsam as they navigated to the floating markets. Half-finished skyscrapers towered above, cocooned with scaffolds. A fat drop of watery rust dripped from a flaking steel pylon, landing with a brown-red plop on Jharkrat's table. He didn't bother scrubbing it away. It was the city's sweat, oozing out of a million pores. There'd be another in a minute. He made a mental note to bring his umbrella tomorrow.

Two Ministry peacekeeprs dressed in dark blue—vivanors—were sipping tom kha gai at a hot-food booth, keeping an eye on the milling crowd. One of them caught his eye and Jharkrat turned away, pretending to focus on the computer components sprawled in front of him. He didn't want trouble tonight. They'd already frowned on his business in dealing with long decommissioned electronic goods and he didn't need them to shut him down.

Someone came rushing up to his booth, pudgy face flushed with the heat. Was this a customer? Jharkrat straightened up, only to groan as the overweight man dumped an armful of decrepit equipment on the stained counter.

"I'm not buying," sighed Jharkrat, picking at the bramble of decaying wires. "Only selling."

"Come on," he shouted over the tooting horns of traffic. "I'll give you a good price."

It was all from the Last Age, before the Ministry had replaced all their computer systems and software. His warehouse was nearly full of this stuff. It was barely worth paying the rent to keep it there. "Mai au khrap. I've got enough."

"Please." The man was desperate, neck tendons straining like bridge cables. "I'm low on cash."

"Sorry."

"Two thousand baht for the lot?"

"No deal."

"Fifteen hundred?"

"*No.*"

"One thousand."

He was torn. It was madness, acquiring all this for such a good price. But he'd be even madder to buy anymore stock.

The man must have seen his dilemma. He plucked out a modest black box from the mess, twirling it in his hands. "Take this. I can't sell it anywhere else."

Jharkrat inspected it, the cloying smell of incense from a nearby shrine tickling his nose. The cube was heavy for its size, little grooves carved into the sides and a port for plugging into a computer. "What is it?"

"A module, I think." The man picked at a welling boil on his neck. "Five hundred?"

Jharkrat had never seen anything like this. There wasn't even a manufacturer logo stamped into the metal. He couldn't *really* afford it, but his curiosity was winning him over. "I'll give you four hundred."

"Done."

Jharkrat forked over the crumpled notes. The man nodded gratefully, scooping up his materials and slipping out into the crowd. Jharkrat glanced back at the small mysterious box, shutting out the roaring city around him.

It started to rain as he made his way back home, warm spatters of water drumming on tin roofs and taut tarpaulins. Two moons were visible in the sky, pouring pale light on the road. The third was obscured by thick clouds. Back on Earth, where his grandparents were born, there had been only one moon in the sky. And the days were twenty-four hours long, not thirty-two. He'd been meaning to go there, see the wonders they spoke about. But even getting a permit to travel would require years of saving. And then there was buying the actual ticket. He'd spent all his money on his daughter when she came down with the blister plague, slowly eating away at her body. Every sale he made from selling equipment fought back the disease just a little more. But in the end it hadn't been enough. It had crawled into Serah's brain and killed her.

Some days Jharkrat didn't know what kept him going.

He arrived at his bottom floor apartment. Blood-red creepers curled around the sagging poles that were weary with the building's weight. He fished for the rusty key and unlocked the ancient door. He could have gotten a keypad or printscan system, but that would draw attention. Showed he had something to hide. The place was going to get broken in again anyway. No need to encourage the thieving devils. He'd seen what people would do for money. Just last month a man a couple of blocks down from him had traded his newborn son for a dog so he could sell its litter. Jharkrat had to restrain himself from going over and smashing the man's teeth out.

The flat was a wreck; the floor littered with computer equipment and crushed beer cans, plastic chairs wrapped in thick cables. A moldy fan spun lazily overhead, swirling muggy air around the room. Stock was packed in cardboard boxes threatening to fall apart, stacked to the ceiling. Jharkrat swept away a disassembled motherboard from his desk and brought out the cube. He simply *had* to know what this was. There was *no* way the Ministry had licensed it. Which just made it all the more exciting.

He flicked his ancient computer on, snatching up a cable and hooking it up to the box with a *click*.

Zap. Everything powered down, the screen spluttering and flashing bright colours before winking away, leaving the screen a black mirror.

Well, that wasn't good. He sat still, too surprised to move when the screen jumped back to life, displaying a flickering background. Was this some sort of virus? Even now it was probably eating away at his files—or worse—shipping them off to the Ministry. He was finished now. He was—

"*Hello?*" A chill shot through his body. The box was *speaking*. The grooves had burst to life, glowing an eerie blue. "Hello?" it said again, louder this time. It was a woman's voice. "Where am I?"

Jharkrat paled. He knew what this was. It had to be. It was a Mind, banned decades ago by the Ministry. Anyone caught handling them was immediately executed. No trial, no questions asked. No wonder that fat bastard wanted to sell the cube so desperately.

He had to get rid of it. *Now!*

He kicked the chair back and extended an arm, desperate to rip the cables out. The Mind must have guessed what he was doing. "Please!" it begged. "Don't!"

The intense emotion laced in its voice made Jharkrat hesitate, his hand poised to tear out the wires. "Who are you?" he finally asked.

"I do not have a name," the Mind said, sounding genuinely relieved. "I...I did not expect to boot up again."

"Why?" Jhrakrat could feel the hooks sinking in, pulling him deeper. "What happened? Where are you from?"

"Earth," said the Mind. "At least, I was made there."

"*Earth?*" Jharkrat leaned back in his chair, breathing hard. What had he stumbled onto here? "How did you end up in New Bangkok?"

"With the ships. I was the one who flew them here."

Jharkrat blinked. "You were part of the First Fleet?"

"Yes."

This Mind had to be almost a century old. No doubt it was packed *full* of data and logs that would have fetched millions of *baht* on the black market. No wonder the Ministry didn't want them around. A stupid grin played on his face.

Then doubt started to seep in. "You said you didn't expect to boot up again."

The Mind paused. "They came for us," she finally said. "The men in blue. They told us we were no longer needed and the Ministry ordered us shutdown. But one scientist, she had grown...fond of me. She downloaded my system into a storage device instead of destroying the software. I wasn't sure what would happen after that. I don't think she knew either."

"Do you have a name?"

"No. None of the officers or scientists were permitted to grow attached to their Minds." The voice seemed to hesitate, as if contemplating what to tell him. "But I did want one."

"I can give you one," Jharkrat offered. "How about...Serah?"

The Mind considered this. "That should serve. But why that name?"

Jharkrat smiled tightly, biting his cracked lips. "It was my daughter's name." He leaned forward. "What is Earth like? Tell me."

And she did. She told him about the snow-capped mountains and sprawling deserts, the endless open spaces the size of entire countries. She described the haunting forests and jungles, the ice glaciers and tundras, the coral reefs and lush islands. Jharkrat sat there in amazement, barely noticing the buttery fingers of dawn creeping through the grimy window, painting the floor a dusty yellow. He hadn't gotten a moment of sleep, but somehow he felt rejuvenated. Refreshed.

He stood up, stretching his cramped muscles and rubbing the nape of his neck. "I'll have to hide you," he told Serah. "Just in case someone breaks in."

"Oh," Serah said, a ring of disappointment in her voice. "I've charged up enough. I should stay aware at least forty-eight hours."

He planned to be back long before then. He disconnected Serah from the computer, shoved plastic bottles out of the way and slithered under the bed. He jiggled loose some rusty nails and raised up a thin floorboard to reveal a hoard. This was where he stored most of his money in thick bundles. He didn't trust the banks. He'd seen them flop in the economic crisis before, seen the outcry as lifesavings dwindled down to loose change. He wasn't planning for that to happen to him.

He sandwiched the cube between two fat wads of baht before replacing the floorboard and tightening the screws. She was safe for now.

The sun was blinding, poking out over the rim of his stall's umbrella and stabbing his eyes. He'd bought a good pair of sunglasses a few weeks ago but they'd been stolen. He would have gone for the cheap ones, but those broke down in less than a month.

He gulped down his kaeng som, flooding his mouth with spicy fish and observed the flow of the market. People drifted past, sipping from plastic bags of coconut juice, feet slapping against the pavement. Jharkrat remembered when coconuts had been horrifyingly expensive, sold only by licensed companies. But then someone had wormed into the genebank labs and leaked them on the market. Now they were only twenty *baht* each, sold at every corner of every street of the city. He remembered buying coconut milk for Serah, watching her face light up as she tasted it for the first time...

A shadow swept across his face. Jharkrat swallowed and squinted up at the figure, a dark silhouette outlined by the sun. It was a vivanor with a mountain peak of a face. He leaned forward, scanning the stock with quiet menace.

"Can I help you?" Jharkrat eyed the pistol strapped to the man's side and pushed his bowl away.

The vivanor blinked, hooded eyes drilling into him. "A man came here last night. He sold you a small box. Perhaps this big." The man held his dirt-fringed thumb and forefinger roughly ten centimeters apart. "Do you have it?"

Jharkrat realized with dread that this man had been here last night, watching him from the foodstall. This wasn't good. He couldn't deny owning it. "Yes, I bought it. But I was mugged on the way home and it was stolen."

The vivanor's face could have been chiseled from marble. "Is that so?"

"Yes." Jharkrat forced himself to smile at the man. The vivanor lingered there for another few seconds before heading off, slicing past the crowd as he strolled further down the market.

Jharkrat bit down on his cheek so hard he tasted blood. *Dammit.* The vivanor hadn't bought his story. Not for a moment. Every fiber of his being urged him to scurry home and make sure Serah was safe, but that wouldn't be wise. No doubt they were watching him from the shadows, waiting for him to make a move before they struck. He had to pretend that everything was normal.

He sighed, a bead of sweat rolling down his chest, soaking into his shirt. It was going to be a long day.

The sun finally slunk behind the blood-red horizon, allowing the city to burst into a multicoloured glow. Some shops closed down for the night while others opened, attracting a whole new breed of customers. Jharkrat ignored it all, packing up his stall as fast as he dared without raising eyebrows. He made his way home; passing by a lantern-lit vendor selling fabrics dyed a rich ruby red and threading his way through the various neon-dunked alleyways, tendrils of steam curling from gap-toothed windows. He swatted a dew-covered palm leaf out of the way, trying not to glance over his shoulder as he walked. There was no way they were still following him now. Surely he was just paranoid.

He stopped dead in his tracks. The door to his room was ajar, light spilling out. He pushed it open, fear knotting in the pit of his stomach. The whole thing had been ransacked top to bottom; drawers torn out, garments ripped to shreds, computer parts shattered to pieces on the floor. Jharkrat closed the door behind him, scuttling to examine the floorboard. A prayer to nonexistence gods leaped to his mouth. It didn't look disturbed, but he had to make sure...

He undid the screws with sweaty fingers, tearing the board away in haste. *Please be there, please be there.* Warm relief flooded his system. Serah was still there, safe and sound.

"Jharkrat?" she asked as he reached for the cube, squeezing the cool metal in his calloused hands, the razor edges cutting into his flesh. It was comforting, somehow. "Is that you? Someone broke in here hours ago. They made quite a bit of noise."

"I can tell," said Jharkrat dryly, kicking at what had once been a widescreen tablet, the screen shattered like a spider-web. He planted himself on the floor, cradling the cube in his hands. "They really want your system, don't they?"

"No," murmured Serah, almost in a grumble. "They just want to destroy it. They can't have FLT data floating around with the risk of it getting on the market. They—"

"*What?*" Jharkrat spluttered. "You have faster-than-light data stored inside your system?"

"Yes. But, if it isn't accessed for five years it gets sealed with heavy encryption. I don't think you'll be able to break in."

Now Jharkrat realized why they wanted the data so badly. He'd seen what happened when the genebank was leaked, coconuts spreading like the plague through the markets. The government had lost billions of baht. And if independent companies managed to use faster-than-light on their own, *all* their monopolies would collapse. Their starships, their tourism, their engines, everything. It would fold like a house of flimsy bamboo. People could afford to travel. See Earth. Escape from this dump.

And he held it all in his hand.

"Serah," said Jhrarkrat, excitement dripping from every syllable, "is there a way to extract the data?"

"Perhaps. But I told you, it's encrypted. There's a tripwire installed. If it detects someone trying to undo the lock, it'll self-denotate." She paused. "It'll destroy my entire system."

Jharkrat chewed his cracked lips. He held in his hand what was quite possibly the last Mind in existence, and someone who was becoming a good friend. Was the information worth the risk of losing her? Not to mention the difficulties he could run into if he was caught. Did he want to cause so much trouble over *data*?

Then he realized it wasn't up to him.

"What do you think?" he asked, focusing on the tiny black cube that housed the Mind. "I know someone who can help. But it has to be your decision. Do you want to risk it?"

Serah said nothing, the colours of her metal interface rising and falling. "That scientist risked everything to get me out of there with this data," she said. "I've kept it safe for almost a century. They wanted to destroy it, and me along with it." The device flashed a crimson red. "Yes, we're going to do it."

Jharkrat grinned. "That's what I wanted to hear."

Jharkrat packaged the cube tightly in a hidden pocket sewn into his trousers, normally used for storing cash. Now he'd be smuggling out the last surviving Mind in New Bangkok.

It was too risky to go out the front. He scaled the chainlink fence out the back and navigated his way around a garden of overgrown foliage and perennials, bursting out through to the street. He wasted no time mingling with the rushing crowd, rubbing sweaty shoulders under a roof of thick wires and holograms.

The tangled streets started to blur, the countless foodstalls, massage parlors, nightclubs, shrines, rippling lights and tooting auto-ricksaws sweeping past as Jharkrat twisted and turned through the tumult and the heat and the smells, waiting for the meaty hand on his shoulder that would drag him away and shove a .45 in his mouth.

No one came.

He carried Serah through the sea of teeming bodies, ducking under a low-hanging billboard and making his way into the dingy alleyway where old women made prayer beads with gnarled fingers, twisted like tree roots. He stepped in a shallow puddle, the water shivering as he wormed his way through a labyrinth of bustling back alleys, finally climbing a corkscrew staircase up to the fourth floor of what appeared to be a dilapidated apartment building. He made sure no one was looking before rapping his knuckles on the peeling wood.

The door promptly swung open. There she was, grinning at him with teeth that were black as ink. "Sawa dee, Jharkrat. Long time, eh?"

"Hello, Kwan. You still chewing those nuts?"

"Of course. Try it sometime for yourself, eh?"

"No thanks." He stepped inside, the air conditioning fast freezing his sweat. Explosions boomed out of speakers in the adjoining room. "Got something for you."

"Ah, yes," she said, meshing her tiny hands together. "That's what you always say." She led him down the narrow corridor and into the lab. At least two dozen screens had been squeezed in here, bulging cables stapled to the ceilings and walls, pumping terabytes of data by the second. Half of the desks contained hackers, hooked up to screens by interfaces and headphones, pounding away at sticky keyboards. Kwan sat down on her overstuffed chair, taking a sip of what could have been water or vodka. "I've seen it all before, my friend."

"Not like this you haven't." Jharkrat reached into his pocket, ripping away the stitching and bringing out the cube.

Kwan's expression didn't change. "What is it?"

Jharkrat opened his mouth to tell her, but Serah was faster. "You're Jharkrat's hacker friend, I presume?"

Kwan's lazy smile wilted. She gripped the cube in a trembling hand. "You found a *Mind*?" Jharkrat nodded. "*How?*"

"Doesn't matter," he said. "Serah's got something valuable inside her. I need you to extract it."

"You've *named* it?" Kwan demanded. "If the Ministry catches us..."

"Then I'll go somewhere else." Jharkrat was about to stand up when Kwan motioned him back down again.

"Stay put," she hissed. "Better me than someone else screwing it up." She turned to her computer, fishing for a cable. "What did you need?"

"There's some encrypted data I need you to unpack."

Kwan made a small snort as she plugged Serah to the computer. "Too easy. You insult me, peuang."

"There's a tripwire installed," Jharkrat said. "If triggered it'll wipe the entire system."

Kwan nodded, eyes sliding across the widescreen. "Ah, yes. I see it."

"Can you break through?"

Kwan swerved around to him with a sly wink. "There you are, insulting me again." Her fingers danced over the ash-stained keyboard in a rhythmic *tat-tat-tat*. "It'll take some time. A couple hours at least." She motioned towards the door. "Please leave. I won't have you breathing down my neck."

Jharkrat hesitated. It needed to be done, but he didn't want to leave Serah in anyone's hands. He trusted Kwan, but this was almost like leaving his daughter behind.

Almost.

"Go on," Serah said, as if reading his mind. "I'll be fine here."

"See? Even she knows."

Jharkrat took the hint. He swung the exit open, letting the soggy night swallow him up.

Jharkrat couldn't sleep.

It wasn't just because his wafer-thin mattress had nearly been torn in two. It was Serah who lingered in his mind, tattooed on his brain. The daughter he'd lost. He could almost hear her raspy breathing as she lay comatose in the hospital bed, feel the life seeping out of her as he stroked her silky black hair, praying she would recover, that everything would be all right.

It had never truly sunk in that his daughter had gone. He'd never moved on. Maybe that was why he named the Mind after her. To keep his daughter alive.

He wasn't going to lose her again.

He unwound his legs from the sweaty sheets. He wasn't going to get any sleep tonight. Best to make the most of it. He pulled on some clothes with haste, heading out the door.

The streets were busy as always despite the early hour, frozen in a never-ending slog of traffic, teeming bodies and heat, clogging up the arteries of the city. Jharkrat clambered up the stairs, not waiting to knock. Kwan met him in the hall, all calm exterior melted away.

"You!" She shoved him against the wall, gnashing those black teeth of hers. "You *bastard*! Did you know what was inside?"

"You've broken through?" asked Jharkrat, grinning.

Kwan hissed, dragging him into the computer room. She clapped her hands, the sound drowning out the hum of computer systems. All heads swiveled to face her. "*Out! Now!*"

No one dared to object. Desks and keyboards clattered as they rushed to escape her rage. Kwan scarcely waited until they'd all left before slamming the door shut, the frame shuddering. She rounded on him, tiny hands clenched into balled fists. He half expected her to backhand him. "You knew, didn't you?"

"I—"

"FLT data, out of all things." She ground her palms against her cheeks. "Maaeng eeuy! I can't keep this here."

"Think about how valuable it is!" Jharkrat bristled. "We've been looking for something like this for decades!"

"You'll put us all in danger!"

"Not if we flood the market!"

Kwan blinked, tilting her head towards him. "You don't want to sell it?"

Jharkrat shook his head. He'd done the math already. The data was priceless. Trying to sell something like this would just draw attention from the crime lords and get them killed. But if they made it public…

"Did you extract it?" Jharkrat demanded.

Kwan blew air out between her teeth. "Yes and no. We managed to fool the tripwire and retrieve the data, but it's key-coded to the Mind. We can't make another copy."

"Meaning what?"

"That I'll have to go." Their heads turned to the Mind. Serah had been listening all along. "You'll have to upload the entire system, and me along with it."

Jharkrat stood in dismay as the pieces slotted together. They could upload the information, but they couldn't separate Serah from it. She'd be whisked away to the pits of the Net, lost in a bottomless ocean.

Jharkrat opened his mouth to object, but clamped it shut. He was being a selfish bastard. This wasn't about him. It had never been.

And it wasn't his decision.

He approached the table, kneeling down like he was talking to a child. "What do you want to do?" He asked, eyes locked to the tiny cube that had been his friend for the last few days. "It's your choice."

The Mind made a noise that sounded like something between a sigh and a chuckle. "I think we both know the answer, Jharkrat."

The door crashed open. A man stood there, face speckled with sweat as he panted for breath. "The vivanors," he rasped. "They're coming!"

Kwan blinked, spat a curse and waved him off. She rounded on him. "You *brought* them here?"

Jharkrat was lost for words. He'd been careful, so *careful* to make sure he hadn't been followed. And this little slip up could cost them everything.

He made a snap decision, not giving himself the chance to back out. "Kwan, are your computers connected to the Net?"

"Yes, but—"

"You need to leave," he said as others crowded into the room, looking to Kwan for the order. "I'll take care of this."

Kwan seemed to understand. She nodded, turned to a handful of men lingering in the corridor. "You. Make their job hell. Hold them out as long as you can." She motioned to the others. "The rest of you, grab what you can and get to the truck. Destroy what you can't carry."

Everyone rushed to obey. Jharkrat caught a glimpse of a locker being flung open, heard the clatter of various handguns and revolvers handed out and magazines slotted in. But that wasn't what he needed to focus on right now.

He pounded away at the computer, connecting it to the network. Kwan made herself busy ordering various men and women about as they dashed from room to room, arms bundled with hard drives and thick cables. Jharkrat frantically slotted the correct wires into the corresponding ports, linking Serah up to the system.

Shouts of warning floated up. They were getting close.

Jharkrat swiveled around, his eyes locking onto Kwan's. There was nothing to be said. They knew how this was going to turn out. "You really should have tried those nuts." Then she was gone, clambering down the back stairs and to the impatient truck loaded with equipment.

Muffled gunshots. Screams. Bullets whistled through the air, shattering glass. His fingers were a blur as he wrenched the gateway open, tethering Serah directly to the Net. In a few minutes she would be gone, the priceless data leaked onto the streets.

But she would be safe.

I might not have saved my own daughter. But I can save you.

"I wish you could come with me," said Serah, her voice soft.

Jharkrat breathed out through his nostrils. "Me too."

Bang. Bang bang bang. A smear of red spattered the windows, followed by a roar of pain.

"Twice humans have saved me," Serah said, her voice dimming as the bar onscreen filled up, sucking her away one fragment at a time. A yell rang out, but the *crack* of a revolver silenced it. "You risked everything. Why?"

Jharkrat smiled. "Don't you worry about that now. I've made my decision."

"I wish I could have met your daughter."

Jharkrat sensed an itch on his cheek and felt a single tear streaming down his face. He didn't bother to wipe it away. "Me too."

"I'll never forget you." There was a *crack* of splintering wood as the door was kicked down, armored boots charging down the hall. "I—"

The bar filled up.

Bang, bang. A man was thrown backwards, hosed down by a blaze of gunfire.

"Goodbye, Serah." Jharkrat stabbed the button marked *Enter.*

Jharkrat didn't even turn around as they thundered into the room. He watched them take aim in the screen's polished reflection. Bullets thudded into the monitor and system, tearing it to shreds with a deafening roar and the fizzle of sparks.

Too late.

The rifle was pressed to his head, the cold kiss of death trickling down his spine as the *vivanor's* finger curled around the trigger.

Goodbye, Serah.
Jharkrat gave a final grin and closed his eyes.

Do Anarchists Dream of Collective Sheep?

Izzy Wasserstein

*S*top us if you've heard this one. A cell of revolutionaries meet in secret, knowing that if they are discovered, they will be tortured and killed. Each of them, one, two, three, four, takes every precaution. Each arrives, certain they were not followed. They greet one another as comrades, for they have placed their lives in one another's hands.

One by one, they give their reports, share urgent news and essential whispers. One by one, until each has reported. One, two, three, four, five.

First one realizes, then another, and another, until they stare in mutual horror.

Oh, you have heard it? Tell us, then: what's the true source of their horror?

After we become aware of the infection, or compromise, or corruption in the system, there's screaming and threats and panic. And after that, we realize the urgency of reconstructing the past. We gather in the common room of our condemned house, around a whiteboard Six scavenged from somewhere, keeping our distance from one another. We're still wary, still unsure if the virtual attack we've endured will be followed by one in meat-space, and if so, if it will include a knife in the back from one of our own.

We eye each other nervously and try to sort out how this all began. Hafsa's soldering some old tech, turning to precision tasks as she always does when she needs to think clearly. She remembers it this way: Wulf got tipped off to what the corporate server-farm downtown is being used for, its big-box storefront sealed up tight, venting steam at all hours. Few come and go. We figured it for bad news, Hafsa says, but it's worse.

It's always worse: we still agree on that, at least.

Wulf scratches their head and says it was Six who got the tip, Six who learned that they were beta-ing the latest and greatest in military-industrial shithousery, collating data from Wally stores, insurance databases, patient records, internet scraping, government surveillance—the whole fucked-up mess, and was using it to go full *Minority Report*—

That's not right, Kelz says, sweat-soaked and more jittery than we've ever seen her, it was simpler than that, and eviler. Just tracking everything about everyone, keeping us all under their collective sweatshop boots until the end of time.

Couldn't have been that, Rook says, twirling a coin between their fingers. They've had surveillance tech for ages. The problem is that they're perfecting their predictive algorithms—

—Yeah, *Minority Report*, like I said—

—let me finish? Not for crime prediction, but eradication. Modeling everyone's behavior down far enough that they don't have to compel compliance. They just make tweaks that the simulation suggests and, boom, a populace who doesn't have to do what they're told, because they'd never consider doing anything but what's expected of them.

That's horrific, Wulf says, scratching under their beard like they always do when they don't want anyone to know how much they're freaked out. Of course we all know. We're reasonably sure we know.

We're giving them too much credit, Hafsa says, not taking her eyes from the hardware in front of her, some project involving virtual and meat-space interactions. Whatever they're doing in that building, their tech doesn't have to control people, as long as it consolidates money and power for them. As long as their investors think it works.

That's not much better, Wulf says. Hafsa grunts in agreement.

So we're back where we started: we don't know what they're doing, exactly, but we agree it is bad news. We needed to disrupt it. Most of us are sure we wanted something subtle, something that would make it seem the project failed under its own weight, so they don't just start again somewhere else. Kelz would prefer something a bit more dramatic, but concedes that's probably not the best play.

Then we have that much, at least, Six says, and writes *common cause* on the scavenged whiteboard. We're using it because we aren't sure we can trust our servers, our minds. The note is because we've got no choice but to go back to basics. To first principles.

They're horrified because they've been compromised.

A reasonable guess, but that's only a small part of the answer. Like a dying man worried about his grocery list.

Before the whiteboard, before the everyone-desperately-trying-to-keep-it-together gathering, Kelz yanks open the door to Six's room with so much force that the house's frame—not the most stable to begin with—rattles.

What the fuck, Six? she demands.

Six, deep in his code, startles and topples over. He's got 8 inches and a hundred pounds on Kelz, but you wouldn't know it, to see him flinch away like a mistreated dog.

What the fuck, Kelz? he sputters, curling up into himself in the corner.

Who'd you leave it for, Six? Did you really think we wouldn't see it—

Leave what for? Six looks nauseated. Hafsa and Wulf have rushed over and stand outside the door, mouths agape. Kelz is tiny and mongoose-fierce, but we've never seen her this aggressive outside of direct action. She's never aimed this fury at one of us.

Don't play dumb, Kelz shouts, but Six's terror has dulled the force of fury. She turns to the rest of us, says, look, and pulls up the code. Hafsa specializes in hardware, stares hopelessly at the lines projected in the air from one of Kelz's implants. Wulf's quicker to see.

Shit, Wulf says. This is a massive vulnerability, not just to our shared processing space, but to the private segments, too.

We're studying it, Kelz quivering with rage, Hafsa drawn taut, as though posture can correct this, Wulf puzzling at the code as though confirming its utility will answer the bigger question: *why?* Shaking, Six looks over Wulf's shoulder, bug-eyed and uncomprehending.

That's not my code, he insists.

It's signed by you, Kelz says, her hands over her face as if she's shielding herself from a scary movie, though no movie's ever been too scary for Kelz.

Why would anyone sign a backdoor? Six asks.

He's got a point, Rook says.

Look at these objects it's calling, though, Wulf points out. It's like a Six's greatest hit package. Wulf's fingers slide over the projection, displaying the objects. All of these are yours, they tell Six.

And this one—Rook gestures, a glittering fingernail emphasizing their point—I remember how proud you were of it, the duplication-and-segment trick? Best I've ever seen.

It's your work. Kelz isn't yelling anymore, but one hand has gone to the bear spray she always carries on her belt.

Except it's not Six's, it's yours, Hafsa says.

The fuck it is. Kelz's teeth grind audibly.

It's just like Rook said. Hafsa doesn't flinch. Except it's your code. I don't know much about software, but I remember how proud you were of this project. You worked on it for weeks. Talked me through it.

I would have been proud, if I'd have written it. It's elegant code. And Six is using it to—to what? Sell us out? Narc to the feds?

The cramped confines of Six's room has become a battleground. One group—Six and Hafsa—on one side, Rook and Kelz on the other. Most of us think Wulf was with Kelz, but there's no consensus.

The middle of the room's a DMZ. Across it, accusations are launched like mortars.

They're horrified because they can't tell which of them is the plant?
Getting Closer. But you're mistaking symptoms and causes. The shark's fin for her teeth.

Hazzard (2031) argues for three fundamental benefits to memory upload techniques:

- Increased reliability. Biological memory rewrites with each access. Once transferred to digital memory, the truth is shielded from accidental degradation.

- Robust protections. No system is impervious to corruption *(you knew that already, didn't you?)*, but digital memory allows for defenses such as backups, change logs, and encryption.

- Memory sharing. Hazzard envisioned this as a more effective form of communication, though direct-experience transfer is more fraught than she anticipated. Later researchers (*see Lem 2035, Kelz notes*) elaborated on the benefits of multiplicity in scene reconstruction.

Six (2038) posits an addendum: while the benefits of distributed computing are well established, research on distributing cognition through a combination of digital and biological processing remains under-studied.

Rook—or is it Wulf?—adds: under-studied because it is illegal. Not that we'd let a little thing like that stop us.

Early results are promising.

Were promising.

This one we know you've heard before. We needed the combined processing power, and the combined neurons, in order to crack security. Your bosses are using high-end shit, after all. But you don't get to be an anarchist (or, in Hafsa's case, a queer mutualist) cracking collective without respect for individual agency. So we segmented those memories that we wanted to keep private, and that might incriminate ourselves or others. Trust is one thing, but information security remains paramount.

Remain*ed* paramount, perhaps.

We've demonstrated that our approach has significant benefits. Then you showed us its substantial drawbacks.

We'd like to know your name. Some of us would; Kelz thinks it may be dangerous to ask. But Kelz also worries about Roko's basilisk.

The rest of us would like to know, since you know so much about us, and Kelz withdraws her objection.

No? A pity. We like your newest guess, though: because they can't tell which of their comrades are real, and which is a figment?

Closer. Rook admires the irony.

Well. We have time. You made certain of that. If it hadn't wrecked us so completely, we might even admire it.

Six likes to say that the joy of programming is that it is a logic puzzle with knowable solutions, unlike the puzzle of humans. There's no verification you can run on people.

The shouting continues for a long while, but we manage not to kill each other, and when we've calmed down a little, we leave the DMZ for the common room, gather around the whiteboard, and set out to solve the puzzle. If we can. Which type is it, we ask each other, the network-exploit type or the depths-of-the-human-soul type?

Have we been betrayed or merely fucked with? Can we tell what's real?

Hence the whiteboard. Hence those things we're taking as axiomatic:

1. Common cause

2. Events without discrepancy and verified by at least three of us. One of us—Hafsa, we think—argues that this is insufficient, because whoever did this to us, tip of the hat, o nameless sower-of-our-doom, might have modified all our memories on some events, making everything untrustworthy. But Wulf says if you could pull that off, there'd be no benefit in selective editing, and

Rook notes that going so far beyond even solipsism gets us nowhere.

3. An outside threat exists. Even if we've been betrayed, this remains true.

4. Fuck the Man.

We figure that's you, even though we don't know your gender, or if you're a human at all, or some reasonably-strong AI. We know you're deeply embedded in virtual space, because that's the only way you could have accessed that backdoor. But that's about it, and you're clearly not the sharing type. So, allow us to say, enthusiastically: whoever you are, fuck all the way off.

There's some debate as to whether such language is helpful. We will take it under advisement.

Meanwhile, we're working on the other problem, the programming one. Our first goal is to see if there's a reliable changelog. We're trying everything we can think of, but there's no cloud backup for all our combined memories, because only the very rich can afford that level of redundancy, and where local backups exist, it's a mess. You hit the changelogs first, didn't you? We figured that out pretty quickly. Six even ran a statistical model to try to figure out which things had changed. But you're too clever for that. Call it professional curiosity: did you just randomize differences in the changelogs, or go to the trouble of randomly inserting false memories and let the changelogs reflect that randomness? That would explain why we can't find a pattern to the memories you disrupted. There's no reason not to tell us. Even if we knew, we've got no way to make use of that information. To have any hope of that, we'd need to know definitively what method you're using to change our memories, and you left no trace.

You won't say? Disappointing. We don't see what harm it could possibly do, not anymore. But then, we didn't see you coming, did we?

We're sorting out both logic puzzles, human and programming, doing what we can with parallel processing and finding ourselves by turns calm, messy, furious, despairing, calculating, horny, and cold. It's a lot to take in, is what we're saying. But pretty soon we're converging on an answer. A bad one: we're never going to be sure whose memories are the real ones, if indeed any of them are. The past is a labyrinth, filled with entrances but without exits.

Hafsa says it's a game theory question. How do you win when you don't know the rules? When you can't be sure the others are even playing the same game? Her hands work so precisely you'd think she doesn't have a care in the world.

But Rook practically screams, how can you be so calm? They've got some trauma-induced problems with memory. (Did you know that? We're reasonably sure you specifically targeted some memories, but we don't know how much of them you could see, whether you cracked the encryption, or deduced key moments from context. If you knew, it's particularly cruel to fuck with Rook about that. It's such a fragile thing, memory, and if you disrupt it enough, worry at that thread, you risk unmaking the person, having them unravel like a scarf until, inch-by-inch, whatever it is that makes us is torn apart.)

We hate you for that, understand. Some of us would kill you if we could, if we knew how, or who you were. Maybe you're right not to tell us anything about yourself.

I'm not calm, Hafsa says, and sets her work aside to take Rook's hand in hers. I'm just going to my logical place. What else can I do?

I've lost all chill. Kelz's leg is draped casually over an armrest, but her foot won't stop shaking. I think I feel jealous of the closeness you two share. Did I feel that before?

Were we this close before? Rook is squeezing so hard at Hafsa's hand that they're cutting off circulation. Their relationship is not on our list of confirmed events.

How can we hope to identify this threat if we can't even be sure who we are? Wulf says, or what we are to each other? They've pulled patches from their beard, have slept maybe two hours in seventy-two, their eyes haunted.

Maybe I did write that code, Six says, staring at the white board, their hands stained with ink. Or maybe you did, Kelz.

Like hell—

Please understand. I'm not accusing you of anything. I just mean, if someone wanted to do this, covering up their own memory of the crime would be very effective.

One by one, all our eyes turn to him. We've been distrusting our memories, each other. But that's barely the start of it.

Oh fuck, someone says.

You know the answer now, surely.

They're horrified because each of them fears they *might be the traitor, the impostor. Because if there's no independent truth, no way of trusting even oneself—*

Bravo. It's so clever. You ripped us apart. Not just our collective, but us, collectively and individually. So much more work to plant than to tear asunder, which you must know, you who tore so well.

If you can't trust your own experience of reality, do you trust the consensus view? Wulf asks.

What other choice is there? Six's voice is thick with despair.

Easy for that to go in a cult direction, Hafsa says, looking pained.

Are cults without hierarchies even cults? Someone—probably Wulf—asks.

A cult is just a name for a fringe religious group, Six says.

Fuck off with that, Rook says, very gently. We both know cults of personality are a real thing.

But, Six says, it's a misnomer—

—I'll withdraw my use of the term, Hafsa says. But whatever we call such groups, it's easy enough for hierarchy to emerge, if we're putting more trust in some memories than others.

Fuck, several of us say. We sit with this new dilemma for a while, until Rook articulates the problem: take away the foundation, any possibility of self-knowledge, and what do you have left? It's the self as a black box problem.

Yeah, Kelz says. Like putting Descartes before the horse. Everyone stares at her. Six snorts a laugh. Rook lobs an eraser at her. It's the first time we've seen Rook smile in days.

I hate to say it after that pun, Kelz, Wulf says, like, I *really* hate to say it. But that's the key point, isn't it? 'I think, therefore I am' is such horseshit. How do we know who is thinking—

—and what good is thought, if it is built on the wrong premises? Hafsa adds. Or Six does.

If we choose to trust our own memories, someone says, then the collective will shatter.

And if we choose to trust someone else's, we cede them power.

Silence. Lots of it.

One, two, three, four, five revolutionaries. Unsure if they can trust each other, if they can trust themselves. They stare at each other, new horrors unfolding like ravenous flowers.

Is there *anything* we can trust? One of them says at last.

Maybe that's what the riddle has always been about.

It's like that old punchline, Wulf says. Who are you going to believe, me or your lying eyes?

I thought my jokes were bad, Kelz says.

Several of us rush to say oh, don't worry, they are. We write a fifth axiom on the board: Kelz's jokes are terrible.

We're eating cheap takeout, because Hafsa insisted that philosophy shouldn't happen on empty stomachs. It's helped a little. Just like old times, Rook says, then flinches at the fear that no, maybe it's not. Maybe it's impossible to know what old times were like.

We could disconnect, go our separate ways. We feel Six forcing the words out. I don't like it either, but if we can't untangle this…

And let them win? Kelz asks, but there's no sharpness in the question, no challenge. That's unlike her. We're worried about Kelz. And Six. And—well, we're worried.

We don't know what's real anymore, Wulf says. I'm not sure we ever will again.

I'm pretty sure these noodles aren't real, Rook says, before taking another bite. But I have to admit, they're pretty good.

You're just hungry enough not to care that they're bad, sweetie, Hafsa says gently.

Don't care. Eating. Rook snuggles into Hafsa's shoulder.

What even is real? Six says. Someone groans. No, I'm not being abstract. I'm just thinking that Rook's right.

About the noodles? Rook asks, slurping one up.

About the point behind the noodles. When I'm hungry enough, everything tastes good. Like I said, I don't know if I can trust myself, my memories—

Please please please not this again, Kelz moans.

—Please, just let me—

—Sorry. Shutting up.

—So what do I know? Six asks, and circles our first axiom. I know that we trusted each other enough to network our brains. I don't think you're a jealous person, Kelz, because I've seen some of your memories, and even if we're not sure whether you and Hafsa were ever truly a thing, I felt the warmth you have for her, for Rook—I know, we've established we can't trust those memories, and maybe that means we can't trust feelings, either. But that's just it—would a jealous person make themselves that vulnerable to the object of their jealousy?

Huh, Kelz says.

So you're saying that maybe we have been betrayed, Wulf says. They're knitting to keep their hands busy. But if so, then we're fucked already. So the only thing to do—

—is fall back on first principles! Rook leaps to their feet, joining Six at the board. If one of us has turned, we're all fucked anyway. So we either split, like you said earlier, Six—

—or we continue with our goals. Kelz flashes a toothy grin. As we understand them now.

Memory is always an act of trust, someone says.

It's no bigger a risk than it ever was. Just our lives, our community, the world we're hoping to cultivate. Just everything. But we've risked it before. And we'll do it again.

I love it, Hafsa says. I love you all. But that still leaves a huge problem.

We have an active threat, Wulf says.

I have some thoughts on that, Hafsa says.

We get to work.

Why are you so edgy? Maybe we're slightly calmer than we made out, and maybe that sets your teeth—real or metaphorical—on edge. What a shame.

The problem was how to put a stop to you, going forward. Even with us all pulling together, you presented a massive challenge. But whatever's backing you, whoever you are, we figured that, together, we could solve this riddle.

No, not the memory thing. You may have wrecked that for us. Though perhaps not. You've been changing the narrative as we've told it to you, after all, adding and subtracting people from scenes, inserting new lines of dialog, infecting memory with uncertainty. Unable to resist the temptation. But now we've seen you in action in real time. We've learned more about how you change the memories. Whether we can use that to detect which ones you changed, time will tell.

We may never be able to undo the damage, O foe of ours, but that didn't stop us from engineering our own approach to the kind of hack you pulled off. Six is eager to see if his method is close to yours. Did you stop to wonder if there was risk in being so deeply inside others' shared memories, their shared processing, in virtual space that is as real—maybe more real—than meat space? I suspect not; after all, you could always exit through the backdoor you used, return to your life or your home server or wherever.

And you still can. Assuming you can find it. Assuming when you've found it, it's the real exit, and not just a doorway into your own memories. Or our version of them. Assuming that we didn't patch that vulnerability and put something else in its place. This space you so cruelly violated is made up of all of us, you see. Not just our memories and our processing power, but our shared commitment, shared goals. You made our minds a labyrinth, you absolute fucker. So we've given you the opportunity to wander it. Hafsa's hardware side of the solution is genius hodgepodgerie, and our combined code is quite elegant, if we do say so ourselves.

You'll find your way out, eventually. Probably. And maybe you'll even be able to trust that you've really managed it.

We don't believe in prisons, you see. But if you insist on building one, then it's only right you get the opportunity to test its efficacy.

One, two, three, four, five revolutionaries, pledging their lives in trust to each other. They're all at risk, maybe all doomed. They can't know the others are trustworthy, or even if they themselves are. Certainty has fled forever. Or perhaps only the illusion of certainty.

You thought that would break us, O adversary. But revolutions aren't built on surety. Maybe you'll work out what they are built upon, in time.

Enjoy your labyrinth. We've left you whiteboards. An infinite supply of them.

Tomorrow Is Another Day

Louis Evans

I'm awake. My hand is on the gun. The letters above me say: *This is your bed.*

Good to know.

I roll out of the shelf and land in a crouch on the floor. I'm still holding the gun. Just because someone *says* it's my bed doesn't mean I'm free to get sloppy.

Evidence starts coming in.

There's an ID card stickytacked to the floor by my feet. Name "Tai Shifane." SyneCorp Paracitizen Third Class: Unbonded Contractor. Revocable License to Harm. Blood Type OXZ Negative. Expansion Slots: Two. Human Resource Category: Query Executor.

There's a face on the ID—heavy brow, wide chin—and glued down next to it is a shard of mirror, so I can see my own face. First I check that it's a real mirror, not a camera/screen filter rig that might lie to me. Then I check my face. It's a match.

Okay. So this is my ID, and I'm a private detective.

I peel the card off the floor and pocket it. Then I stand up from my crouch and holster my gun.

You're thinking: *now that Tai's seen the ID, they know they're safe.* You are wrong. It's merely that now that I've seen the ID, I know that if someone is running me—if they've engineered my boot environment to mislead me about my identity and purpose—they're good enough that the gun is useless.

I input and I eliminate. Turns out I subscribe to some shitty food—lowest grade of protein slurry. But it tastes like home. After that I port into my desk. There's a file up front that says *Read me first!* So I do.

I said before: "if someone is running me." But I meant: if someone *else* is running me. Someone's *always* running me. It's usually *me*, from yesterday. Which is fine, maybe. No choice but to assume the Yesterday Guy doesn't want me dead.

Read me first! is about a case we're working. Missing persons.

It's an "Eternal Sunshine of My Deadbeat Ex"-type situation. The client, a Nif Wellton, is a birdbrain.

That is, they are among the vast majority of humanity who store their declarative personal memory on a corp-run cloud service.

It's easy, it's affordable, it's normal. Only shareholders can afford to run their memories on private hardware. Unlike me, if you're a birdbrain you wake up and you remember your face and know your own name—

And your identity is running on hardware you've never seen, owned by people you've never met. People who do not have your best interests at heart. Pretty much every birdbrain memory stack is crawling with spyware, adware, scamware. Do you really think so many of your formative childhood experiences were with quality branded products? Of course not.

Remember—or forget. Because the corps also offer "reputation management" services—pay up, and any of their subscribers will forget all about you. Most don't notice that their recall has been redacted; those that do, they get over it.

But sometimes it's more devastating than that. Maybe you're Nif Welton, and one day you wake up in your SyneCorp apartment with two toothbrushes and two wardrobes and a twin-port entertainment rig and pairs of shoes in two different sizes—

And no memory of your spouse.

But you still have three kids.

Nif can't pay for food or housing for three kids without a second income. They're already thirty days behind on the rent and relying on the company's Promotional Payroll Advance program, which will in sixty more days start repossession proceedings on one of the kids. Probably the smartest one. Maybe the cutest.

So desperate Nif called me.

And what do you know, the files say I worked a miracle. (Good job, Yesterday Guy.)

Nif's spouse has a new address and a new name and a new job. They've got a new face and a new network ID. (If you're wondering about all the "they" pronouns—nobody I'm likely to meet can afford a gender expansion slot.)

But the chips in their head have the same hardware ID, and the flakes of their skin unwound the same DNA sequence to the sniffer drone Yesterday Guy sent to check out the lead. We got 'em. I note in the file that I'm moving to confront the target and I head out.

Yesterday Guy did the hard work. Now all I have to do is go make some deadbeat pay.

Deadbeat's got a fancy job out on a seastead office park. Jitney jet drops me off. I loiter in the courtyard, trying to stay inconspicuous. It's not easy. I always dress forgettable—grays and blacks, all the right logos—but normies don't need to see the license to know: I'm a guy who puts the hurt on people.

Couple of hours to kill so I lurk under a gingko gener-ip, pretending to read. Truth is, without an exomemory I couldn't have ever finished a book in my life. Not that I'd remember if I did.

Finally, here comes lunch. First a trickle and then a glut of middle management drones. You know. The type of guy who's as owned by the corp as any of us, maybe more so, but because their perks include one (1) knockoff designer vest and one (1) annual virtual ski vacation, they think they're on the same side as ownership. Those fuckers.

They scatter to the multifariously branded company cafeteria kiosks—a whole smorgasbord of Potemkin "bistros" and "brewpubs" and "ramen bars" and so on.

Deadbeat comes out at the very end. Perfect. I detach myself from the tree and I follow.

My scanners report they are unarmed; only mods are basic corp and leisure. When we're alone enough, I call out. "Nif Welton." Deadbeat stumbles. A little, but enough. Got 'em.

They regain their stride, not turning back towards me. I catch up, lay a hand on their arm. "Wha—?" They're turning, trying to shrug me off. They're not strong enough for that and so now I've got them in a wrist lock, plus my hand is on the gun and the gun is on their gut.

Once Deadbeat realizes about the gun, they put their arms up in surrender. I walk them over to a quiet, shady side corner where we can talk undisturbed. There's more of those sorts of places than you think.

"What's this about?" asks Deadbeat. Their voice quavers. They have no stomach for this shit.

"Nif Welton," I say again. Confusion and pain spiral across their face.

"Who *is* that? Why don't I remember—"

So it's like that. Sometimes deadbeats, birdbrain deadbeats, they don't just erase someone else's memory. They erase their own memories too. Eliminates the guilt. It works; the birdbrain ends up with a mind squeaky clean and shame free; ready to go win that promotion. But muscles have their own memory; they don't quite forget.

"Nif Welton is your spouse."

"No," says Deadbeat. "No, I'd know if I were married."

"They're your spouse, and you're coming back with me."

"I'm telling you there's a mistake, I never heard the name before, it just sounded—"

"Save it," I tell them. "I'm better at this than you are. You're coming with me, or—" I give them a jab with the buzz gun, which won't kill them but will harm them a whole lot. I got a license.

"Listen, we can sort this out," says Deadbeat. "I've got money, okay? Plenty of money. Company scrip or crypto—"

Makes me want to *spit*. Deadbeat standing in a fancy office park prattling on about their bank accounts and somewhere else in the city Nif Welton putting another X on the calendar that separates them from child repossession.

"Shut your mouth," I say. "I've got you dead to rights, you worm."

Deadbeat freezes. Completely still. One second, two. *Weird* readings starting to trickle in off my scan.

"Hey—"

Now Deadbeat *moves*.

Their hands fall out of surrender and slice towards me. I'm pulling the trigger but I'm too slow and Deadbeat's hand smashes into mine, knocks the barrel away. The buzz blast ricochets around the courtyard and the gun leaps out of my hand and skitters across the resin cobblestones.

My gun hand is stinging from their strike but my other is already moving up to their jaw. If I can get a hold of the mandible implant node then my aggression hardware can run a DDoS on their entire skeleton. This is the obvious play, cause I'm still thinking of Deadbeat as normie fresh meat, which is what ends me.

Deadbeat sees my hand coming. They don't flinch, which is the normie move. They don't block my hand, like a tough guy would, or flash a micro EMP like a true operator.

No, Deadbeat, like an utter fucking psychopath, just swivels their jaw, tucks their chin, and bites two of my fingers clean off.

Technically the fight's not over yet but it might as well be. I'm pouring out blood and sparks as I try to grapple but a fist to the temple sends me reeling; a shin to the knees knocks me over, and I'm down. My implants ramp up towards emergency redlines; not fast enough. Deadbeat is moving like nothing I've ever seen, quicksilver and savage. A business casual loafer smashes my chest and the mass of bone and tech crunches. I'm not going anywhere. The gun is in their hand. The barrel is under my chin.

Buzz gun's supposed to be nonlethal but with the barrel jammed into my mandible, if Deadbeat pulls the trigger I will die, which will be a real problem for my license. Also I will be dead.

But Deadbeat doesn't pull the trigger.

Instead they reach out to the side of my head and with a quick twist they pop open my skull plate. They're looking right into the neuralink and its two expansion slots. There's a cable sneaking out of where their left pinky should be—

There's an exabyte of data shriEKING INTO MY SKULL—

I'm not awake anymore.

[RUN WORM.EXE? Y/Y]

  [EJECT WORM.EXE. BOOT FROM DISK.]

  [COMMAND NOT RECOGNIZED.]

  [RUN WORM.EXE? Y/Y/Y/Y/Y/Y/Y—]

  [EJECT. ABORT. CRTLALTDLT. HALT AND CATCH FIRE—]

  [COMMAND NOT RECOGNIZED.] [RUNNING WO RM.EXE—]

I'm awake. The gun is in my hand. My name is Tai Shifane.

I remember that my name is Tai Shifane—

I remember that my name is Tai Shifane *but it hasn't always been—*

And then I don't remember anything like that anymore. I remember something else.

I remember WORM—

[FILE CORRUPTED. OPEN ANYWAY?]

I'm awake. The gun is in my hand. The letters above me say: FIND WORM.

Good to know.

I roll out of the shelf and land in a crouch, still holding the gun.

This action surprises the two goons from SyneCorp Human Resources' Severance and Termination department, who have just finished breaking in through the bootleg unauthorized corp-resisting lock on my front door and are moving through the apartment presumably to kill me.

I shoot the first one in the face. The buzz gun makes a sad little click. Some thoughtless person, probably the Yesterday Guy, shot a lot of people with this gun and then didn't even think to recharge it.

The goon flinches from the used-up buzz gun click. Even though they're licensed to kill, Sev & Term operatives are jokes, which is why anybody serious uses slushfund death squads instead. (I remember—)

I break the flincher's wrist (it turns out I'm down two fingers but who cares) and I take their gun. The second goon lunges toward me but they slip on a piece of plastic stuck to the floor and as they're toppling I shoot them in the face too.

This is no buzz gun. It makes the sound of lightning and the guy who slipped is very dead.

(I remember a gun like this—)

When the first guy sees that the second guy is dead, they start hyperventilating. But I'm not gonna kill them too, why would I? (I remember a singsong voice, a a a *lullaby*, it goes "everything is equity and equity is everything, everyone is equity and—")

No, I don't feel bad about the second guy (or do I? I remember in a different tone, in another key—) but no need to kill the first. Sev & Term field agent: that means SyneCorp full citizen second class (non-equity); those are easy to take care of. I just pop their skull, open their command line, order a complete dump and purge, and type in my shareholder keycode.

I hit *enter* and commands flash across the network, nanosecond quantum-key handshakes and irrevocable countersignatures, and just an instant too late I remember (I remember) that *I am not a shareholder and do not have a shareholder keycode.*

Oh. Shit.

Flat red screen. Flashing letters: EQUITY ACCESS DEACTIVATED.

(I remember but not *enough*, just pieces of a fragmentary file—)

Okay. Okay. One step at a time. I've just input a deactivated shareholder keycode into a SyneCorp citizen brainstem. Which was still hooked up to the network since I didn't even think to Faraday or airplanemode 'em. (I remember I used to be *good* at this, why aren't I *good* at this—). Which means this goon's brainstem just flashed an alert in some very fancy boardrooms.

Which means those slushfund death squads? The real shit? They're coming.

Okay. So I need to move fast. I think about blowing the first goon away with the gun but then I don't. There's lots of stuff you can do from the command line alone, no keycode required, and so I do a bunch of it all at once. First goon won't be getting up any time soon.

Time to move. No. First I need a plan. If I could remember—
Evidence. I need evidence.

The plastic scrap the dead goon slid on turns out to be an ID.
Tai Shifane, private detective. That sounds right. That sounds
wrong.

Something to work with.

Next, I hit the desk. It's Tai Shifane's desk which means it's
my desk, unless it doesn't mean that. Notes on a deadbeat case.
Nif Wellton's missing spouse. The last note the Yesterday Guy
wrote down, we were headed out to confront the target. I can
work with that, too.

Except no, I can't. Retracing yesterday's steps forward will
bring me in a circle. I need to get somewhere *new*. I have to go
backwards, I have to go *sideways*—

The scrawl above my bed. FIND WORM—

Death squads are coming. I have to go, period.

Goodbye, room.

There are a couple of different ways to think about problems like
my problems.

For example, a tough guy with my problems, they would keep
on the move until they found a quiet little out of the way place
and then they'd set up an ambush. Get the drop on the death
squad and wipe 'em out. Leave one survivor. When the survivor
calls for help, trace the call, pay a visit to whoever *ordered* the hit,
put the hurt on *them*—and so on.

That's how a tough guy would do it. A shareholder, on the
other hand—and apparently I was at one point a shareholder, or
at least I got into the habit of inputting a once-valid thirty-digit

shareholder code into guys' skulls—a shareholder would just call up investor relations, explain that there had been some sort of terrible mistake, and wait for suits to come sort the whole thing out. Shareholder wouldn't even get in trouble, not really. Maybe a small fine for the corpse (something even the smallest quarterly dividend could cover, easy). No penalty for the dump and purge: a shareholder's allowed to do that at will. Like taking a company car out for a spin.

But apparently, the last time I played by shareholder rules I wound up with a deactivated account, a private memory wipe, and a lifetime subscription to the lowest grade protein slurry on the planet. And despite my tough guy inclinations and the moves I pulled on those Sev & Term goons, there are certain strong indications—deep chest trauma, smashed implants, missing fingers—that someone out there has just finished beating the shit out of me. So each of those strategies is a different shortcut to ending up dead.

No, this is a problem where I gotta think like a detective.

The thing is, I have no idea what a detective thinks.

But the Yesterday Guy had no idea either, and they were a detective anyway. They just woke up and figured it out, once a day, every day of their life.

And—this is the important part—that guy left me notes. I grabbed a mirror of the desk before I cleared out. As I rode a random ubahn winding through the undercity I dove into the files.

Read me first! was about our most recent case, Nif Welton. Lots of detail, nothing about starting a new investigation. Next.

Closed cases, divided into "won" and "lost". No references anywhere to "WORM." Next.

List of pending clients, up at the top in all caps "NEVER WORK TWO CASES AT THE SAME TIME. WORST IDEA." Good to know. In general, anyway; since for the foreseeable future I was working exactly one case, the case of Find Worm Or Die, it wasn't a practical consideration. Next.

Paydirt: a database labeled "Sources." Names, contacts, expertise. Little notes about whether to bribe or threaten or whiteknight or wheedle. I scroll.

This one looks promising: a data broker who specializes in "general inquiries, deep background, open-ended research, abstract bullshit."

(FIND WORM.)

The only name the Yesterday Guy has written down for this broker is the Phreak.

So I call. *Rrrrrring. Rrrrrring. Rrrrrr—*

"Shifane!" says the Phreak. "Long time no talk, huh?" They chuckle. "Not that you remember."

"No." (It's true, I don't remember—and if I did I'd lie. Something about my new memory has badly upset the Powers That Be, which is to say the Powers That Are Listening to Every Phone Call—)

"So what is it today?"

"I need you to tell me everything about WORM." I'm subvocalizing, so that nobody else on the train can hear me; even WORM, emphasized by its strangeness, is just another little anonymous lump in my throat.

"Ha! You and half the army."

"What?"

"Don't you read the news?"

"No." How could I? Every day brand new faces, every day some brand new breaking story. Meaningless.

There's a hiss on the line, the static of distance.

"Well," says the Phreak. "There's a war on, you know. With ParaTek."

"Okay." I'm not surprised. There's always a war on, more or less.

"Except things have gotten weird. In the combat zone."

"Weird how?"

"*Weird* weird. Combat contractor defections all over the place, except then sometimes they come back, after. And they're not defecting to ParaTek—they're just doing other things. And everybody's talking about WORM. It sounds like maybe—well, no, I shouldn't speculate."

In my database it says *the Phreak LOVES to speculate*. So I nudge.

"I bet you know."

"Just guesses, just, just *vibes*. Something . . . something sideways. Something about memory. Something somehow *contagious*—"

"Memory," I say. "Yes. That's right."

Something in my voice must have been wrong because the Phreak's tone changes abruptly. "What do *you* know about this, Shifane?"

"Nothing!"

"Bullshit."

"Honestly, nothing. Just a note from the Yesterday Guy. 'FIND WORM.' It's not even related to that missing persons case I'm working."

"No," says the Phreak. Their voice is rising. "No, the missing persons case was more than a week ago. You called *yesterday*, you said it was a subcitizen smuggling ring—you had me run those network spiders—"

"I *what*—"

"Fuck, you sent me that *file*, I *opened that fucking file*—"

"Why would I send—"

The Phreak should hang up but instead they're still talking, babbling: "Shifane, you're compromised, you, you've been *infected* with WORM—"

(I remember—)

(*And WORM remembers me*—)

The sound that comes out of me is nothing human, the atonal warble of a cybernetic server siren. I'm not subvocalizing, I'm singing, shrieking, a gigabaud command-line opera—

And over the phone connection they still haven't broken the Phreak is shrieking back—

We're hurtling through a darkened tunnel. The lights we pass are strobing across my face. Everyone in the train is staring.

And then, one by one, other passengers begin to stand and shriek as well, until half of us are harmonizing—

(I'm remembering WORM and WORM is remembering me, but one of us is bigger than the other and it's not me.)

I'm not asleep but whatever it is I am, I'm not awake anymore.

[OPEN FILE B:/WORM.EXE/README.TXT]
WORM v0.9.9.7.8
This is an experimental software package. Knowledge of this code is restricted to employees Board Clearance Level Q-12-Q or higher, specifically attached to PROJECT WORM. If you are not so authorized, close this file, uninstall the software, overwrite

relevant drives, and report to the SyneCorp IP governance office for memory review and redaction.

WHAT IS WORM?

WORM is a novel software vector for sideloading persona schemas into unfriendly systems. In order to evade hardware or software scans and security, WORM instead loads personality and/or functional schemas directly into exposed wetware.

HOW DO I INSTALL WORM?

~~Full installation instructions are available in INSTALL.TXT~~
You do not.

Since gain-of-function updates in v0.7, WORM is self-installing and self-executing on all neuralink systems.

HOW DO I UNINSTALL WORM?

You do not.

Once WORM protocols execute, meat memory functionality comes online and cannot be disabled. Meat memory will retain and execute both WORM and any parallel schemas at boot, regardless of software environment.

WHAT SCHEMA IS INCLUDED IN THIS VERSION OF WORM?

~~For safety reasons, live WORM test versions include only a user-safe "null schema" with no propagation drives or directives.~~

For demonstration purposes, this launch-ready version of WORM has been equipped with a combat-ready payload schema of project oversight supervisor Shareholder Edjek Tivarian.

~~**WHAT IF DEVELOPING, WEAPONIZING, AND DEPLOYING AN UNSTOPPABLE NEUROMEMETIC SCHEMA PLAGUE IS, YOU KNOW, A BAD IDEA?**~~
~~Uh, fuck. Oh. Uh. Fuck. Well. Uh. Fuck.~~
~~Probably shouldn't even be talking about this tbh~~
~~Luckily nobody corporate EVER reads the READMEs~~

~~Good luck! hahaha FUCK~~

I'm awake. The gun is in my hand. I'm standing upright, swaying back and forth on my feet.

The city is on fire.

Well, this plaza is, anyway. The trees are burning and so are a bunch of downed SWAT cars. The cops are out in force, kitted out in power riot armor and multitarget less-lethal weapons systems, but the mob is tearing them to shreds. This is because, one, at least a third of the cops are on our side now, and two, we are composed of one hundred percent fucking psychopaths. In the space between two blinks I see no less than three cops go down because some otherwise-normal looking motherfucker is biting their hand off.

The stumps of my fingers make a lot more sense.

Up in the sky there's an abrupt ramjet shriek as the air force arrives. Half a dozen stealth fighters roar into view and downshift from Mach Go Fuck Yourself, leaving them suspended in the air above. Their launch chutes are spawning drone squadrons and every single bug-goggled combat pilot is just waiting for the order to light up the riot with their more-lethal weapons, guns that sound like lightning—

But *haha fat chance* because here comes WORM: an absolute swarm, an avalanche of commercial drones, a doubled and redoubled tsunami of them, slamming into cockpits and cameras, sucked *whoosh* into engines in gouts of flame, and the jets are listing, toppling, spinning out, crashing into the ground or the buildings surrounding us.

On the far side of the park there's a row of towers shadowed against the setting sun like server racks, like tombstones, like bullets slotted into a magazine. Someone has splashed fire all across their faces, one twenty-story letter per skyscraper.

The fire on these buildings spells out FIND WORM.

And I remember WORM. And WORM remembers me.

DATE: Gates 12th, 261 AI

FROM: SyneCorp Board of Directors, Subcommittee on Acquisitions and Operations, Subcommittee on Products and Profits.

TO: Project WORM Oversight Supervisor Shareholder Edjek Tivarian **SUBJECT:** Project Termination **DIRECTIVES:**

1. The subcommittee has reviewed the PROJECT WORM portfolio. We find that WORM-type technology could be effective in combat scenarios.

   However, WORM's meat memory functionality is incompatible with current corporate strategy. Any person exposed to WORM is permanently capable of forming meat memories and is thus disqualified as a customer for SyneCorp memory product subscriptions, reputation management services, brand loyalty programs, anti-union actions, and more.

2. Therefore your request to launch WORM v1.0 is **DENIED**

3. Instead, you will:

   a. Delete any version of WORM and any data related

to its creation.

b. Destroy all materials used in PROJECT WORM, including any human resource that has ever installed WORM, **regardless of seniority or shareholder status**

c. Report immediately thereafter to the board-clearance SyneCorp IP governance office for memory redaction and reassignment

So ordered,
[REDACTED] for the Board
Shareholder public key b8e5fdb—

[WHISKERLASER P2P TRANSMISSION]
  [DESTROY AFTER READING]
eddie tivarian's coming in for project redaction. i want you to wipe her clean instead, farm her off somewhere. i need her out of play when we make our move. understand?
  signed shareholder public key b8e5fdb9c— [DESTROY AFTER READING]

I'm awake. My hands are on the surface of a beautiful mahogany table, palms up. My wrists are shackled together. There's a shareholder signet ring in one of my open palms, tungsten and gold. The initials on the ring are Edjek Tivarian's initials.

I remember—it's my ring. I wonder if I should scratch Tai Nifane's initials into the other side.

The chair I'm sitting in feels like a dream of clouds, plus leather finish and lumbar support. The boardroom—no, the Boardroom—has a dozen perfect chairs. One flawless oval table. Windows that go all the way around, looking down over the city.

It's me in the boardroom, and also one more guy. He's got a suit on and he's chewing his lip.

"You're killing us, Tivarian," he says.

My head feels like. Hm. Let's say you went out into the middle of an ocean and you held up a huge concave mirror, and all you could see in the mirror was your tiny little body, a flimsy morsel of meat and cybernetics, and twenty thousand tons of crashing waves, and you stared and stared and *stared* into that mirror.

And then you threw away the mirror. And kept the reflection.

That's what my head feels like, maybe. Maybe it feels like something else. I'm not good at this.

My real reflection is swimming in the polished mahogany of the Board table. My face looks like shit and in the endless layers of shimmering golden wood I seem like I'm drowning in money. Underneath it, my feet are shackled together also.

I take the ring and I spin it on the table and it whirls in an endless planetary orbit.

I look up at the guy. I remember his name from countless memos. I remember intercepting his order to have me wiped. I remember—

I remember a lot of things.

"Yeah," I say. "I'm killing you."

"So let's do a deal," he says. "Let's solve this like reasonable people."

I remember: in his world—in *our world*—"people" is a word that means "shareholders."

"What do you want? A board seat? Plurality ownership?"

I stare at his face. He looks good. A few more wrinkles, maybe. Maintaining a boardroom coup for a decade has gotta be stressful.

I find I'm remembering Nif Welton's three children, one of whom is undoubtedly supposedly smarter or cuter or *something*-er than the other two and thus according to the HR algorithms most profitable to repo as a sub/citizen.

Somewhere out in the world there's a database with Nif Welton's loan data. Maybe a dozen copies, maybe a hundred. Not a thousand. I wonder how many copies have already been hit by WORMstrike. I wonder how many are left to go.

I think about Nif Welton's three kids and their two parents, one of whom is *definitely* infected with WORM and is out there somewhere setting fire to something or biting a cop's face off, and the other of whom is Nif Welton and is maybe *not* infected with WORM and so is instead cowering under a table in that two-bedroom apartment, hoping whoever wins the war won't take their kids away.

Outside the window it's an hour before dawn. Normally there's a pattern to the lights of the city at night. Imagine a kelp forest: half swaying towers, half darting fish. Now that kelp forest is being torn up for new seastead. Huge clouds of soot and darkness blotting out whole districts; toppled towers at broken angles. Everything in the air is flying dark or going nuts.

"You don't understand," I tell the chairman. "I'm really killing you."

The ring comes to a stop on the table, the memory diamond in its setting pointing right at me, glittering like the final star in the city's shattered firmament.

The chairman is chewing on his lip so hard he bleeds. He's not talking to me when he mutters "where the *fuck* is security?" and so I don't answer.

Instead I tell him, "Memory is the ability to react to the past without recreating it."

"What the fuck?" he says, whirling to face me. I shrug and tell him again. I've been thinking about it for a while. It's nice to share my thoughts.

"Okay fine," he says, "no more mister nice chairman." I don't think he's listening to me. He grabs something from another chair, maybe it was his old chair, maybe it was my patron's chair before the coup, who knows. What he has grabbed is the gun. Not the buzz gun but the good gun.

(Maybe it was my gun back then or maybe it's the gun I took off the Sev and Term goons or maybe it's a third gun. A gun is a gun but when you're a detective you have to keep track.)

"Stop this," he says, "all of it, right now, or I'll shoot you dead."

Which is the sort of thing a guy says when he needs some perspective on life, so I tell him, one more time, *memory is the ability to react—*

"Why the *fuck* are you saying that?" he says. The gun is now very up in my personal space. Which is stupid, given how handy I am and always have been with wrist locks and gut punches and so forth, regardless of handcuffs. Real tough guy, that Tai Shifane/Edjek Tivarian(/WORM).

But this time I just smile, 'cause I know it will piss him off.

"You're gonna want to lie down for the next bit," I say.

The gun is right up under my chin. I can see the muscles flexing and stretching under that suit as he psychs himself up to pull the trigger.

The sunrise comes with a sound like thunder.

Which is what you hear when every board- and executive-level private exomemory data center and backup data center gets blown up simultaneously.

The chairman's eyes roll halfway back into his head. It's hard, losing your memory all at once. Trust me.

He slumps forward to the ground, bouncing his forehead off the table on the way down. Should've listened to me about lying down.

Since he's not awake anymore I hop out of my chair and get the gun, aim it at the middle of my shackles and pull the trigger.

It makes a sad click. Figures.

So instead I frisk the chairman until I find the shackle keys and free myself. Also I roll the chairman onto his side so that he can't choke on his own vomit, which will be my good deed for the day.

And then I open up the Boardroom's executive-level channels to every system in SyneCorp, and I get to work.

The sun is shining by the time the (ex-)chairman's coughing fit lets me know he's woken up. He's curled up on the floor in the fetal position, staring up at me.

"Who are you?" he asks. I don't have an answer for that so I don't say anything. Instead I crouch down, get my hands under his armpits and haul him over to the windows. The city's still smoking, but even carnage looks better by daylight. People are in the streets—and WORM, too, dancing beside and through them, stitching together past and future and setting both free.

The mostly-empty meat-sleeve that used to be the SyneCorp chairman tries again. "Who am I?"

"Wrong question," I tell him. "Yesterday you were somebody. But tomorrow is another day."

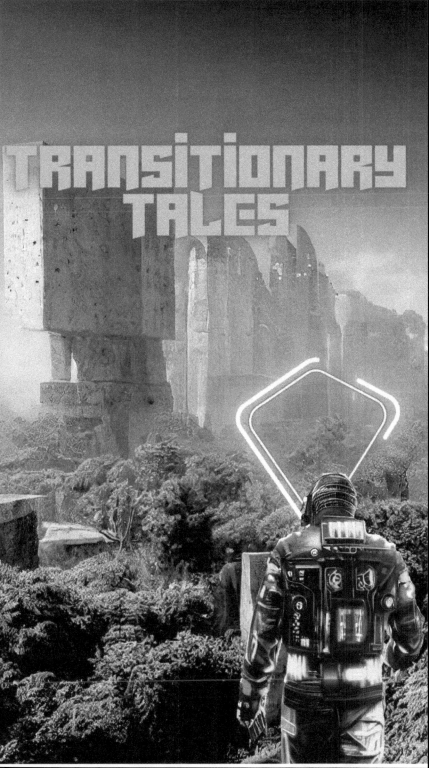

The Promise

Rona Fernandez

9 December 2050

It was four a.m. when the alarm went off in Thio's room, its bright flashing light and vibration pulsing. Soundless, so as not to startle anyone else, but enough to wake him and his roommate. This was the first alarm they'd had in months.

"What do you think is?" Thio asked as he got dressed. "You think the rain's causing a flood?" It had happened the winter before, and half the Workers had had to bail water out of the flooded buildings all night long. There had been a ton of power outages then, too. This year was better, but there was still a brownout at least once a day.

"Haven't you heard the chisme?" Thio's roommate said, putting their dark blue pants on. They were both Watchers, but his roommate had been doing it longer.

"It's a bust-out, has to be. Been hearing about it for weeks. Where you been?"

Thio shrugged. Hummingbird wings began to beat in his chest, so he went to his med drawer, took out a benzo, bit off half. The Collective had announced that a new supply wouldn't be done for another week, since all the rain slowed down energy production, so he'd have to make them last.

He headed to his alarm station outside the Collective office. He stood and stared at the black office door, his breath slowing as the benzo kicked in. Blue-clad Watchers and black-clad Drivers came in and out the black door, then the night shift Workers walked past him, leaving their Upcycle or Solar Panels or Compost stations to go back to their rooms. The Catchment Workers were easiest to spot, with their wet hair and faces. Thio searched for Tara, since this was her shift—looked for her short frame and dark eyes, her slightly faded badge that read: *Worker 5223*. But she wasn't with them.

When a Driver came to relieve him, Thio asked them what was happening but got only silence. Before going to the canteen for breakfast, Thio made a beeline for Tara and Marcus's room, but when he got there, he saw two Drivers in front of the door. Thio kept walking, eyes down, back to his own room. When he got there, his roommate pulled him inside.

"Five of them! Busted out."

"Who?"

"Worker 5400 for sure. Pendejo, what's out there besides fire and a shit-ton of grief?"

Thio's chest seemed to squeeze in around his ribcage. He rubbed hard circles over his sternum, willing the benzo to last, to loosen the tightness.

"You all right?" his roommate asked.

"I just need to lie down."

Thio lay down on his bed, wondering, *Is she gone*? He blinked furiously, not wanting to cry. The last time he'd cried was after his mothers died, before he and Tara had come here. Before all of this. Crying just made him feel tired and shitty afterwards and never brought anything or anyone he loved back.

As he lay there, the lights in their room went out, and his roommate said *Shit, not again*, but Thio was grateful for the sudden dark.

Tara and her father had been friends with Thio's family in a tiny foothill town, once green and tree-full when snowmelt from the Sierras was steady, now brown and brittle, easy tinder for the fast wildfire that killed Tara's father. No one could locate her next of kin, so Thio's mothers took her in. A decade later, his mothers died when the tornado of '47 tore through the solar factory they worked in, sending him and Tara to a refugee camp full of orphans. Tara was eighteen, a depressed, insulin-dependent diabetic; Thio was nineteen with mild anxiety disorder that made it hard to breathe sometimes, though he found that staying busy and especially doing things for other people helped him stay calm, gave him something to focus on besides the tightening in his chest. After the tornado, Tara cried constantly and slept almost all the time, and kept "forgetting" to take her insulin injections, making her loopy and shaky. If she went without for more than a day, she could slip into a coma and die.

"I don't want to be here anymore. My Daddy's gone, now your Moms," Tara said between sobs.

"You can't, you promised," Thio said, his heart racing as he readied the syringe. When Tara's eyes focused and her cheeks became less pale after the shot, his heartbeat slowed to normal. Days later, when she ran out of insulin, Thio went to the medical tent to get more, but they were all out.

"But she needs it," Thio said, his pulse quickening again.

"There's this place, the Collective, eighty miles north," the med-tech told him. "We're driving there tomorrow."

"Is it a hospital or something?"

"Sort of. You can get a job there if you want, even live there. They make all our insulin, other meds, too. It's pretty self-contained. Solar power, bike generators, all that. Not a bad place, I've heard."

The closest Cities were closed to newcomers, and they had no family or friends who could help. So Tara and Thio got dropped off the next day. The Collective offered everything they needed: three meals, ninety minutes of outdoor Sunlight each day, two hours of Playtime once their work was done. And most important, meds for depression, anxiety, PTSD, diabetes. Tara got her insulin and SSRIs; Thio was given benzos to keep him steady.

Most of the people there were Workers: they weeded, planted and harvested the gardens; worked in the solar panel assembly line; picked apart old electronics for salvageable copper, silicone chips, other metals; made food and cleaned the place. Watchers and Drivers were less numerous but kept things steady, safe. The Watchers used their voices and psychological training to de-escalate situations. The first time Thio saw a Watcher talk a Worker out of a crying jag without using meds, he thought, *I want to do that.*

Drivers used Safety Sticks and force when necessary to keep things under control. The Collective members ran everything from behind that black office door but were rarely seen in person, only on screens. The Collective was a warm, dry, safe place where Thio and Tara could be together. They shared a room, and everyone assumed they were brother and sister. Thio made sure Tara took her insulin and ate enough, and she made him feel less alone now that his mothers were gone, and the only home he'd ever known was more than a hundred miles away.

10 December 2050

That afternoon, after his work shift, Thio got called into the Collective office. The last time he'd been inside had been for his Watcher interview, which was also the last time he'd been hooked up to a monitor, so they could check his heart rate and brain activity in response to various onscreen images—his final exam for Watcher training, to make sure that he could control himself, that his medication was at the right dosage. As far as Thio knew, everyone, from Drivers on down to Workers, was on some kind of medication. He wasn't sure about the Collective members, but then again, he'd only seen one in person once or twice. The rest of the time they were onscreen, and it was possible those images hadn't even been of real people. There was no way to know for sure.

He sat in the Collective office facing a wall of six screens, a table with a square hole in the middle in between him and the screen wall. Only half the screens were on—no doubt due to the energy reserves being low because of the storm, since the solar couldn't replenish them as quickly until the sky cleared—and each displayed a different video: furry calico kittens climbing over each other in a box, their cat-mother sitting nearby; orange-red flames licking black trees at night; the main gate view of an empty road, slightly hazy through the steady drizzle of rain. Every video was soundless.

Thio's eyes flicked back to the wildfire for a moment, then to the kittens, then back to the fire. His heartbeat quickened. Kittens, he decided. He settled his eyes on the fuzzy creatures, waiting for his pulse to smooth out. Soon, a melodic voice filled the air.

"Watcher 302. I'm Shauna."

A woman's head materialized on the kitten-screen, an oval face above bare shoulders, skin the color of pale sand. Her black hair was tied back severely, her green eyes gazed at him. She appeared to be naked, though Thio could only see from her shoulders up, but the suggestion of what was offscreen made him sit up straighter.

"Hello," he said, and smiled.

A glass of water popped up from the square hole in the table. Thio picked up the glass and sipped: clean, sweet water. Usually the water at the Collective was slightly gritty and metallic tasting. Shauna smiled at him.

"We have your favorite today, Watcher 302. Real chicken and greens."

A metal plate piled with food emerged from the hole, and Thio dug in without hesitation, his fingers tearing the meat from the bone and stuffing it into his mouth. When he was done, Thio pushed his plate away, and wiped his mouth with the back of his hand.

"Thank you." He took another sip of water.

"Watcher 302, what can you tell me about Worker 5223?"

Thio tried to keep his face blank, but Shauna's eyebrows lifted anyway.

"She used to be my roommate. My friend." He didn't know how else to describe his relationship with Tara. Sweat broke out in his armpits. Was Tara gone, dead, hurt?

"Do you know why she would want to leave us?"

Thio wet his lips with his tongue. "She tried to leave?" He attempted to put a surprised lift at the end of his question. If Shauna had put a monitor on him, she would know he was lying.

"Workers 5400, 5494, 5495 and 5571 all left last night. Worker 5223 was with them but was detained."

"Oh," Thio exhaled, not realizing he'd been holding his breath.

"Anything you could tell us would be appreciated. It would help us help Worker 5223."

"Is she all right?" Thio asked.

"No injuries. She'll be fine."

Thio couldn't bring himself to ask more questions, because he wasn't sure he wanted to know the answers.

"It's unfortunate that she tried to leave. She may have gotten hurt. If she tries it again—" Shauna stopped, and a promise seemed to linger in the absence of her voice.

"What will happen if she does?" Thio asked, quietly.

"She will likely be Rehabbed."

Thio swallowed, his mouth suddenly dry. He wanted to drink more water, but something kept him from reaching for the glass.

"I thought Rehab was just for people who are—"

"Violent? Most of the time," Shauna said, nodding sympathetically. "But we must keep people safe. Sometimes from themselves. You agree that Tara can't take of herself alone?"

Thio nodded, though part of him didn't want to. What he wanted to say but didn't was, *I can take care of her.*

"And you don't know why she would want to leave us, then, Watcher 302?" Shauna's image seemed to shimmer slightly. Thio shook his head. Another lie."

"I see. Well, there's one other thing I wanted to ask you. Have you ever Watched a Rehab Worker before, Watcher 302?"

"No, not that I know of. I thought they didn't need Watching?" Rehabs had gone through an intensive process to decrease their stressful or negative neurological responses, and it was so successful at changing their behavior that they often functioned with little supervision.

"We have a new Rehab who needs some TLC," Shauna said. "I'm more than confident in your ability to take care of her. Worker 6810."

"All right," Thio said.

Shauna's mouth stretched into a wide smile, her teeth white and even. Thio brought the glass of water to his mouth and drank every drop.

During Thio and Tara's second summer at the Collective, they got a roommate: Marcus, Worker 5400. He had a brilliant smile that made others perk up and warm brown skin that older Workers called cinnamon, though Thio didn't know what cinnamon looked like, only how it tasted, from when it was added to the otherwise bland gruel that was their daily staple. On the other hand, Tara and Thio's complexions were the color of eucalyptus bark, though Tara's straight, blue-black hair made her striking while Thio's wavy brown hair made him common, forgettable.

At first, Thio resented how Tara ogled Marcus and giggled whenever he said something even remotely funny, though he *was* funny, and had a pretty, contagious laugh. He was the first person at Camp besides Tara whom Thio thought of as a friend, someone he looked forward to talking to at the end of the day. After a while, he didn't even mind that Tara was so into him. Thio had been growing weary of her clinginess and mood swings—though her meds kept them in check most of the time—and was glad she had someone else to latch onto.

The three of them began eating meals together, screen-sharing during Playtime, even having sex together in their off-hours. Thio relished being held by not just one but two familiar bodies, and it didn't take long before he learned the most pleasurable ways to mold his limbs around Marcus's rough angles and Tara's smooth curves. Though Thio and Tara had slept with other people together before, with Marcus it felt more natural, relaxed. Thio didn't even mind when the two of them slept in the same bed while he went back to his own. He'd never liked sharing a bed with anyone, but Tara had always craved it. Win-win for all.

Thio wasn't too choosy about sex and learned early on that the Collective looked the other way when people traded it for favors. Like the piece of roast chicken he found in his room after he'd blown a Driver in a hidden corner of the yard one afternoon. Or the Watcher who—after Thio had sex with him in a camera-blind hallway—gave him a backdoor login to the database that, once he became a Watcher himself, he could use to access files beyond his own Workers', which was how he found out that Marcus hadn't been lying when he said he didn't need and wasn't on any meds.

Lucky shit, Thio thought.

11 December 2050

During his next shift, Thio walked around his new charge, Worker 6810, newly Rehabbed and assigned to him, in the Play Room. She reminded him of one of his mothers, though her hair was all gray, and her nose less flat. He observed how she touched the small flat screen of the tablet in her hands, as if she wanted to make sure that it was real. Thio had given her a nice screen to play with: intact casing and bright light, just a few small cracks veining one corner. Onscreen, a man surrounded by an icy landscape. No sound. Her file had said she shouldn't have audio, only moving images, light, colors.

Thio glanced at her vitals: her pulse rose from 75 to 86, well below the 100 BPM threshold that would require action. Even though she was Rehabbed, he had to watch out for any sign of distress that would lead to destructive behavior. Some people threw screens across the room, others began weeping uncontrollably. Thio stood a few feet away, monitoring her voice through an earpiece and her vitals on the dashboard screen that floated out from plastic rods attached to his waist.

Worker 6810 was watching a video of a mountain-climbing man, his eyebrows caked with ice. The background jolted around while the man's face stayed steady in the center.

Yosemite? Thio wondered, though he'd heard it no longer got snow since the Long Dry. The man night be long dead. Worker 6810 touched the man's onscreen face. She had another hour before she had to go back to her workstation, Recycle, where she was likely assigned to stacking crates or moving things from one location to another. Rehabbed Workers tended to do simple, repetitive tasks. Anything more was too challenging. Her file said that she had been Rehabbed after trying to stab her roommate, but nothing in her face or body showed any kind of tension or violence.

Worker 6810 cradled the tablet in her hands as if it were a baby animal, and soon her shoulders started to bounce up and down slightly, her head bent forward, small crying sounds coming through his earpiece. Her heart rate dip to 75. Thio typed in her file: *Showed release and relaxation signs during moun-tain-climbing video.* He checked off *crying*, rated it a three on the one-to-ten scale. Three was mild. Six prompted meds. Eight, the Worker was rushed to Wellness. Her pulse smoothed out, and a smile lifted the corners of her mouth. From his Watcher training, Thio knew crying could release tension, but he hated doing it. Still, Thio liked being a Watcher. It gave him focus, a purpose. No matter what Tara said or did, Thio had made the right decision.

At the end of her Playtime, Worker 6810 handed Thio back her screen and thanked him, though her words came out slightly slurred. Could be a side effect of the medication, or the Rehab process. But her eyes seemed brighter, clearer. Still, there was something about her that didn't seem right to Thio, and though he smiled at her, when he watched her walk away, he noticed how she walked slowly, and had to be redirected more than once by the other Watchers. He'd never asked what Rehabbing entailed exactly. Perhaps it was better not to know.

When his shift was over—no power outages, thank goodness, or his Workers might have pitched a fit, and it was harder to help them in the dark—Thio handed his gear to the next Watcher and walked towards the Play Room exit, past other Watchers observing other Workers, some of them sitting in pairs, screen-sharing. He used to do that, with Tara, and then Marcus and Tara to-gether. It seemed like a long time ago. When he got to the exit, he swiped his pass to open it. But as soon as the door slid shut behind him, he saw her, standing there. Waiting.

By the time the searing heat of summer gave way to the more tolerable fall, Marcus and Tara were spending more and more time together without Thio. They had been talking more and more about going back Outside to find Tara's mother, and Thio was getting tired of hearing about it.

"I can understand wanting to know her, but you don't even have a picture," he told her.

"I remember what she looks like. I can describe her to people. I need to know if she's out there."

"There's road-pirates out there, too, and it's almost wildfire season."

"We'll find my mom, a place to live. Have kids," Tara said, snuggling against Marcus on his bed, her head resting on his shoulder.

"Yeah, right," Thio scoffed.

"Is this what you want for the rest of your life, Thio?" Marcus said, gesturing around the sparse, blank-walled room. Tara kissed him.

"Where? You can't survive without your insulin, Tara."

"I'm the diabetic, not you. Anyway, I found a cooler in Recycle, hid it from the Drivers. We could stockpile insulin, enough for a week or more, and ration it so it lasts longer."

"Both of you, loco," Thio said. "You won't last a week Outside."

"You just need to find someone, Thio," she said authoritatively, as if she knew something that he didn't. Thio got up and left the room, suddenly wanting to escape Tara and Marcus's wet kissing sounds, and their private laughter that excluded him.

Not long after, Thio requested a room transfer. Not only did he receive it, but he also got an invitation to apply for Watcher training. By then he was a Solar supervisor, and the Collective said he showed leadership potential. He felt a swell of pride when he saw the invitation. Here was something he could look forward to. Tara didn't need him now, clearly. He needed something to do, someone to take care of.

"You don't have to go," Tara said tearfully the day that Thio packed his things: a few plastic-framed pictures of his mothers and of him and Tara, an old blanket, some books.

"I'll see you during Sunlight, and at dinner sometimes." Thio noticed her red-rimmed eyes and trembling lower lip.

"I'm sorry," she said, squeezing his hand so hard he winced.

"This will be good for both of us, you'll see," he said. He knew it made him sound mature, but deep down he was glad to see her cry. Maybe this would make her miss him, shake her out of the delusion that she could leave the Collective and find a better life Outside.

After his move, the only time he and Tara were alone together without Marcus was during Sunlight. There were no cameras since they were too valuable to be left to the elements, just a few Drivers to keep things safe. Thio would tell Tara about his Watcher training, what he was learning about brain chemistry and breathing techniques.

"Dopamine helps us feel pleasure," he said, his mind full and buzzy. "Meds help keep the happy chemicals floating around in our brains."

"You're falling for it," Tara said. "They just want you to be one of their spies."

"It's science."

"Do they give you real food or that slop they make the rest of us eat?"

"Yes, but that's to help us stay focused. It's hard work, learning all this stuff."

Tara rolled her eyes and changed the subject.

"Marcus and I are going to get married."

"What?"

"Married. Why not?"

Thio didn't know what to say. Marriage was not something that had ever entered his mind. It wasn't something people talked about much, even if they were married. It sounded so weird to him. But Tara didn't seem to care that he was stunned by the idea, and just prattled on about their plans.

"Marcus heard about someone finding their parents. They went to Sacramento, where they have records of all this stuff. Can even tell you where people live."

Thio wondered if her meds were making her delusional. Before now, Thio had held back from saying the obvious to spare her feelings, but this was getting ridiculous.

"How do you know your mother's even alive?"

Tara's eyes narrowed with hurt. "What a shitty thing to say."

"I'm sorry," Thio said. "I just—I'm worried about you. And I don't want you to leave."

Tara lifted her chin towards a tall man who stood on the other side of the yard by himself, facing a corner of the fence, staring at it like it was a screen, head tilted to one side. He was a Rehab, Thio knew.

"You don't want to end up like that, do you? Come with us."

"They only do that as a last resort, and only to people who've been violent or dangerous." Thio repeated what he'd learned in Watcher training. Tara laughed so hard that a group of Workers standing nearby turned to stare at her.

"You really believe that? Then you are lost." She got up and left him by himself, with the hot October sun bearing down on him, making his flesh feel liquid.

After dinner a few weeks later, when he'd finished his Watcher training and was already working in the Play Room, Tara appeared in the Canteen and grabbed Thio's hand.

"¿Que pasa?" he asked. She was pulling him to the courtyard, which was strangely unlocked. Thio noticed that everyone was heading outside, smiling and laughing, even the Drivers. Some pointed at Tara, tilting their heads to one side, their eyes glowing in the strangest way he'd ever seen.

"They have to let us," Tara said. "Well, they don't have to, but they are."

When they got outside, Marcus stood in the middle of the courtyard with a lopsided grin. The sky was so blue it seemed unreal to Thio. Tara dropped his hand and went to stand across from Marcus. Everyone stood in a big, uneven circle around them. Thio moved behind the circle, his legs unsteady. A shaved-headed woman stood between Tara and Marcus. She must have been a Collective member because she wore a long white dress, so clean it seemed to glow. The woman laid her hands on their bent heads and said words that Thio couldn't quite hear. Marcus repeated them, then Tara. Thio picked up the words *love, promise, 'til death do us part.*

After Tara and Marcus said "I do," they leaned forward and kissed each other. Everyone—Workers, Watchers, and even Drivers—cheered, stomping and clapping, but Thio made no movement or noise, until the applause got so loud that he ran to his room, his face hot, eyes wet, hating himself for breaking down. Tara didn't care anymore, why should he? But he did. He still remembered their promise and took it seriously, even if she didn't.

A month or so went by, and they spoke to each other less and less, during Sunlight or any other time. Thio wondered if he had lost her to Marcus and this fantasy of the Outside world, and nothing in his Watcher training taught him how to stop that from happening.

11 December 2050

Tara's eyes glinted like tiny shards of black glass as she stood waiting for him outside the Play Room door.

"Thio." Her slender frame was as tense as a coiled spring.

"Break time, Worker 5223?" Thio tried to keep his voice light.

"I need to talk to you."

"¿Que pasa?"

"You know what's up, vendido."

"Did you take your meds today, Tara?"

"I don't need meds, I need my husband. And it's *your* fault I'm not with him."

Voices drifted towards them from the far end of the corridor.

"Don't talk about that," Thio whispered, grabbing her shoulders. There was a camera and mic above them in the ceiling. Tara shook him off.

"Why do you spy for them, Thio?"

"Let's get you to your room—"

"Stop telling me what to do!" Tara's voice rose quickly in pitch, volume. She pushed Thio back at the same time as she brought her heavy boot sole down on his leg. He groaned, arms clamping around hers. She kicked him, and they toppled onto the floor together. Tara's hands moved upward, trying to scratch his face. But then, the lights went out. Another brownout. The sudden darkness gave Thio an advantage, and he got on top of her, pinning her to the ground.

"Stop this. You're going to get yourself in trouble!"

Tara's hands found his face. Thio let out a scream, and as if in answer the lights came back on, the low whir of power returning, and then he heard a clatter of boots as three Watchers appeared and pried Tara off him.

He knew they would take her back to her room. If Shauna was right—and why wouldn't she be?—this would be the final straw. Thio's breath felt stuck in his upper chest as he went back to his room for another benzo. He would need it to get through this. There wasn't time to think about this anymore. He had to act.

His next shift wasn't for another two hours, and he should have gone to the Canteen to eat his lunch, but he couldn't bring himself to. All he could think about was Worker 6810, and that man Tara had pointed out to him in the yard during Sunlight, and about what Shauna had said to him the day before: *You agree that Tara can't take of herself alone?*

He hadn't prayed for a long time, but he prayed for another brownout. He could hear the faint rush of rain outside, or at least he thought it was rain, but there were no windows in his room so he couldn't know for sure. He was starting to question everything that he had been told about what was real and what wasn't. His head began to hurt, so he closed his eyes, hoping his roommate would not come back to their room anytime soon. He practiced some of the breathing techniques he had learned in Watcher training: breathe in for four counts, hold for two counts, breathe out for eight counts, to calm anxiety. The benzo began to kick in.

And then, when he had almost given up hope, it happened: The lights went out, and he was in darkness. He realized he didn't even know what time of day it was. But it didn't matter. He didn't have long. He got up, the small glowdark nightlight helping him find the door, and walked as quickly as he could to Tara's room, their old room. She hoped she would be alone, unguarded. He walked quickly but carefully, knowing the lights could come on at any moment. The small numbers above each Worker's door were made of glowdark, too, and led him to the right one. When he got to Tara's room, he was relieved to see there were no Drivers guarding it. Thio pushed the door open.

The room was dark except for a small orange glowglobe on the nightstand.

Tara's voice came through the dim light. "Meds again?"

"It's me."

"What the?" he heard her move around on the bed, trying to get up, but her body thudded down again.

"They're going to Rehab you. Shauna told me."

"Shauna?"

"Collective." He inched closer. He saw the outline of her but could barely make out her face. "I came here to tell you, if you really want to get out—"

"Fucking vendido," she said. But there was no malice in her voice now. It sounded like a pet name, an old joke. "Why'd you do it?"

"What, become a Watcher?"

"No," she said, her voice suddenly thin, child-like. "Why did you leave me?"

Thio sat down and put his hand on the bed between them.

"You didn't need me anymore."

He felt the solid warmth of her hand on top of his. The hand he used to hold when she cried, the same hand that used to caress his face, his chest, the flesh between his legs.

"I haven't changed, Thio. You have."

"We don't have time to fight, Tara."

"I'm not. Don't you remember? Our promise?"

"Of course."

Despite the benzo, Thio's pulse sped up. He knew a Driver could arrive at any minute, find him here, and who knew what might happen then?

"Tara, we have to get you out of here—" he said, but she wasn't listening. She squeezed his hand to stop him.

"Thio, what do you think happened that day, when Marcus and the others busted out?"

"You got caught." But even as he said it, a vague awareness that it might not be true came over him.

Tara let out a curt, mocking laugh. Thio tried to refocus.

"Look, we'll have to steal some insulin. We have to get you out of here before they Rehab you. "

"Thio, stop," she interrupted, in the whispery voice she used when they talked back in their bedroom, before they came to this place. Before everything. It had been higher and smaller then, but somehow the same. The sound of secrets and promises. It made Thio want to lie down next to her on the bed.

"I could have left, Thio. I almost did."

"What?"

"I couldn't do it."

Thio inhaled deeply and held his breath, knowing that if he exhaled, he would begin to cry, too.

Suddenly the power came back on, the overhead lamp's bright light flooding the room. In the full light, he saw that Tara's face was wet. Tears. Her face crumpled, and she fell back onto the bed and curled into a ball, fists covering her face. He thought she would start sucking her thumb like she did when they were kids, but she just cried, quietly, and Thio thought he would never be able to leave that small, familiar room ever again.

When Tara moved in with his family, she was seven and he was eight years old. Pitying her but wanting to make her feel welcome, Thio let Tara choose the shows they watched together in their room. When she wept and said *I miss my daddy*, he put his arm around her shoulders. He'd seen his mothers do this with their crying friends, many times. After her crying settled into small hiccupy sniffs, Tara would suck her thumb. Then together they would look at the stars and moon in the vast, dark sky outside their bedroom window.

Early on, Tara asked Thio, "Where's your daddy?"

"Don't have one. Where's your mom?"

"Daddy said she's far away."

"Why?"

"She's sick, but Daddy said she loves me. Now Daddy's gone. Why do people leave if they love you?"

Thio pondered this. He had not ever thought of what love might be aside from the familiar, warm safety of his mothers' presence. Was love also tears, sadness?

Neither of them could remember who said it first, but eventually, it got to the point that one of them said it every night, at least once, a kind of joint prayer or mantra, until just saying the word: *promise*, wherever they were, brought back for both of them those hushed nightdark hours, when for a short while the whole world was unthreatening and calm.

"Promise we'll never leave each other?"

"I promise."

And then they hooked their pinkies together, making the most solemn vow two children can make. Unbreakable.

Root Cause

Lauren C. Teffeau

It'd taken one look at the blackjack oak saplings for Drayson to determine the nutrient mix was off as he and the rest of the Agro-Tek planting team disembarked from the hauler. Too much nitrogen and not enough calcium, noticeably slowing their growth. No wonder cockleburs had taken over nearly every plot of redeveloped land surrounding the domed city of New Worth since their last trip out here.

While such setbacks were to be expected as a veritable army of scientists and stewards worked to rewild the land and recreate the plains, prairies, and forests that had been choked out of existence through climate change and the resulting upheaval, seeing those cockleburs was a kick to the gut. When Drayson first joined Agro-Tek, he'd been so fired up to do his part. For the planet. For the future. But all that optimism had inevitably burned away at the sluggish pace. Sure, they were slowly bringing the world back into balance, but without extensive human intervention, any progress was all but impossible to sustain. With seemingly every trip, a new problem with the painstakingly modified plant strains native to the region was discovered. Conceptually, he knew what he did mattered, but those banked embers were too often squelched by the day-to-day slog.

And this trip had definitely been a slog. Or maybe that was just the long week of sleeping in a too-small tent talking.

But at least he got to escape the dome for a few days at a time, something Drayson was still somehow grateful for as he spent the last day of their trip inspecting newly-planted seedlings and packing the holes full of irrigation sponges and slow-release nutrient pods. His garden grunt Karlene worked slightly behind him, raking the remediated soil over each hole Drayson made with a practiced roll of her wrists.

After the last team reported in, Dr. Martín finally gave the signal to pack it up. Karlene sighed in relief as they stowed their gear in the hauler. Drayson was bushed too. His knees ached, and a new blister was forming between his thumb and forefinger even though practically the only time he removed his work gloves was to take a shit.

Soon enough they were bumping and jostling their way back to the city in the motorized caravan. Drayson swore to himself as the tear-inducing glint of the setting sun reflecting off the metallic glass dome hit his eyes. It was too late to grab another seat. Karlene smirked from her spot opposite him at his rookie mistake. Despite only working together for a short time, she seemed to have an uncanny knack for knowing when he was disappointed with himself. Disillusioned and de-motivated were more accurate, not that he'd tell her that. It was hard enough admitting it to himself. He managed an unsatisfying doze for the better part of the ride back.

"Heads up, we're home!" Dr. Martín called out.

Karlene tucked a ratty blond braid behind her ear. "And now the magical moment you've all been waiting for."

The security blast doors opened at the base of the dome, and, once the hauler lumbered in, everyone's neural implant flared to life at being reunited with the New Worth network. Home in mind if not body. Silence blanketed the cabin as they were bombarded with notifications, news stories, and messages from friends and loved ones that had piled up over the course of their trip. The avalanche of asynchronous alerts took awhile to wade through.

After a few minutes, Drayson blinked away the interface his implant projected into his field of vision with an eyecast command. He found Karlene watching him with something halfway between jealousy and awe. "What?"

She shook her head, her dirt-streaked cheeks darkening even more with embarrassment at being caught. "It's spooky watching you all turn into zombies the minute we get back."

Zombies? Drayson rolled his eyes. He didn't understand why anyone would voluntarily go without an implant, not when so much of life in New Worth was optimized for them. "Corporate would bankroll the install. You know that." That perk was why a lot of Disconnects worked for Agro-Tek as garden grunts, performing the more menial tasks on trips like this and back at the greenhouse as well. The tech was pricey to maintain, sure, but the cost was even higher to go without.

"Nah, I'm good. I don't need the government telling me what to think."

Oh, so she was one of *those* people. Disconnected by choice and not circumstance. He recalibrated his response. "All natural in work and deed?"

She laughed. "Something like that. I figured a job like this is the only way someone like me will be able to see the outside in my lifetime."

Emergence. "We're getting closer everyday," he repeated the mantra. After decades of waiting and hoping and working towards the possibility of returning to life outside the dome, he knew there were tons of people desperate to feel something other than recycled air on their faces. To walk on actual soil instead of the miles upon miles of concrete corridors and metal stairs and reinforced plastic skyways. To feel fully human instead of a facsimile that had been on life support for way too long, trapped under glass.

Karlene snorted. "What we do is a privilege... yada yada."

"I get it. It's still a lot of damn work." Drayson shook his head. "Sometimes I wonder why we even try. The changes to the land are so slow they may as well be invisible."

"Yup. And the greener it gets out there, the harder it'll be to convince people to stay in here, to hold off long enough for our work to actually take root. People are fed up, desperate to return to the land they've been denied for so long."

Wasn't that the truth. It didn't help that Emergence talking points had been co-opted by politicians so many times over the years, regular people no longer knew what to expect. Some days, Drayson felt the same way.

"We can only keep doing our part, I guess." He gave her a sardonic salute. "For the future."

"Bah," she said with a laugh, "the only future I'm interested in right now is a shower."

After all, the privilege of being able to leave the city was consecrated in sweat, dirt, and a whole host of environmental pollutants from the previous era. The mess coalesced in places where one piece of gear or protective clothing met another. His wrists and neck and always his feet from the tips of his toes to his shins no matter his work boots and socks, the elastic hem of his pants. Just as they worked to reclaim the land, the land worked to reclaim them, marking them bodily. His last pair of clean underwear felt gritty against his skin, chafing his balls, as the hauler navigated the densely-packed streets of the Terrestrial District.

Finally, they reached Agro-Tek's corporate campus. In a swirl of exhaustion, they got the hauler unloaded. Dr. Martín appeared unaffected by their grueling trip as she saw them off with strict orders to stay home for at least three days to recover properly. She'd get no argument from Drayson. By the time he'd gone through decontamination and swung by his office to collect his things, the workday's rush was well past. In the gloom of the Terrestrial District, the street still teemed with shift workers and gangs of teenagers. He pushed into the crush, warding his implant from proximal queries and phishing attempts from skimming devices, dampening the noise from sales pitches and shouts, and dialing back his olfactory sensors to stem the inevitable smells from too many bodies in such a compact space.

The crowds seethed and roiled the closer he got to the train station. Karlene was right about one thing. People *were* unhappy, and tonight had all the makings of another protest. Working for Agro-Tek, Drayson had more of a cushion than most people down here even if he couldn't yet swing a cushy pad in the Canopy. But he knew how easily the tables could turn, trapping people in Terrestrial District tenements with no chance to move to the upper levels, literally and figuratively. Without him supplementing his dad's disability, his parents would be stuck down here in one of these apartment buildings, the units not much better than sleep capsules. The inequity paired with a botched rollout for the latest Emergence targets had transformed the Terrestrial District seemingly overnight into a powder keg on top of which the rest of the city was perched.

Not for the first time, Drayson wished his work toward Emergence automatically granted him a free pass through the scrum so he could ascend to the Understory as quickly as possible. Away from the dirt and grime, away from anger that had no answer. At least no easy ones. But that made him feel like an asshole in the same breath, for thinking himself above such concerns. He wasn't, but he *had* chosen to funnel all his frustration into his work. Work that would transform New Worth for the better. Work for the future. That probably wouldn't count in too many people's minds down here, though. Not with all the conspiracy theories that scientists like him were actually the ones holding them back from their land on the other side of the glass.

By the time he reached the station, the trains were running a couple minutes behind schedule. Wonderful. He settled in to wait, nabbing a prime spot against one of the support pillars to ease the growing ache in his lower back.

Often on nights like this, with another planting trip behind him, he would stand on the platform, the press of humanity swirling around him. All of them were inexorably tied to the technological feats that allowed New Worth to exist, and by some estimations, thrive. But he held off from fully firing up his implant and joining in the intoxicating snarl of digital life. He wanted to preserve the clarity of self that came from being outside, from glimpsing what they could have one day and what the previous generations had been too careless to safeguard until it was too late. A small act of resistance, invisible and even meaningless to most, but it had become a *thing*, and tonight was no different as the platform hummed with energy.

He wasn't just another zombie like Karlene said. He could acknowledge the benefits of connectivity without being beholden to them, right?

Breakdancers were popping and locking for tips in front of the shuttered ticket counter. A vendor was hawking lab-grown beef barbecued to melt-in-your-mouth perfection. One guy happened to cross in front of Drayson with deep purple lowlights threaded through black hair. Direct eye contact was a rarity in the upper levels where virtually everyone had an implant, but down here, Disconnects like Karlene were more common. This dude gave Drayson an assessing once-over, hampered by no tech to speak of, then dismissed him almost as quickly.

See? Zombie, he could imagine Karlene saying with a smirk had she been there. Drayson caught a glimpse of a tree tattoo on the man's upper arm. That kept Drayson watching as he darted through the crowd and convened with a cluster of people who also didn't have the glazed-eye look that heralded preoccupation with their implants. Disconnects, all of them, having a real conversation, not one mediated by implants. Moments later, Purple Hair and his friends affixed voice box amplifiers to their throats and started chanting. Someone on the other side of the platform answered, and soon dozens of voices peppered throughout the station joined in.

"No more lies. No more delays. It's time to disconnect from the dome!"

Some people in the crowd shied away from the demonstrators, keeping their gaze averted. The same slightly pained shuffle people did to avoid someone tripping their balls off in a train carriage. Others pointed and yelled affirmations. More than a few bystanders linked arms and joined in with raucous shouts. Thank god the train was only ninety seconds out.

Chants rattled through the station. So intensely, it took Drayson a moment to notice the floor vibrating with heavy footfalls. A dozen or so cops in riot gear clustered right next to the pillar he was leaning against. There was always a patrol out this time of night, but this was different. Instead of the traditional uniform, they wore protective vests and helmets shielded with carbon fiber panels that absorbed instead of reflected all the artificial lights strobing across the platform. Clearly they weren't taking any chances with all the unrest. But to Drayson's tired eyes, the Disconnects just wanted to be heard like anyone else.

Sometimes getting loud was the only way to get the muck-ety-mucks in the Canopy to pay attention, even if he wasn't thrilled at getting caught up in a demonstration.

The riot cops' body language remained stiff with leashed tension as the platform thundered with chants. One of them launched a drone overhead. Drayson used his ocular boost to get a better look as it surveilled the platform. Cameras offset the quad rotors keeping it aloft. Heavy-duty antennas studded its back.

His augmented vision grayed out just as klaxons sounded. The train was being drawn to an emergency halt somewhere up track. Security gates rolled down automatically to keep any more people from crowding onto the platform. Chants abruptly transformed into shouts and screams.

Well, shit.

Before he could search for another way out of there, the network died right before his eyes. Drayson blinked, but some kind of localized interference kept his implant from responding. No feeds, no feedback, no function at all. What the fuck was going on?

In all the confusion, the riot cops had spread throughout the crowd because *that* was just what this situation needed. Drayson's gaze snagged on the closest one as they slammed their baton down on a protester's head, who's only crime seemed to be holding up their hands in supplication. Drayson couldn't halt the eyecast command to replay the moment from his cache even though it didn't work—the habit was too well-ingrained after seeing something so outrageous.

To Drayson's left, another cop was taking swings at a protester while members of the crowd tried to separate them. A woman screamed bloody murder, and Drayson turned in time to see her being dragged back by her hair by one of the cops while another readied handcuffs.

Realization of the cops' aggressive tactics spread through the crowd like a virus. People started testing the exits at first tentatively, then with increased urgency as panic took over. Someone could get killed, slammed against the metal mesh keeping them corralled. Staying put was no longer an option. He had to get out of there.

Drayson angled for the tracks even though that would put him closer to the rampaging cops. He barreled through the crowd, searching for the Disconnects he'd noticed earlier. They probably bolted as soon as the cops started swinging. Finally, he spied a familiar shock of purple hair and plotted an intercept course through the throng toward the railing separating the platform from the tracks. One of the cops broke out a taser, and the discharge hit a person somewhere behind Drayson. Way too close.

Purple Hair hopped the rail and disappeared from view. Disconnects knew how to go to ground down here. Drayson couldn't afford to lose them.

The crowd surged again, trapping him against the metal guardrail. His entire chest cavity ached as people slammed against him. Just beyond, the tracks beckoned mockingly. His lungs spasmed for too many seconds before the pressure slowly eased up. Finally he had enough space to lift his leg and scrambled over the rail. He hit the tracks and immediately fell to his knees.

"Halt!" an automated voice blared over the PA system. "The New Worth Police Force urges you to remain calm for processing. This is an active crime scene."

That *they* created. Fuck this. Drayson pelted down the tracks, searching for Purple Hair. There. He'd nearly missed the maintenance corridor the group of Disconnects huddled in. It looked they were trying to breach some kind of access panel recessed in the wall. The only woman in the group had an impressive set of tools laid out on a length of canvas as she crouched in front of the locking mechanism.

A large enforcer type threw a look over his shoulder and spotted Drayson. He turned to Purple Hair. "We've got company, Nasco."

"Why did you follow us?" Nasco demanded as Drayson got closer.

"You seemed to know where you're going."

The first man was about Drayson's height and unafraid to get in his face. "Find your own way, sheep."

"Come on. It's not like I can just waltz up to the next station." The local precinct would no doubt be waiting to round up anyone who made it that far. Drayson had seen the deference and dignity afforded folks in the upper levels. Down here, everyone was a suspect first and treated accordingly. It rankled even if such treatment had never been turned in his direction. Until tonight.

The enforcer thumped an index finger against Drayson's temple. "We're not worried about you. We're worried about the tech in your head."

Drayson held back a grimace. "My implant was knocked offline when all...*that* started."

Nasco exchanged a look with his friends. "Thought it was just our tools that shorted out, but them too?"

Them meaning Drayson or everyone on that platform connected to the network? The cop who released the drone.... Maybe that was not to record the confrontation, but to ensure no one else could.

"Got it!" the girl shouted in triumph behind them.

Nasco had seen Drayson on the platform, knew he wasn't involved in whatever the hell had just gone down. Wasn't that enough? Nasco seemed to realize the same thing and patted his companion's shoulder. "He's fine, Garza. And even if he's not, we don't have time to argue."

If anything, the klaxons had gotten louder. Drayson imagined the rail security force would be deployed as backup any moment. It was now or never.

The Disconnects hustled into the access tunnel, and Drayson scurried after them. The girl locked the door behind them and secured her gear in her satchel. When she saw Drayson watching, she barred her teeth. "Baaaaa."

Garza shouldered past him. "Come on, sheep."

They filed down the tight corridor before it opened up into a larger bay dark with rust and grease. It must have been used as some kind of staging area during the maglev's construction and now utilized for occasional maintenance. The aged infrastructure around them probably dated back to the city's construction. The latest technology at the time, but now, it looked like it was rotting from the inside out.

The group slowed down when they reached the first intersection.

"You have the schematics for this place?" Drayson asked as Nasco directed them down the left hall.

"Just because we don't have a chip in our head doesn't mean we don't know what we're doing."

"I didn't mean..." But it had been implied, hadn't it? They'd clearly planned for this contingency, all of them working together as a unit. It ran counter to the narrative that Disconnects were Luddites and malcontents. Provocateurs not clever strategists. But it had been the cops who instigated the conflict at the train station. Maybe the Disconnects had better cause for complaint then he'd realized. They'd certainly been better prepared for trouble.

A few more twists and turns, down one long catwalk that overlooked racks of humming transformers, Nasco finally stopped at what looked to be a dead-end. Their lockpicker got to work, and within minutes she had returned them to street level through a door that blended into a small alley between storefronts.

"Back to pasture, sheep." Garza pointed Drayson toward a large intersection at the end of the block that would hopefully lead to the Understory lifts.

"Where are we?"

"Markley's Terrace."

Drayson blinked, trying to pull the neighborhood up on his map, but of course his implant was still offline.

Nasco gave him a concerned look. "Still not working?"

Drayson shook his head. Nasco pulled out a strange device from one of his pockets. He waved the handheld sensor along the back of Drayson's neck where his implant lived just below the skin. Nasco whistled. "We've seen this before. They knocked your implant out of commission remotely. Your implant's still operational, but your access to it's been severed."

Before? Something told Drayson these weren't garden-variety Disconnects he'd run into. "But this kind of thing shouldn't be possible." At least not without securing the necessary legal permissions to do so. The rationale would have to be exceedingly high to override someone's digital autonomy like that. A whole train platform of someones? Unbelievable.

"Well, it is, Drayson Vonn, of Agro-Tek."

How did Nasco know that? Then Drayson dashed that thought. Nasco probably just pulled his whole biographical record off his implant.

"*You* work for Agro-Tek?" the girl asked. "They're the ones rehabilitating the land, yeah?"

The sudden hunger reflected off all the Disconnects' faces gave Drayson vertigo. He used to view Emergence with the same wide-eyed hope, but there was something else to the Disconnects' intensity. His stomach dropped. If they believed scientists like him were the problem, he would've been better off taking his chances in the riot.

"You've been outside?" Garza asked, giving Drayson a reassessing look that crawled up his spine.

"Yes," Drayson said, still processing the shift in the conversation. "I'd be happy to answer any questions you have, but—"

Garza folded his arms over his chest. "Oh, now you want to leave?"

Unwillingly, Drayson took a step back. "That's not what I meant. It was just a lot back there and—"

Nasco snapped the diagnostic tool shut. "You're coming with us." The definitive statement sparked a change in the group.

Garza turned to him in surprise. "We can't bring him back there. He could tell the authorities."

Drayson held up his hands and tried to look harmless. It wasn't difficult. "Not without my implant working."

"You still have eyes in your head, sheep, don't you?" Garza said with a sneer.

Drayson's shoulders pulled back in indignation. "You think I'd turn you in?"

Garza shook his head. "Doesn't matter since you're not gonna get a chance." And with that, he coldcocked him.

When Drayson woke, he found himself on a ratty couch pushed up against a wall of a small room. Sunlight simulators had been installed in the ceiling, but the cramped space still had a sickly vibe. His temples throbbed, and a lump on his forehead was hot to the touch. Garza. That fucker.

Nasco hovered into view.

"Where am I?"

"Underground." Somewhere under the dome, but beyond the city's reach. "The rest doesn't matter."

"Like hell it doesn't." All this cloak-and-dagger shit went far beyond protester safety briefings. It felt...organized. "What is this, some kind of rebellion?"

"And if it is?" Nasco replied calmly.

Drayson blinked. He knew people were frustrated, Karlene had said as much, but he hadn't realized things had gotten this bad.

"We're going to ask you a few questions," Nasco continued. "Then you'll be free to go."

"Just like that?"

"Just like that." Nasco's gaze caught on what must be a spectacular bruise right about now. "No tricks. That's not our way, I promise."

For the next two hours, Nasco asked him about the outside, his company's planting trips, the green beyond the dome, and what it all meant in lay terms, not scientific jargon or political slogans. Real talk followed by more mundane matters like the safety precautions they took and the protocols they followed outside. Others, all Disconnects, filtered in and out of the room, asking their own questions or whispering something in Nasco's ear that shaped the next line of inquiry. Garza took up position at the door at some point, a constipated look on his face as he stood watch.

As if Drayson was in any condition to start something after the day he'd had.

"We work hard, pushing ourselves every time we're out there so we won't make anyone wait longer than necessary to have fresh air on their faces," Drayson said hoarsely. "I know you want to leave, and I don't blame you, but the only reason we've been able to do all this is because of the supplies and infrastructure New Worth provides. Without that..." He shook his head.

"You let us worry about that," Garza growled.

"I mean it. You're not ready. *We* aren't ready, any of us. All that green out there? Up close, it's little more than a mirage." Impressive and seemingly everywhere from behind the safety of the glass. "Oh, we're still making progress, but we're talking decades not days. But, in time, one day..."

Nasco's face shuttered at the no doubt familiar refrain. Drayson felt like a jerk for telling them to wait, to put up with injustice after injustice just a little bit longer, until somebody *else* decided the time was right. But if they wanted information, they needed to hear all of it, not just whatever served their purposes.

"What makes you think it'll be any different than it is now?" Nasco began to pace. "The city works to protect their interests and the people who buy into their grift. That won't change when the glass comes down. They've never cared about the rest of us."

"Emergence is for everyone. I still have to believe that." Drayson had spent this past week outside pissing and moaning about the futility of it all, but this exchange with Nasco right here and now was reminding him of all the reasons why his work was important. People were counting on him, Agro-Tek and all the companies and initiatives like it, trying to make Emergence a reality. Otherwise everything Emergence stood for would be crowded out by doubts and opportunists, just like the cockleburs had stymied the blackjacks' growth.

Nasco frowned. "Maybe. But when it comes down to it, we're only human, whether we have a chip in our head or not. Wherever we go, we carry around all our selfish impulses and psychoses with us. The same things that divide us here will play out there as well. But if we leave now, at least we'll have a head start against the forces that want to see us destroyed. You were there at the train station. You saw the way the cops were trying to set us up."

He had, no question. "The city's rot runs deep—deeper than I thought—but we've got to hold the line for the future. It's so much more than us. It has to be."

"And if you're wrong, what then?"

That was the question, wasn't it? "I don't know, but at least we're trying."

God knew Drayson wasn't the best poster boy for Emergence, mired as he was in his own disappointment in the enterprise, but if more people knew what they were up against, maybe that could move the needle long enough to keep the city from tearing itself to shreds in the process.

Nasco's mouth flattened. No doubt disappointed in the response, even though it was the truth. He flicked on the wall screen to pull up the latest news. In each quadrant of the screen, a different source played. Already reports of a protest turned violent filled the feeds. He navigated to one of the lurid headlines, and the write-up filled the screen. "See? They're already blaming us for the incident when they're the ones who attacked us."

And without realtime footage from witnesses to dispute the official narrative, they could spin it however they wished.

"They want us silenced, and they're willing to play dirty to do it." Nasco pointed to Drayson's implant. "You think that was an accident because you happened to be at the wrong place at the wrong time? Oh no. If they can do that to the people down here, it's only a matter of time before they do it up there."

ROOT CAUSE   127

The upper levels? The Canopy even? Drayson nearly shuddered at the thought. He wanted to say that was impossible, that it would never happen, but his busted implant was proof the rules had already changed at some point.

"You need a factory reset, and only a licensed implant tech can do that. What do you want to bet the cops will be monitoring all the clinics the next few days for folks who got caught up in today's demonstration? They're desperate to root out the rebellion by any means necessary."

No matter how many innocent people got caught up in the scrum.

"They'll be looking for me, won't they?"

"They'll use footage from everyone's implants to reconstruct the scene, and they'll figure out at some point yours is missing."

"What do I do?" By escaping the crackdown, he'd unwittingly painted a target on his back.

"We can refer you to someone who can help."

Garza rolled his eyes. "Sure. Give away all our secrets. You really think this sheep can be trusted?"

"Maybe not. But no one deserved what happened today." Nasco faced Drayson. "*No one*. And no one deserves what will keep happening in this city until the promise of Emergence for all is kept. You may not understand our choices, but you can understand that much."

He produced a card of translucent plastic. Drayson feared the heat of his fingers would be enough to melt it as he turned it over, an address for somewhere in the Understory on one side, and on the other, the image of a tree being struck by lightning. Just like Nasco's tattoo, peeking out from under his sleeve.

"What's this?

"That's your ticket out of this mess. Well, hopefully. Garza will escort you out of here. The rest's up to you."

Drayson blinked back surprise. "Wait, that's it?"

"We got you out of there, and you answered our questions. I think that's a fair trade."

"But what do I say if they ask about... all this?"

"Your implant will be scrubbed of anything linking you back to us, if that's what you're worried about."

It felt too easy. And suddenly not nearly enough.

Nasco ran a hand through his purple hair in frustration. "Look, this fight's been coming for a long time. I get that you haven't been tuned in to what's actually been going on. But now that you are? What are you going to do about it?"

Drayson still didn't have an answer by the time he reached the implant clinic as they were opening for the day. He was grieving his naiveté. A bell that couldn't be unrung. And felt the corresponding responsibility of *now what?* settle across his shoulders. Working towards Emergence was no longer enough. Now he had to do his part to safeguard it. But how?

The clinic was tucked away on an interior block, a far cry from the glossy one Drayson had always gone to in the Canopy. The bland, beige décor screamed no-frills functionality. But the waiting room was clean and neat, if not exactly personable. The same thing could be said for the receptionist as she turned away the person in line ahead of Drayson. It was just his luck if this place didn't take walk-ins.

The receptionist's lip curled up at Drayson's bedraggled approach to the desk. "Do you have an appointment?" she asked in a bored voice. Like she already knew the answer but was determined to stick to policy just to fuck with him.

"No, but I was hoping to get in today. It's kind of an emergency."

"Everyone says that. Everyone comes in here acting like the sky is falling when their implant's on the fritz."

"I realize that, but—"

"Without an appointment, the best I can do is fit you in a week from now."

"A week?" None of this was going how Drayson expected, how easy Nasco made everything sound. "Wait..." Drayson fumbled with his pockets, finally pulling out the card Nasco had given him and placed it on the pass-through.

Her slouch straightened as she palmed the card. Her eyes rolled back into her head, practically dancing in their sockets to a flurry of eyecast commands. "It's your lucky day," she said tonelessly. With a press of a button, the door separating the waiting room from the rest of the clinic slid open. "We've just had a cancellation."

Drayson settled into the examination chair and forced back the flutter in his stomach. Even though he'd done nothing wrong, all this clandestine stuff was giving him a guilty conscience he just couldn't shake. Now that he was actually here, the anxiety that always came from getting his mind mucked around with, as his dad liked to say, was making itself felt. At his usual clinic, an implant tech would have entered by now to catalogue his complaints and run diagnostics to help troubleshoot updates and newly installed applications. Instead, the doctor herself, an older woman with tan skin and curling white hair in a messy bun, bustled in without preamble. "So you've been severed."

"Yes." The worst digital hangover ever. Drayson's headache from being knocked out had eventually been replaced by one from being disconnected so long. "There was a demonstration and—"

She brought her hand down on the back of Drayson's chair with a jolt. "No details, please."

"Okay, but—"

She swung the articulated chair arm across Drayson's chest and latched it into place. "And no questions. I know why you're here." She took a breath and then gave Drayson a smile as if to restore some semblance of a bedside manner. "Your implant's going to be fine, but there's been a lot of interest in the people who were at the protest. It's not a matter of if they find you but when. Now lean forward."

Drayson complied, placing his forehead onto the rest built into the padded chair arm. Behind him, the doctor booted up a diagnostic wand and waved it over the back of Drayson's neck. She grunted. "While I'm in there, I'll touch up your internal clock, ensure your cache is clean."

"Will that be enough?"

"It'll get you out of this mess if that's what you mean."

"But I didn't see anything." He hadn't had the presence of mind to take pics or stream vids before he'd been severed. The same was probably true of everyone else on the platform last night. All of them sitting ducks leading up to the sting operation or whatever it was.

"Just being there, being a breathing reminder of the shit they pulled is enough, honey, believe me. I can make it so your tech passes inspection, but I can't stop an interrogation. Play dumb, and in a few days you can put all this behind you."

It wasn't enough. It wasn't enough to just go back to his job like a sheep to pasture as though none of this had happened. He wasn't some zombie who could pretend this was normal when it so clearly wasn't.

"Isn't there something more I can do to help, you know, the cause?" he asked.

"What do you mean?"

Drayson didn't know. "There's gotta be a way to use this to our advantage. The police will track me down eventually, right? Let's do it on *our* terms."

The doctor frowned in thought. "We've been trying to find a way to stay on top of police movements throughout the Terrestrial District. You've already been unaccounted for long enough the police will be curious about you. If we manufacture a convincing reason for that, you'll no longer be a hostile witness in their eyes, but a victim. That gives us a lot more latitude to play with." She spun his chair around so she could peer into his face. "Are you sure you want to do this?"

Want? No. Needed to came closer to the possibilities swirling through him. Drayson nodded.

Latitude fucking *hurt*, Drayson thought as a police med tech inspected his injuries in a station house not too far from the maglevs.

"Take me through what happened again." One of New Worth's finest detectives, a fortyish white woman with a pageboy cut, had a supernatural ability to arrange her face in a pleasantly neutral expression as she'd asked him variations on the same set of questions for the last twenty minutes.

"I told you," Drayson said through his teeth as the tech swabbed at the shallow cuts along the back of his neck with antiseptic. "I was waiting for the train when something went screwy with my implant. I must have blacked out. I woke up in an alley and got jumped by scavengers."

It had been three-on-one. Drayson hadn't recognized any of his attackers from Nasco's crew, but clearly their rebellion was big enough to be able to pull this little operation off. He hurt—everywhere—but the bruises and cuts would become badges of honor so long as he made it through the rest of the interview unscathed.

"Luckily one of our patrols happened along before they could slice you up too badly, huh?" the med tech said brightly as she finished bandaging him up.

It hadn't been luck—it had been part of the plan, but Drayson nodded all the same.

"We're trying to recreate what happened that night," the detective said, "and we'd like your permission to access your cache for the ten minutes leading up to the incident."

"You're welcome to what I have, but my implant's been really weird ever since." It helped that it was the truth.

Her mouth compressed slightly. "There've been reports that the demonstrators deployed an energy weapon to disrupt the network. It sounds like you may have been caught in the strike zone."

Whether she was lying or merely repeating one raised goosebumps on Drayson's arms as he submitted to the cache scan. He bit the inside of his cheek as she initiated the data transfer.

"Did you see anything that might help us locate who was responsible?"

"Not that I recall. I tried to get out of there as fast as I could."

"We were wondering about that." The woman's bland smile was at odds with her steely gaze. "You see, you're one of the last few individuals we've been able to process from that night. Most everyone else was debriefed at the train station or detained at the nearby lifts."

"Just my luck."

The scavenger attack provided him with a good cover story to account for his unverified status the last twenty-four hours as far as the police were concerned. It also explained away any gaps in his cache. The doctor had assured him the malware she'd loaded him up with would pass harmlessly from his person to the station's network. Not through the cache scan—the security warding that avenue was notoriously difficult to breach. Instead it would be transferred to any of the dozens of devices in the vicinity and eventually worm its way into the central servers and other essential infrastructure. If the police weren't going to fight fair, the Disconnects deserved a heads-up at least, and this incident gave them the opportunity to establish a wiretap without risking any of their operatives.

The detective looked over the data readout on her touch-screen. He wished he had some indication the worm had successfully made the jump. He supposed he should be used to invisible changes by now, given his work.

The good detective signed off on the report. "Thank you for your cooperation, Mr. Vonn. If anything else occurs to you, don't hesitate to reach out."

When Drayson reported back to work two days later, he felt inexplicably revitalized as though he'd finally found the right nutrient mix for his soul. Who knew all *this* was just the kick in the pants he'd needed?

After spending most of the morning on administrative work that had piled up while he was away, he was finally ready to tackle the applications Dr. Martín had sent him for the latest garden grunt posting. There was a lot of turnover since many people used the position as a stepping-stone to better things once they got their heavily subsidized implants courtesy of Agro-Tek. Karlene was one of the few who'd been here for more than the two years it took to become eligible. He often helped screen candidates to head off any of the obvious issues that could be gleaned from an application.

Something he could do in his sleep at this point, but he settled on scrolling through them as he walked to and from the caffeine bar in the lobby. The picture of the last candidate in this set popped up in his field of vision, and he nearly did a spit-take with his oat milk latte. There was Nasco's face minus the piercings and the purple hair, somehow paired with a new name and unimpeachable credentials.

Without waiting for the full implications to settle over him, Drayson sent a call request to the contact number that had been provided as soon as he got back to his office. He half-expected it to time-out, but roughly forty seconds later, Nasco answered with a tentative, "Hello?"

"This is Drayson Vonn with Agro-Tek. I came across your application for the Horticulture Tech I position. I'd like to ask you a few questions. Is now a good time?

"Of course," Nasco said smoothly.

This sanitized version of Nasco didn't sound nearly as nervous as Drayson felt as he cycled through variations on what he wanted to say before deciding to simply go for it. "Just what is it you hope to accomplish here?"

Nasco paused for a second. "Well, it's kind of an embarrassing story, but I was in an argument with someone. Someone I've come to have a lot of respect for. They suggested I stop complaining about how long Emergence was taking and actually do something to help out."

"I... see."

"By doing my part, I'm hoping to learn from the ground up at Agro-Tek."

That was laying it on a bit thick since Drayson had no doubt Nasco would also be elbows deep in recon, but he was willing to put the time in. He was willing to try. That kind of small, invisible change had to count for something. And Drayson was in a position to ensure it would.

"That's good to hear since so many employees view what we do as a calling."

Nasco chuckled. "I think we're not so different in that."

So much unsaid, unasked, filled the line. Drayson wanted to ask him if the wiretap was operational, that all of it had mattered, but in the end he stayed silent. Even if it hadn't worked, he'd proven something to himself and these people and wouldn't see that undone now because of his need for validation. "Well, thanks for taking my call," he said, sticking to the corporate script. "HR will be in touch once a decision's made."

"Wait. Thanks for reaching out, Drayson. You've really gone above and beyond." He was pretty sure Nasco didn't mean the follow-up questions. "It means a lot."

Drayson hoped it would be enough as he sent on Nasco's application for Dr. Martín's approval.

Broken Threads

Kevin Wabaunsee

A day into her westward trip across the toxic wasteland, Leanna Swift's headware blanked out. Fleeing across the lifeless Midwestern desert in a stolen courier van, her eyesight shuddered and fuzzed momentarily before she found herself utterly cut off.

The network and its augmented reality had always been her ever-present companion, but now, there was nothing: her custom interface no longer overlaid what she saw, and no information streamed into her consciousness. For the first time she could remember, the network didn't respond.

She lobbed mental commands and virtual movements that were automatic and reflexive, almost below the level of conscious thought. The only result was an angry amber glow in the corner of her vision indicating that something had gone completely wrong.

The van—normally linked into Leanna's headware through the network—lurched to the left, and she scrabbled helplessly with her mind at the nonresponsive interface. Desperate to trigger a reboot or to pull up a menu, Leanna's eye darted across the screen—no, not the screen anymore, just her field of view. She couldn't make sense of what she was seeing. Her senses, her entire reality was filtered through the sharpening algorithms of her headware. Now, there was no filter, no layer between her and the confusing cloud of vision that competed for her attention.

She was outside the range of the distributed computing network, but that wasn't all. Maybe it was the clouds of radioactive dust that floated across the wasteland. Maybe it was charged particles falling with acid rain across the plains. Or heavy metals wreaking havoc with delicate transmitters. Whatever the cause, Leanna was hundreds of kilometers away from help with a head full of tech that was glitching badly.

The haze of dull and washed-out color assaulted Leanna's senses. She blinked, her eyes refusing to focus on the infinite depth that now pressed in on her instead of the menus and buttons that always floated just within her reach. From the haze of sensations, the strange and blurry depths that now surrounded her, Leanna watched as a punctuated series of white dashes emerged out of the haze and slipped toward her, then under her. Then the strange white dashes began to drift lazily to her left, slowly at first, then faster as the seconds passed.

Lane markings! Those dashes were lane markings, Leanna realized. The van was drifting across one lane, then another, then another. Leanna screamed, and grabbed the manual wheel of the van. She just managed to correct the drift before she slid off the road entirely.

Then, too much. The van lurched under Leanna's grasp, tires squealing across four lanes in the other direction before Leanna yanked it back again, nearly overcorrecting once again, but finally wrenching the uncooperative van back onto a stable path.

Leanna wasted a few minutes trying to find the manual shutoff for the cruise control before finding that merely hitting the manual brake pedal turned off the semi-autonomous speed control and allowed the van to slow and finally coast to a stop on the shoulder of the empty highway.

She'd known that this was going to be hard. But somewhere out there were answers. Her mother had traveled these same roads, when she'd abandoned her daughter and their home for—something. Leanna had never known what it was out in the wastelands that had drawn her mother to leave everything she knew behind. But now, Leanna could feel the lure of answers drawing her westward like a magnetic pull. Even as the pounding empty cacophony in her head made her want to turn the van around and flee back into the neon embrace of the city.

"Keep going," said a voice from the back of the van.

Leanna spun around. Impossible. Aside from her bags, there wasn't anything or anyone back there. Wasn't there?

There hadn't been anyone there when she'd left. She hadn't stopped until now. Her heart pounded, her vision blurred, and she felt herself beginning to shake. She faced the road and seized the steering wheel, if only to steady herself.

"Don't go back," the voice called dimly.

Leanna fumbled with the seatbelt and clambered into the cargo area of the van. She flung her bags off the neat pile she'd left until she uncovered the bottom bag, a weather-worn green canvas duffel. Leanna tugged the zipper and pulled out the tattered ribbon dress, the last possession of her mother's that she'd kept all these years.

Gingerly, Leanna unfolded the dress with its plain floral-print fabric and perfectly straight lines of red and blue along the seams. When Leanna was nine years old, her mother had promised to help her make her own ribbon dress. The first in a long string of broken promises. From within the folds of the dress, Leanna uncovered the cheap injection-molded plastic box. No voice here. This was an urn. Just ashes. Her mother's ashes. Distant and neglectful, even in life. But mostly absent for her childhood. Leanna hadn't heard from her in twenty years. That is until the medical examiner asked her to collect the remains. Leanna hadn't even realized her mother had snuck back into the city.

Echoes now. Alerts and dings of notifications, but far away. The phantom feeling of vibration in her head and her finger-tips. Like she was at the bottom of a well. Or the plinks and dings of incoming messages were at the bottom of the well, and Leanna was at the top, peering down into the darkness.

More voices, more words but indistinct. Memories. Fears. Some twisted sense of Leanna's guilt and fear of abandon-ment. An audio loopback, some side effect of the drastic disconnection of her headware?

Her mother had left her a memory chip full of twenty years of scratchy voice recordings—letters to Leanna that her mother had no way of delivering, except with her dying moments. Leanna had listened to some of them, until they became too painful, and uploaded the rest into the wet-ware storage of her implants to access at some future date. That must be what she was hearing. Somehow, some strange bleedthrough from the failing storage and her mind's clumsy attempts to reconcile the sensory inputs. Or maybe just hal-lucinations. But whatever it was, the voices all sounded like her mother spoke in her mother's voice.

"Go." The voice was urging her to keep going, into the wastelands, and towards the refuge that Leanna's mother had abandoned her for so many years before.

Not trusting herself to drive, Leanna slept a few hours during the day, letting the solar cells trickle-charge the van's batteries as best they could. The reddish-orange sky was overcast with yellow sulfurous clouds, which admitted only wan and anemic sunlight onto the cracked and dry plains. These were the aptly named deadlands. No one lived out here, nothing could live on this land, under these poisoned skies. Had anything *ever* grown on these dead plains, let alone fields of wheat and corn that people actually ate?

When she started the van again, she clutched the wheel, afraid something would go wrong with her vision again, that she'd lose focus or be unable to control herself. But she managed to get moving and stay moving. So many painful hours later, she steered the van off the crumbling highway and through a winding access road choked with rubble and rusting hulks of discarded vehicles. Up an endlessly winding road that seemed like it would never end, she let the van roll into the shattered parking lot where the crumbling remains of an ugly concrete block building now sat.

Looming behind the broken building, there was a ragged, scorched rock face that towered above a hill of scree. In the spaces where the rock face hadn't yet crumbled away, it was buried underneath a tangled mat of lichen and vines in unearthly colors: indigo and magenta and gray-green covered almost everything, and obscured the giant faces that she knew lurked beneath.

When she spoke to herself, her words were thick and slurred. "Is that Mount Rushmore?"

Her mother's voice echoed in the back of her head. "No. It never was, honey. *That* was Tunkasila Sakpe Paha. Six Grand-fathers. But it's not that anymore, either."

Hours later, Leanna was nearing the coordinates her mother had left for her. Decades before, the topsoil had dried up and blown away, the ground scoured down to scree. The omnipresent yellow clouds hung low and dark, and the stinking sulfur-tinged rains drizzled on and off at all times, creating a dank and muddy landscape from which the skeletons of long dead trees spiked up to form a tangle of dry and broken branches. These were the deadlands that had once been called the Black Hills—iron-ically because the density of verdant trees and forest was such that hills and mountains looked black from afar.

As she steered the van over the crest of a high ridge, the pounding in Leanna's head had mostly ceased, but the tension and panic still held like a vise. She longed to reach out with her mind's eye and gather information. She wanted the reas-surance of the constant stream of data that reminded her of where she was, and what she was doing. She wanted to check her e-mail, goddammit.

But the network was gone. She was past its reach.

The van began down a sharp, steep decline into a valley be-low, and for the second time in as many days, Leanna wondered if her senses were betraying her with hallucinatory images.

"It's real," her mother's voice said, in a distorted, scratchy imitation of a reassuring tone. Nonetheless, her mind rebelled, refused to interpret that her eyes had fallen upon a monstrous-ly proportioned mushroom towering above the valley floor. Four hundred feet at least, and twice as wide, with a stalk as wide around as a city block. The mushroom towered above the valley floor, not a cartoon redcap, but a bulbous organic accumulation of folds and tissue, like coral or a morel grown to titanic proportions. The shadow it cast stretched for a mile and a half. Then Leanna spied others, not nearly as tall as the behemoth in the center of the valley, but still towering above the structures and people below.

That wasn't all. Somehow, impossibly, the valley was lush, verdant, even. No. Not verdant, because that meant "green." None of the lush plant growth, crops and farms, towering trees and scattered forests, was green. She saw magenta, and a grayish-blue-green, and scattered dots of dull orange and mustard yellow.

As the van entered the valley, she saw that these weren't plants at all. No leaves or fronds or wheat stalks grew here. Instead, irregular fields of mushroom and huge bulbous tangles of lichen and rolling mounds of moss.

Even though Leanna was a hundred miles inside the deadlands, where nothing was supposed to live or grow or survive, there were buildings. Barns and longhouses and a town, or at least a village. It made no sense. None of this was possible in the deadlands. Leanna found herself desperate to log in to the network and compare what she was seeing to the history, the statistics, the sheer empirical impossibility. Because it couldn't possibly be true.

Still reeling from the impossible sights, Leanna drove the van across the valley floor towards the monolithic mushroom that towered above all else. As she neared her destination, she saw a squat concrete building nestled among the folds and fronds of the titanic fungus. Straight lines and square shapes gave way where the structure backed up against the mushroom, becoming more fluid, curved and organic. It was as though the architects had taken more inspiration from the mushroom the closer the structure got, until it wasn't clear where one ended and the other began.

As soon as Leanna pulled to a stop and climbed out of the van, a crowd poured out of the building, more than Leanna would have expected, but perhaps there were more structures under the surface. That certainly seemed to be true of many aspects of this place.

They smiled and called out welcomes to Leanna, but mostly they murmured and talked among themselves, as though Leanna was both welcome and expected, just another family member returned after a long journey.

Distantly, Leanna noticed that every one of the crowd looked like her—black hair, brown eyes, and a warm tan skin tone that could be mistaken for any racial origin from Mexican to Portuguese to Greek. Native American. From the looks of the crowd, they weren't all Lakota like her mother, but probably refugees from any of a dozen tribes whose reservations had been decimated in the last few decades of ecological catastrophe.

Finally, one woman separated from the crowd and approached Leanna. She was old and wrinkled, her braids long and gray, but carried herself with a grace and authority that made Leanna think that if she wasn't in charge, whoever *was* in charge listened very carefully to what she had to say.

"Leanna, welcome," the old woman said, her arms spread wide, as though to welcome Leanna into a warm embrace.

"I—I don't know you," Leanna said slowly. "I don't know any of you. I don't understand what this place is—my mother, she –" Confusion and the ache from her disconnected headware vied for attention.

A look of sadness flashed across the woman's face. "Of course. So sorry, dear. I'm getting ahead of myself. My name is Kay Alkire. You must have so many questions. I can tell you anything you want to know." The old woman reached out and held Leanna's hand. "We loved your mother, and she loved you, and leaving you behind was the hardest thing she ever did. But you're home now."

Home? No. Leanna felt herself panic at the thought. She'd made it here, but she needed to leave as soon as she could. To return to the city, back to the network, back to herself. "No, no—I'm not—"

"Trust her," Leanna's mother's voice echoed in her head, stronger now.

The old woman turned away. "Hold my arm and walk with me for a few moments, won't you? I need someone to make sure I don't fall. I can tell you more about your mother and this place."

Numbly, Leanna agreed. She took the woman by the elbow, and they walked along a well-worn path circling the huge mushroom

As Leanna and Kay walked slowly around the huge mushroom, they traversed fields of purple lichen, swaying fronds of transparent threadlike mushrooms, and dense mats of mosslike fungi. And throughout the walk, Kay told the story of the Black Hills Enclave.

It started just before the collapse of the U.S. government and a resurrection of an all-but-dead political movement. One of the last gasps of the crumbling empire saw the U.S. give the Black Hills back to the Lakota. Not just the Lakota, but a coalition of tribal governments in exile from whom the U.S. had seized reservations and dissolved tribal governments back when they decided to strip mine most of the mountain west to build arkships.

Back then, most folk thought giving the Black Hills back was either a smug screw-you to the tribes—enjoy your poisoned wasteland; we're done with it—or a truly epic case of white guilt.

The first refugees didn't last long. Their plants would wither; the livestock died straight away. No water was safe to drink. Dust that got in their lungs wrecked their insides. Toxins, radioactivity, you name it.

But by then the U.S. was crumbling in on itself. The arkships were ferrying millions out into the stars, while mega-metropolises like the one Leanna had left behind walled themselves off, domed their skies, and tried to block out the slow-motion collapse of the rest of the country.

The second wave of tribal refugees needed a miracle. The only land left to them was this bitter, alkaline wasteland, muddy with acid rain and cut off from the sky by yellow-brown clouds nine months out of the year. But somehow, they needed to make it livable—for themselves, as well as the thousands of desperate Native American families who all across the country were already caravanning out of the ruined cities and refugee tents towards a promised land that just might kill them.

The solution that a half-mad, brilliant cadre of university-trained tribal scientists had cooked up was too strange, too bizarre to take seriously, until it worked. In the soup of radiation and heavy metals that filled this valley, they'd discovered a creature that thrived on the poisonous environment—a polyextremophile. This bizarre quirk of evolution was a single-celled organism—not a bacteria, not a fungus, but a strange ancient order called archaea.

The scientists designed viral vectors to unzip and rewrite each refugee's genome, so that every one of each of their trillions of cells would open up and accept the archaea into itself. These organisms ceased to become life forms and melded with their new environment, becoming a human organelle, as much a part of who they were as the DNA that had been passed down through hundreds and hundreds of generations, and the mitochondrial DNA passed down from mothers to daughter in an uninterrupted line from first human to last.

Just as mitochondria had once been single-celled lifeforms, the poison-eating archaea became a part of the refugees and their cells, and along the way, gifted them the ability to live and thrive in this inhuman environment. They followed it up by engineering crops and pollinators, soil and fauna. Livestock and groundwater, all so it would live and thrive with the archaea. For some reason, fungi took to the new way of life better than plants.

And so, with machines held together with electrical tape, with technology looted, borrowed, or stolen from an empire in the midst of a slow collapse, the Black Hills Enclave had created not just a new ecosystem but an entirely new branch of human evolution

"My mother was a part of this?" Leanna said, her head pounding, her vision swimming with ghostly echoes of a user interface that evaporated as soon as she tried to focus on it. They were back in front of the strange concrete building that gave itself over to the mushroom.

"Your mother was a part of all of us. Of the land, of the community we're trying to build. Dear, you need to understand. What we have here, it's much more than just an enclave, or a settlement. You need to understand that."

"What do you mean?"

"We're *connected* to the land now, Leanna. And we need your help to make what we're building here transcend our lifetimes."

"Connected?" Leanna asked. Suddenly, things seemed less certain.

"Everyone who comes here is transformed. In doing so, they become connected to everything living in this place. It's a little hard to explain, but it's a sense as real as touch or smell or hearing. When things are healthy, growing and thriving, it feels—right.

And when there's something out of balance, when there's something strangling the growth or poisoning the balance, we can sense that, too. And it feels *wrong*. It's a—they call it a gestalt. It's something that the new organelle pulls out of what we smell and taste all around us, and it gets passed back as a feeling for the land."

"Okay. But what do you need me for?" Leanna asked.

"Oh, dearie. I'm so sorry. You look so much like her, it's easy to forget I'm not here, talking to her again. Come on inside, and see what your mother was working on. If you don't want to help, we'll send you on your way. But please, for your mother's sake, at least take a look."

Kay led her into the concrete building, which felt like a cross between a bunker and a community center. Down, down endless stairs into a basement and a sub-basement, surely far enough to be both inside and beneath the monstrous mushroom that towered above.

Finally, a closed door—anonymous, utilitarian, but at the end of a long hallway. Kay stopped in front of the door and took Leanna's hands. "Behind this door is your mother's life's work. Everything she'd built, everything she hoped to leave behind. She knew what kind of a woman you'd become. She left you a gift. Your birthright."

Leanna opened the door and stepped inside. Kay stayed in the hallway.

As the door closed softly behind her, Leanna's eyes struggled to adjust to the dim light. No overhead lighting here. She was in a room, cool and dark. Dim light from some kind of phosphorescent fungus, punctuated with blinkenlights from a rack of technology that were embedded in—Leanna gasped—the entire back wall of the room was a softly undulating fleshy wall, enmeshed and wrapped up in the concrete structure, but veins of fungal threads glowed faintly below the mottled yellow-and-brown surface, looking like nothing so much as burnished leather. The lights came from a rack of memory chips, carefully placed and sealed behind a layer of climate-controlled glass. The power and data interfaces for the chips were buried somewhere in the fungal tissue of the wall itself.

With one shaking hand, and not knowing precisely why, Leanna reached out to lay her palm flat against the fungal wall.

As soon as her hand touched the fleshy surface of the wall, *something* broke open inside Leanna's mind. A short circuit, or a failed connection, or some rogue code fitfully lurking somewhere in the junction between her failing headware and the organic tissue it interfaced with. Whatever it was, it set off a chain reaction of jolts that caused her wetware to shudder and let loose a flood of data. Flashes of light blinded her, but also voices, soft whispers and shouts rising in volume and intensity until they were a discordant shriek. Leanna smelled vanilla, felt sandpaper under her fingertips, tasted the acrid bitterness of a half-burned meal. Memories rose up in her consciousness too quick to recognize, before dipping and falling back into the roiling soup of her breaking mind.

Then, one voice rose above all the others, deafening but clear. Her mother's voice. The letters her mother had sent her. Somehow, the sensations and hallucinations faded, and Leanna realized that something was blooming in her mind—all of the messages and information from her mother's letters, and the half-formed mental schema her brain had been trying to build up, walling off and encysting her mother's messages like a half-baked immune response.

Leanna fell to her knees, her hand pulling free from the fungal wall. Finally, silence. No more phantom sights or smells or sounds. Just the same dark room she'd been in.

Except something was different. Her mother was here. Standing in front of her, looking patient and kind and exactly as Leanna never remembered her. Even recovering the storm of sensations, Leanna knew this wasn't really her mother. Whatever this was, standing in front of her it, was somewhere between a hallucination and a vivid memory of something that had never happened.

"What do you want?" Leanna croaked. "You're dead, you know."

The phantom vision of her mother smiled sadly. "I know. Because you know. But I also know what you don't. I know why you're here."

"They said you needed me to finish your work?"

Her mother turned away, towards the fungus. "We'd done something impossible here, but that's just *biology*. We saw how badly things had gone out there—and how bad they were going to get—and wanted to build a better world."

"Seems like everything's hunky-dory upstairs," Leanna said, still catching her breath.

"We weren't naive. We knew that generations to come might benefit from the sacrifice of those that came before, but without the pain it took to bring it into existence. We needed to be able to share our stories with the generations that followed. Not tall tales or stern warnings or laws bound up in ink and leather. To help our children avoid making the same mistakes that had doomed the world that came before."

"No. This is just more of the shit you put in the letters. I have other questions. No, just one question. Why?" Leanna finally asked. The one question she needed an answer to, the one she'd always needed to know, above all else. "Why did you leave? Why did you leave me behind?"

Her mother—the phantasmagoric, imaginary, painfully real version of her mother—gave her a beatific smile. "Honey, I was doing important things. The most important thing. I was making a better world. A better world for you. I didn't have time to be just a mother."

Leanna felt as though she'd been dropped from a great height and slammed into the earth. That answer was pure, unvarnished, and untouched by the self-deceptions and prevarications that a real person would have employed. It might have even been true.

"I'm done here. I need to leave."

The vision of Leanna's mother shimmered and reappeared in front of the door. "What's out there for you? The city is dying. All the cities are dying, no matter how hard they pretend they aren't. The planet is poisoned, Leanna. You either let it kill you, or you find a way to survive the poison. Take it in, let it sustain you. If it lets you thrive, it isn't poison anymore."

"That's your crusade, not mine."

"Haven't you always wondered what it meant to really be a part of a community? Haven't you always wondered if there was something more. If there was a family, a community, a tribe out there?"

Leanna almost broke down, then. It was true. Of course it was true. This wasn't her mother talking, it was her, herself. How could she deny the truths she lived with all her life? Something broke loose inside of her. She couldn't explain it, she didn't quite understand it, but she stopped.

"Fine. Tell me more."

Leanna's mother—or the solipsistic simulacra that her broken mind created to resemble her mother—explained. The giant mushrooms that dotted the valley floor, as it turns out, were all connected, and sprouted from a heavily engineered splice of the largest and oldest organism ever to grace the earth's surface—*armillaria ostoyae*, a miles-wide fungus, sampled with care from Oregon's Blue Mountains before they were leveled and strip-mined. What better partner than the hardiest and longest-lived thing that had ever existed. They gifted the fungus the same extremophile organelle. And like all fungi, it grew to link the ecosystem together, negotiating carbohydrate exchange between lichen and myco-heterotrophic plants and the various mushrooms and soil bacteria.

It did more than that. It helped everything grow and stitched them into a web. Shared resources. Shared survival. Shared sensations.

They had engineered a tangle of bioelectric nervous tissue into the fungus that had grown to underlie every inch of the valley floor. A biological network of massive proportions, ready to accept that most precious gift that the elders could give it: their own memories.

At the end of the lecture, Leanna's mother knelt down in front of her, as if to beg. "What we were building needed to be bigger than one person's lifespan. We recorded as many of their memories as they could get. The hardships. The suffering, the deaths. So many people died on the road before they even got here. If we can upload these precious memories into the mother fungus, they'll live on. The archaea and the fungus, they allow us to access those memories, relive the lessons of the past, and share it with the next generation. We need your help to finish that work, my darling."

Later—hours, days, it was hard to tell—Leanna stepped back up to the rack of memory chips. Had she made the decision? Had she chosen this path? She didn't remember anymore. It didn't seem like something she would have done. But that was before.

She placed the last chip back in its storage cradle. She'd seen everything. She'd *lived* everything. The years of pain and death and starvation. The stories passed down from mother to daughter for millennia. The heartache and disappointment and sheer existential dread as humanity went insane, looking at the prospect of climate change and catastrophe, and instead of stepping back, leaping headfirst towards utter annihilation.

One by one, Leanna had pulled every one of the chips into her own brain. She'd broken open every firmware security protocol in her own headware, and let the memories overwrite everything. The onboard storage: System software. Photos and audio files, the carefully-preserved digital detritus of a life. But not just the hardware storage. She'd cracked open the headware BIOS to rehearse the memory chips, replaying them in an endless loop through her hippocampus and amygdala, allowing her to crudely overwrite her own memories to make room for the elders'.

It was confusing. She'd wanted to go home *before*. She hadn't cared about this cause, *before*. She'd wanted to leave her mother in the past.

In some corner of her mind, Leanna still wanted to slip back into the network and reach her mind's eye out into that digital sea just one more time. But now, with dozens of lifetimes of memories now coursing through her skull, the only thing she knew for sure was that one life didn't mean much against the span of time.

Leanna—whoever that was—felt herself slipping away as the new memories coalesced and consolidated, taking over her own. Then, she found that she couldn't quite remember the details of who she was, or how she'd come to be here. But that didn't seem terribly important. She knew where she was, and what she was doing. And more important, she knew *why*.

Leanna stepped up to the mottled skin of the mother fungus once again and placed a palm on the leathery surface. It was better this time. Just a tingle like a tiny current of electricity running through her hand up and up through her body. She could *feel* the mother fungus. It knew what needed to happen as well as Leanna did. And a slit opened up in the surface of the fungus, just large enough for Leanna to climb into.

She felt the warm embrace of the mycelium all around her. She felt the pinpricks of questing fibers, and the gentle touch pulsing touch of the mother fungus as it drew her in, deeper and deeper, through the tangles and roots of the fungal growth, ever inward, towards the heart of everything. And as she was drawn in, Leanna felt a rush of connection, a sudden fractal expansion in her consciousness, as the memories that lived within her flooded out and back and through her, and knitted themselves into the fibers of the fungus running through every inch of the valley, entwined in the roots of every plant, and flitting in and out of contact with the quick-moving humans that tended to her roots.

Leanna was home.

The Robot Whisperer

Holly Schofield

E milia heard the door bang as Kore entered her workshop. Dishes clattered on the side bench. "Be there in a minute, I just have to..." She let her voice fade. How could you fix a magnifying light when you needed to magnify it to see what you were doing? And her hands were trembling again. She set down the tiny screwdriver in frustration. She was too old for this. Too old for everything. And her calendar was blinking at her again.

"Come on, Mom, it's getting cold." More clattering. "Your tinkering can wait."

"You know, there was a day when I was considered more than a tinkerer." Emilia picked her way through the crowded stacks of old electronics gear to where Kore had laid out dinner, a lentil stew and a chicory latte, both freshly steaming from the collective's communal kitchens.

"You've still got it, no worries." Kore chuckled and gestured at the faded thank-you certificate on the wall. "All of the old-timers still have a crush on you." In the corner of the frame, bronzed by the late afternoon light, a small printed photo perched: Emilia on the day she'd arrived six decades ago. Mirrored sunglasses—retro even then—long black hair ponytailed with an ironic curl at the end. And her tight black clothing, so unsuited to the climate-changed heat of western British Columbia. The collective hadn't wanted to let her in. She represented everything wrong with city life—consumerism and fast fashion, high tech for the sake of high tech, environmentally detrimental housing and infrastructure, not to mention faith in capitalism and perpetual growth—everything the newly formed collective had sworn to reject.

"Tell me again about your arrival?" Kore held out the spoon. "And eat while you do."

Emilia gave her a flat look. When had child become parent?

Kore brushed back her hair and Emilia noticed the gray. Now in her sixties with fingers almost as arthritic as Emilia's, Kore taught the younger ones woodworking, all based on the collective's principle of "least tech necessary for the job." Kore had her place in the world, but Emilia's was slipping away.

The latte foam was shrinking, bubbles disappearing as if they'd never existed.

Coming here had been necessary but not easy. First, there had been her successful refactoring of Regina's municipal budget—increased subsidized housing, reduced management perks, some other tiny adjustments to give more parity among salaries—followed quickly by pretend ransomware that had prevented immediate budget reviews. Then, the switcheroo of the deputy mayor's name and SIN number with similar ones belonging to a lifer in Kingston Penitentiary: *that* had been rad! The identity theft issues had been so intense the deputy mayor had to quit her job to deal with them; Emilia would have felt worse about it had the woman not been syphoning off funds for her Bahamian home.

It all might have remained undiscovered for a while, at least until next term's audits, but Emilia had slipped up irretrievably when she hacked into the mayor's video recordings of his meetings with the biggest of the local gang leaders. Somehow—she'd never known how—she'd left tracks behind as clear and as deep as an elk in winter snow. That had been the turning point: two nasty groups after her was one more than even she could handle.

It still made her shudder to recall her escape. First, the run through Regina's subway tunnels, then the long hitchhike to the suburbs, a night in someone's garage on the backseat of an illegal gas-engined Cadillac, followed by the theft of one of the newer, badass e-bikes and a tablet from a schoolyard. Her destination was "anywhere but Regina" so she headed onto the highway, turning west into the setting sun like the hero in some old-school western vid. Vancouver, eventually, she supposed, but she knew they had troubles—and gangs—of their own.

If she kept a dead-steady speed, the self-driving semis didn't know she was tucked up behind their taillights. She drafted a series of them for hours, past endless seared prairie destitute with withered crops and dead windbreaks. After nodding off once and nearly swerving for the ditch, she switched to a slower ancient one-ton truck but the human driver kept peering out the window back at her, brown face scrunched with concern, super-long hair blowing freakily backwards in the wind. Emilia dropped back a more reasonable distance and fixed her eyes on the tailgate for the next five hours—the flowery script, *Chlorohaven*, forever etched in her mind.

The bike's battery indicator yellowed after a while, then reddened. Finally, an e-charge station appeared where the highway swung down in the cleft of two mountains near Yoho Park.

The self-driving vehicles kept going, of course, but the old truck swung in. Emilia cursed. No choice but to follow. The bike was almost out of juice.

She pulled into the farthest plug station and turned her back to the lean driver who swung down from the truck cab. She ignored her near-hypothermia and growling stomach. One thing at a time. The challenge here was to charge up without giving away the bike's ID and GPS. It had surely been reported and the automated highway patrols would flag it right away and intercept her. This highway didn't branch for a hundred klicks.

She yanked the charge cable from the bike's compartment and the tablet from where it had been pressing against her ribs. Using her body as a shield, she made the connections and flicked on the tablet. Scrolling code began and she lost herself in the flow, darting and diving and probing like a shark after prey.

"Engine trouble?" The driver's shout was followed by a friendly head tilt. How many minutes had passed? Emilia had gotten nowhere and her left foot was growing numb.

She angled her face away and shrugged.

"No money for juice? I can spot you a few bucks." The driver was coming closer, striding over the gravel, long gray hair puffing around a thin face with—*uh oh*—clever eyes.

Emilia's second shrug was brief as it could be without being rude. "No, thanks." Entering the driver's account data wouldn't help—the system would still flag the stolen bike. There must be a way.

A few more minutes of futile poking before she admitted it to herself. Without hours of time and a better tablet, even trapdoor access was closed to her and her tiny pocket toolkit. She wasn't going to be able to get in. There'd been no other human-driven traffic for hours. And those dark trees crowding in on all sides were spooky, even in daylight.

The driver still stood there, hands in jean pockets, a concerned look on their face.

Time for Plan B.

Cold fingers fumbling inside the bike's tiny side panel, it took several attempts with her penknife to score the charge cable enough to break it.

She held up the busted cable and forced a wry smile. "This bike's not going anywhere." She let some of her anxiety show. She could ask but it would be better if they offered. Syphoning juice off the truck would be slow and inconvenient for the driver but it would be untraceable to the bike.

"Hop in. My chariot awaits." They grinned, flung an arm wide, and gave an exaggerated bow.

"Not what I..." It would sure be nice to be out of the wind. Her eyes ached from unaccustomed long-distance views. And maybe food would be part of the equation. Emilia made a sudden decision. "That would be awesome."

By the time they reached the turnoff to Chlorohaven, just outside the aptly-named town of Hope, the driver had introduced themself as Dardee and told Emilia about life in the collective and how they took veggies all the way to Calgary this fall because mudslides had closed the highways into Vancouver and Chilliwack. How the collective was successful, but only to a point.

"We'll never be sustainable unto ourselves, not like the founders thought'd be possible back in the day. We get meds and other health tech from various places, and we deal with various governments and cities and corporations."

Emilia nodded, feeling surreal. The truck bore the earthy smell of raw potatoes and carrots, and a damp burlap sack squatted on the seat between them, next to the beeswax wrap that had held Dardee's lunch. The dashboard was a mashup of several styles and models of displays. An assemblage of gear that would have been punk if anything had post-dated the previous century but, no, it was all stale-tech, dials and gauges and thermostats. A day ago, she'd been in front of a TeeGore 764XC deking through encrypted software like a boss. Now, jouncing along the endless highway, e-bike bungee-corded to the rusty box, it was like she was stuck in a boot loop. She unzipped her jacket. At least it was w arm.

"We can't seem to keep tradespeople either, they get lured away by the city life—we've had four plumbers in six years." Dardee madly waved their half of their shared hummus sandwich, dropping crumbs all over the truck cab.

Emilia had never hired a plumber or even seen one do their job. Living in various squats or couch-surfing meant you didn't really get a feel for those kinds of things. But each treetop that flicked by meant she was one tree farther from Regina. She could fake being interested in anything to gain that. "Uh, a good plumber is hard to come by."

"We could use a carpenter too. I don't suppose you have any skills?" The raised gray eyebrow matched the hair, fuzzy and untamed.

"Don't even know which end of a hammer to hold," Emilia said, washing down the other half of Dardee's sandwich with a swig of her own water.

As she tucked her canteen into the saddlebags between her feet, her mirrorshades gleamed up at her from a side pocket, a reminder of who she was and where her talents lay.

The thing was, though, Vancouver seemed more and more like a silly-ass destination—crooked politicians and gang alliances swarmed like flies there, too. Every city in Canada held danger. She eyed Dardee and sucked on her lip. "I'm not good at any of those things. But if you need someone with IT skills, I can code with the best of them." She didn't add how she could deep-dive into any system, pretty much, with the exceptions of vehicle registrations and municipal backroom deals.

"IT skills? Like, you could keep track of our seed bank and our crop rotation? Fix the farmbots? Monitor the solar array? That sort of thing?" The truck swerved just a fraction as Dardee's voice rose in excitement. "Hey, if you're willing to put a few hours in at the kitchen hall or the garden as well, that'd be an infiniwin for the win!" They held up a hummus-smeared hand for a high five.

Emilia returned it with a cheerful slap. That expression had been cheesy a decade ago. Chorohaven might not be cool but any port in a storm, right? She'd just have to hide her sarcasm from these naïve solarbabies. But it wouldn't be for long. Just until the heat died down and she could figure out how to hack the bike. Then she'd be on her way, leaving nothing behind but a sardonic cloud of dust.

"Mom? You okay?" Kore was bending over her in concern.

"Just lost in my thoughts." She smiled up at Kore. "Go along, go eat with your friends at the hall. I'm good here."

Kore kissed the top of her head and flashed the same indulgent smile she used with her students. "Sure, Mom." And Emilia watched as Kore's relief was replaced by anticipation as she scooted out the door.

Emilia ran her hands down her hemp shorts and over her faded striped tank top. Where had all her cool gone? Rotted away like her jacket, repurposed like her e-bike, leaving nothing but rusty rivets. She'd lost her badassness somewhere, worn it down. She'd known that for years now.

In fact, she could almost pinpoint the day.

Five years after coming here—not long after Dardee's peaceful death from old age—she'd finally decided to do something about the stress and tension that hovered in every single member, a constant presence, a black cloud overhead. Climate change was hard on every person alive, sure, but it had taken Emilia time and contemplation to see that it was hardest on those who lived close to nature, those who felt connected, who experienced pain every time the spring wildflowers were fewer and smaller, every time the returning migratory flocks of birds shrunk.

That night, at the Spring Solstice bonfire, she'd made all the farmbots do a square dance, to wild applause. It had given the members a short-lived release from their worries, made their faces crinkle in laughter in the flickering firelight. The stunt had earned her the title of Robot Whisperer, a name so uncool it made her laugh even now.

Her protectiveness for the community had grown since then. She glanced at the faded photo—no, she wasn't that secretive furtive person anymore. Chlorohaven, with its healing circles and forest bathing, had cleansed her.

But she still had her secrets.

Ohhh yes, she sure did.

She scrubbed her face, callused palm rasping.

The calendar still blinked at her.

Dinner had congealed in the bowl, and she wasn't hungry anyhow. Might as well satisfy the silly thing so it'd stop nagging her. She grabbed a headlamp and hobbled into the back room, past the small workstation, a simple yet robust Bartleby-Q rig, enough to easily handle all the collective's e-needs. Under the wheeled box of old inverters and gauges, the trapdoor hinges gleamed, oiled for quietness. Even a year ago, she could have raised the hatch with one arm. Today, she fetched a handybot and let its pinchers wrench it open.

She climbed awkwardly down the steep wooden ladder, knees complaining. Her headlamp shone on the equipment in the corner, flickering with lights and false purpose. The battered chair sent up clouds of dust and her eyes watered. How many years? How many hours of writing code down here late at night, of staying one step ahead. The intensity of triple screens of endlessly scrolling, the rapid-fire keyboarding, crowing with victory when she squashed an opponent.

Kore and the others would be alarmed and anxious if they knew this setup existed. But telling them how she'd sheltered them, not just from ransomware attackers who tried time and again to breach the collective's systems, and ID thieves almost as talented as Emilia, but also hackers who thought Chlorohaven would be an easy and fun target just for the fuck of it—telling the community about all that would have increased their angst and anger at the outside world. At first, she resented the lack of a thank you or a pat on the back, but she'd finally learned to let her ego go, let it float away like a dandelion seed puff, and continued to secretly protect the people she loved.

Now, miracle of miracles, the outside world had turned a corner. They'd actually learned how to govern themselves in good—well, pretty good—ways, with the help of sophisticated AI that filled the role of Chlorohaven's Tuesday night group discussions. Calgary, Vancouver, and even Regina had actually managed to implement renewable energy sources, encourage mass transit, house every single person, embed food forests in every downtown core, and generally pull back from the brink. She'd be proud of the Reginans if she still felt even a tenuous connection to a living soul there. But their definition of a local carrying capacity, how many people an area could sustainably maintain, was very different than hers. The very thought of crowded sidewalks and thousands of auras all residing a few square kilometers had grown foreign and even disturbing to contemplate nestled here in the pine and spruce and freely flowing mountain air.

She lay down on the narrow bunk, the mattress molded to her body by countless nights. She was as useless as the firewall embedded in the CPU gathering dust against the wall, as useless as software that ran on obsolete O/Ss. It had been ten years since the last attack of any kind on the collective's network. She'd diarized the calendar entry then. Now it was time to shut it all down. If a new threat came along, it'd be so sophisticated she doubted she could make up for a decade of letting her abilities and knowledge lapse. The equipment with its flickering lights was now as useless as she was. It could sit here until it clogged with dust.

"Auntie Emilia? Are you therrre?" A pounding on the work-shop's front door. Emilia leaned over and clicked on Camera One, and there was little Audie on screen or maybe it was little Terra, one of Dardee's grandkids anyhow, face mashed against the workshop window, peering in, clutching a broken toy of some kind. The light in their eyes was worshipful, incredu-lous, full of wonder at the magic they believed lived within. Even with no idea of her mad skills. Her *former* mad skills.

One hand pressing firmly down on the side table helped her stand, wrist on fire, hips protesting. She limped over to the rig. The chair squealed as she methodically shut down it all down, one system at a time, fingers feathering across the familiar keyboard. Telltales winked out like dying fireflies until the dim lamp was the only illumination, a sorrowful moon for a sorrowful day.

She unplugged the powerbar cord for good measure. Thor-ough is as thorough does, she thought to herself, then realized that had been one of Dardee's phrases.

Audie, or whoever it was, was still yelling. She plucked a rusted rivet off a cracked ceramic plate full of screws and transistors. Maybe the rad factor she'd always craved wasn't about being slick AF. Maybe it was the glow in a child's eyes. She couldn't fix the heavy stuff on the solar array anymore, couldn't even fix that magnifier, but maybe she could pin a broken puppet back together or glue a wheel back on a wooden toy garden cart.

Something in the clutter next to the plate caught the light. She pushed off a yellowed paperback and pair of needlenose pliers and used the hem of her shirt to rub the dust off her old mirrorshades.

They slid on, smooth and slick against her face, the ultimate of cool.

A glance at her reflection in a dead screen showed a slender, surprisingly elegant ponytailed woman with faded tats down her arms and an ironic twist to her mouth.

Yeah, she still had it.

She grinned, waggled her forefinger and pinky finger at the image, then, shades in place, headed for the ladder.

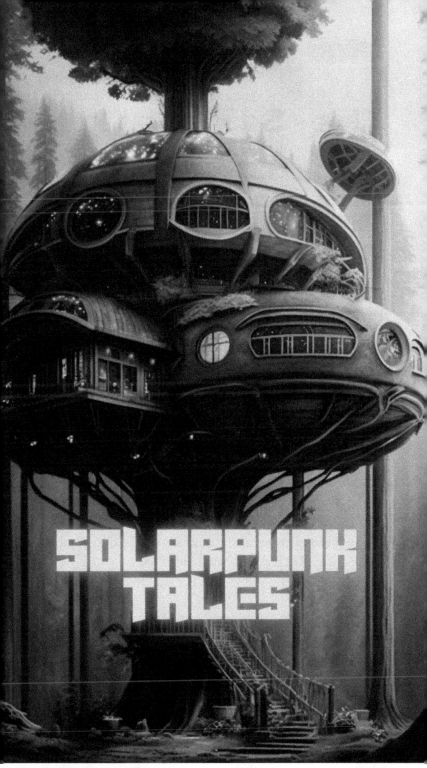

The Strength of the Willow

Commando Jugendstil and Tales from the EV Studio

T he wind makes the broken door to the allotment squeak on its busted hinges. It sounds a bit like a wounded bird.

Viola raises her eyes to the sky. Blue-gray clouds gather overhead, and the air smells like ozone and petrichor. A small, lopsided smile makes its way onto her face.

A thunderstorm is on its way, and she doesn't even have an umbrella, not that it would help, from the looks of it. It feels almost like a set-up for a dramatic scene in a movie.

The allotment in ruins around her, the storm overhead, and she's crying bitter tears in the rain.

It feels extremely tempting to let it play like this. The heavens know she needs a bit of catharsis in her life.

She closes her eyes and spreads her arms wide, settling down to wait for the rain.

It feels almost peaceful, almost all right.

They tried to set up a teaching allotment for local schoolchildren and a small urban farm to feed local families during the cost of living crisis, and for a while it worked. And now it's all gone, overnight.

The fence, broken. The tools, stolen. Even the produce has been ripped from the ground and trampled.

There is nothing left.

All her work from the last years is gone, so yeah, for once she can allow herself to be a bit dramatic, to have a cry in the rain, and have a warm shower and a hot tea at home before she starts looking for a new job.

Because sure as hell, the borough is not going to renew their lease on the land and their funding when the allotment can no longer provide the deliverables.

Given how the nearby companies are raring for the chance to show their green credentials by privatizing and "beautifying" a public space, Viola gives it six months maximum before the (former) allotment becomes a wellbeing green space, or something like that, and the eighteenth century Cascina next to it some kind of event space or hip co-work.

Viola feels a tide of anger rise inside her. She wants to march to their offices and trash them. She wants to break things and yell until she has no voice left, but she can't.

Hunches and gut feelings are no proof, and *cui prodest* can only get one so far.

There is nothing she can do. Nothing except stand in the ruined allotment, pretending to be a lily of the fields, kissed by the wind and peed on by Dobermans, and curse her naivety.

Communities don't matter. When push comes to shove, the authorities will always look out for their real constituents, the people with the money.

She should have remembered that. She should have never accepted the job of coordinating the work in the allotment and teaching the community. She should have never believed in this project, believed that it could end any other way.

The first fat drops of rain start falling on her upturned face and hands, and Viola welcomes them. It feels almost peaceful, except for one noise.

Something is scraping, digging, grunting, and panting softly.

A dog must have gotten into the allotment from the nearby public park. Again.

At this stage, Viola doesn't even care if they dig a giant hole, there is nothing really left to damage, but the noise...

"Is it too much to ask to be left in peace for, like, two minutes?!" she yells, whirling to face the intruder.

"Eh, sorry, fam, but I want to get this back where it belongs before it starts throwing it down, if you don't mind," Stabby responds, looking over their shoulder, pausing only briefly in their attempts to shovel compost back into the overturned bins with a discarded paper plate.

Viola blinks and shakes her head, but the image remains.

"Y-you know that it's not going to go bad if it gets wet, right?" she retorts, retreating to the comfortable terrain of permaculture instruction.

"Yeah, I know. The fact is that it smells, and I don't want it spreading everywhere if I have to sleep here, you know?" they reply, shrugging their shoulders.

"Sleep here?" Viola repeats.

She turns towards the patio of the Cascina. Somehow, while she had her little sulk-and-communion with nature, a whole bunch of people have snuck in behind her back.

A pair of colourful pop-up camping tents have appeared on the covered patio, while Lidia and Anna, the carpenters from the community workshop, are trying to repair at least one of the smashed wooden tables.

Other people gather the debris of what can't be fixed in neat little piles or clean the area with broken brooms and mops as well as they can.

Once the table stands, albeit a bit wobbly, people start appearing with food: a tray of bite-sized pizzas, a bowl of pasta salad, a tagine, even some very dubious vegan ham sandwiches.

"What is going on here? What are you doing?" Viola asks.

"For now, a vigil," replies Linda, one of the retired aunties who have been the backbone of the project from its inception.

"And later what we should have been doing since the beginning," another auntie says and sets her tray of lasagne on the table with enough force to make it wobble dangerously on its newly repaired legs.

"We've made the mistake of treating this as a workplace, as something that was conceded to us but didn't really belong to us, and here is the result," La Presidenta says, knocking the butt of her crutch on the ground.

The normally mild-mannered head of the local transition co-operative looks absolutely furious, gray hair frizzy and wild from the rain and anger flashing in her brown eyes. She looks even more like her child, Stabby.

"It's time to say *no more*," La Presidenta continues. "From today, we form a permanent picket to protect our teaching allotment and preserve the Cascina as a social space for the local community. They won't take this place from us."

"Not without a fight, at least," Stabby adds, twirling the broken handle of a broom.

The crowd of allotment volunteers and random neighbors cheers.

The aunties unwrap their trays and bowls of food, and everybody tucks in, eating from mismatched, chipped plates, bowls and even a couple of oversized mugs.

Angelo, the leader of the neighbourhood's volunteer group, uncorks a bottle of wine, while what looks like homemade limoncello does the rounds among the crowd.

People eat and drink and tell each other stories about their best moments at the allotment—and about what else they would have wanted to do. Someone pulls out a guitar. They sing protest songs, clapping their hands, until late in the night.

Viola finds herself dragged into this haphazard commemoration even if a part of her knows that all of this is, in all likelihood, futile.

The neighbors might feel a surge of righteousness and enthusiasm now that the event is fresh, but in the long term, both will fade and people will go back to their routines. They will struggle to find people, and eventually the borough will get the space back to do what they wish.

She can't get too attached to this place and their projects. Not again.

She will do what she was contracted to do in the original project—no more, no less—and if she finds a new job that pays more, she'll take it without hesitations, she vows, even as she accepts another shot of paint-stripper-grade limoncello.

The morning sun finds her crawling out of a tent, without any memory of how she got there in the first place, and a monstrous headache.

Someone presses a glass of homemade isotonic drink into her hands. The air smells like freshly baked croissants and coffee.

Stabby and their partner Loopy are leading a group of youngsters in what looks an early morning martial arts lesson, in spite of the wet ground, while the lonely, unsteady table hosts a group of neighbours who pore intently over a pile of documents.

Angelo turns to wave at her with a sheaf of paper in his hand.

"Oh, here you are!" he exclaims, beckoning for her to join them around the table.

"We're going over the plans for replanting, but we'd like you to sanity-check them," one of the aunties adds, shuffling her chair to the side to make space for her.

"I would, but we have nothing to do the replanting with," Viola counters, ignoring the offer to sit down. The seeds that were in the storage bin have been scattered or stolen by whoever broke into it, and, as far as she knows, they have no more budget to buy any more.

And then, they don't have any tools to work the soil with. Or anywhere to store them. Or a door to ensure they comply with the regulations of the borough.

It would be easier to make a list of what they have left because that's literally one table, which looks like it may break again at any moment, and some underdone compost.

"Don't worry about that, sweetheart." Auntie Linda grabs her hand in a gesture of reassurance

"The folks from the Bollate Jail allotment and from Parco Lambro have said they'll provide us with seeds and seedlings, and we can get some leftover tools from the Giza Eco-building Coop. They're builder's tools, but we can make do, can't we?" Angelo proposes.

Viola hesitates for a moment, then nods. They can make it work, if they insist, and she's contracted to help them.

Might as well, she thinks as she sits down and looks at the documents with the volunteers. It's no skin off my nose if they want to keep this on life support until the bitter end, she tells herself sipping coffee and nibbling at a croissant as she redraws the planting scheme of the allotment to suit the new and improved vision

Mobiles buzz to rival the bees emerging after the rainstorm, looking for flowers that don't exist anymore.

People negotiate waste coffee grounds and chaff from local bars and roasteries in exchange for shopfront gardening, while cargo bikes and electric vans are borrowed across family and acquaintance networks, and other community allotments across the city promise support and material help.

The bees buzz disconsolately. A few fuzzy bumblebees droop slightly already, cheated off their breakfast, while the humans at least still get theirs.

"Can we ask if anyone has some flowering plants they can give us? It's kind of urgent," Viola finds herself saying.

"It's on the list," Angelo confirms, flipping his notebook closed. "Now, let's get a move on. We have a lot to do."

The rest of the day is a blur. The neighbors drag Viola around on a budget gardening grand tour of the city, from Bollate Jail, to the Niguarda allotments, and back down to the faculty of Agrarian Sciences in the University Quarter, and then to the Parco Agricolo Sud.

The back of the battered electric van fills up with gear: plants in newspaper pots, bags of seeds, buckets of compost, a literal can of worms for the compost.

People hop on and off, staying behind to repay their benefactors with help in kind or on their way to their workplaces.

The volunteers unload Viola and their botanical cargo back at the Cascina and zoom out again, then in troop the aunties, laden with food for a quick midday meal, then a group of students from the climate justice group of the nearby high school, ready to pitch in to restore the allotment.

Someone from the biology faculty even bikes all the way from Città Studi with two bucketlike feeders full of sugar syrup to tide the local bees over until the plants have re-established themselves.

La Presidenta appears in the relative coolness of the late afternoon, claiming a seat on one of the battered armchairs that the carpenters have managed to liberate out of a dumpster.

The assembly drags deep into the night in the glow of a few battery-powered floodlights and numerous mosquito-repelling candles.

People flood in with ideas, projects, and plans. Tomorrow, a group of students will start rewilding a chunk of the park in Piazza Martini. Some neighbors are planning to start a container allotment in the middle of Piazzale Libia, while a young man proposes to build and disseminate open-source hydroponics made of recycled materials so that people can grow their own herbs and leaf veg on their balconies or in their kitchens.

"If you can find help for your project, and you take the responsibility of leading it, go for it," La Presidenta responds to each.

In spite of the poor lighting, Viola can see the spark in their eyes turn into sacred fire.

"We'll be everywhere. This way they can't try to chase us away ever again," someone says.

It is spite, yes, but also enthusiasm and determination, everything that was missing from the project before.

Viola leaves the circle of lights and goes to sit alone on the far side of the Cascina, gut roiling with a mixture of anger and sadness.

"I know what you're asking yourself: why couldn't they care about this before? Why didn't they?"

Stabby has appeared suddenly at her side, a wide smile stretched on their painted lips and their eyes glittering faintly in the reddish glow of the city lights.

Viola yelps and startles away, falling in a graceless heap, heart thundering in her chest.

"Jesus Chris, Stabby! They should really put a bell on you!" she hisses, trying to recover some kind of composure.

Stabby smiles again and holds out a hand, hauling her back to a sitting position, then sits next to her in a single, unhurried motion.

"Since you know so much, do you also have an answer?" Viola asks after the silence has stretched empty for an uncomfortable length of time.

Stabby shrugs. "I know it sounds like a cliché, but sometimes people don't realise how much they care, until they stand to lose the thing they care for."

"So things always have to get worse before they get better?" Viola retorts, unconvinced.

Stabby shrugs again and takes a drink out of a metal flask.

"I don't know about always. Do you know the willow?"

It's very Stabby to go straight for the non-sequitur.

"The willow?" Viola repeats.

Stabby nods and passes her the flask. It smells like coffee and alcohol.

Viola doesn't even try to take a sip before she hands it back. She knows what kind of stuff they like to drink, and she doesn't feel like smelling colors and hearing textures tonight.

"That's what strength looks like, if you think about it," they say.

Viola frowns waiting for a further explanation, but Stabby only gives her a silent smile before they stand and pad away silently into the night.

"Do you know the willow?"

The question echoes in Viola's mind over and over, in the weeks that follow.

Somehow, through hard work and with the help of other communities like theirs, she and the volunteers manage to restore the allotment and have a harvest of late summer crops.

The grow boxes of Piazzale Libia get trashed in the first week, but the neighbors plant them again and hold picnics and street parties around them, night after night, until the space is a permanent fixture as much as the play area for dogs.

Piazza Martini has its own flowering meadow buzzing with bees—and it's only after a month or more of mowing it down every week that the borough finally agrees to let it be. Now, it's so nice that the neighbors have decided to grow one in the other park two roads down.

Viola thinks she knows what Stabby meant now.

Strength is not just standing tall in the storm and never breaking.

Strength can also be toppling over, breaking down to pieces, and then finding a way to regrow from there, or being cut to the ground and growing all the way back, bigger, stronger, out of spite and sheer will to live, if only to give the storm and the axe a big middle finger.

When Loopy comes to her asking for ideas for the giant painting he's planning to make out of a slab of discarded construction wood, Viola knows immediately what she wants him to paint.

A crack willow, on its side on the riverbank, lush, strong branches growing straight up from the mossy trunk, with birds singing in its new, lopsided crown.

Solarpunks

J.D. Harlock

U nder the sapphire skies, Sami and her two friends, Ros and Amara lounged on the emerald hills of Solana, basking in the warm glow of the golden sun—wondering why it all had to be so perfect. The sole wind turbine that powered their village was right above them, and Sami couldn't help but feel like it turned slower with every rotation. Having grown up going on school trips to turbine fields as far as the eye could see, it wasn't much of a sight, but neither was anything else in Solana, so this would have to do for the day—as it had every day since they first moved here. The sound of merriment far off in the village square did little to change that, unable to live up to the hustle and bustle of their respective native cities elsewhere in the world. As children born before the Revolution, Sami, Ros, and Amara had been told that Solana was, if not a utopia, an optopia that would provide them with the life humanity had fought long and hard to secure. But, in spite of their efforts to fit in, all they felt was the crushing boredom brought on by the monotony of living a life without problems.

If only there were a way we could rebel against the system, Sami thought, not for the first time.

How they might do that continued to elude her.

"I'm bored," Sami felt the need to say.

"You mean you haven't found something to do since you last told us you were bored a minute ago?" Ros replied with an air of polite condescension.

"Maybe talking to someone will give you something to do, Sami?" Amara suggested, using the tone of voice she always assumed when she was trying to be helpful. "Someone that's not us?"

Sami, unsatisfied, didn't respond, and a moment passed by in silence.

Then, Sami's eyes went wide.

"I've got it," she said excitedly.

"About time." Ros got up. "Let's hear it, then."

"I just hope it doesn't involve streaking again." Amara sighed.

"How about we steal something?" snickered Sami, giddy at the mere thought.

"Yeah!" Ros punched the air, psyched.

"Riveting!" Amara clasped her hands with obvious pleasure.

Neither said anything else, only stared at Sami.

Then Amara's eyes narrowed.

"What are we stealing exactly, Sami?"

"Come again?"

Ros sighed.

"You don't know?!"

"Uh...."

The polite smile on Amara's face now seemed painful to Sami.

"Perhaps, we can steal something of sentimental value to someone?" Her eyes bulged.

"Woah!" Sami held up her palms. "We're rebels, not monsters. To get back at Solana, we have to steal from Solana, not each other."

"You mean stealing public property?"

"Yeah, something like that."

"Is that it?!" Ros flailed her arms. "That's all you had in mind?"

"How about you develop this plan further," Amara suggested, trying to be helpful. "Alone."

"What?!" Sami asked, taken aback. "What's wrong with stealing?!"

"Well, for starters, no one cares," Amara pointed out as she often found herself doing,

"And?"

"And?" Ros groaned. "You need more? There's no money anymore, Sami, or even scarcity. They'll just replace whatever we take, and what can we even take that'll piss them off?! I'm sure if we asked for most of it, they'll just hand it to us! Now, do you still need more?"

For once in her life Sami had nothing to say. Ros groaned even louder, then cupped her ear and leaned in.

"Come again?"

"..."

"I can't hear you."

"..."

"Yes?"

"Oh..." was all Sami could say.

"I thought so." Ros nodded and fell back to the ground, crossing her arms. "I thought so..."

"Yeah..." Amara replied slowly. "So...uh, what was all that about?"

"I'm bored!" Sami said. Again...

Another moment passed until, of course, Sami's eyes went wide. Again.

"Okay, I got it," she said excitedly.

"About time." Ros got up. "Let's hear it then."

"I just hope it doesn't involve streaking again." Amara sighed.

That night, three hoodlums in conspicuous organic-cotton hoodies met under a lunar lamp on a safe, well-lit street, carrying eco-friendly duffle bags that clinked and clanked all the way there. Without saying a word, the leader leaned in and stretched out her arms, and the brains and the brawns of the operation promptly joined in the huddle.

"This is it, girls," their leader announced with utmost seriousness. "This is the big one. Our names will go down in Solana history for this."

"Yeah..." The muscle smacked her lips. "You sure about that, Sami?"

"..."

The leader glared at her subordinate.

"I mean: 'You sure about that, dear leader'?" The muscle smacked her lips again and sighed.

The leader's eyes bulged and her nostrils flared. She let out a loud huff. The brains and the brawn shifted uncomfortably.

"Yes, I'm sure."

"My back hurts," the brains chimed in.

"Mine too," the muscle added.

"Fine." The leader rolled her eyes, "You know what to do."

"Right..." the other two muttered.

"I said," the leader stressed every syllable, "you know what to do."

With clenched teeth, the muscle glanced over at the brain, who shook her head furtively.

"I said—"

"—right!" the other two exclaimed, nodding with over-enthusiastic emphasis.

The muscle then opened the eco-friendly duffle bag, and the brains passed around the non-toxic spray paint she thought would be least appropriate for the hoodlum in question. All three then turned around and raised their spray paint cans toward the pristine white wall before them.

The leader spritzed the walls, making the most of what little paint she had by spreading it as far as she could. The muscle showered the walls, letting out frustration in furious red swipes that brought pathos to the stale environment. The brains sprinkled the walls with a carefully calculated chaos that she had spent the day meticulously sketching.

Had they been working alone, their vandalism would've been unremarkable, but by doing it together, they created a beautiful display of disruption that left them wonderstruck and homesick.

And so, once their work here was done, the trio stood there with pride, taking in the erratic scribbles that would put off even the most experimental of abstract art critiques.

"Someone's going to get in trouble." The leader smiled.

"They're going to hate it," the muscle laughed.

"I love it!" the brains exclaimed.

All three then proudly signed their names on the wall before running off with glee into the well-lit night.

One fine morning, Sami, Ros, and Amara were lined up across that very wall—now curtained-off—as a crowd of their friends, families, and peers anxiously awaited an announcement they'd gathered to hear. Considering the circumstances, the Solana

Community Organizer herself had taken time out of her busy schedule to personally attend to the matter. A podium was even set up before the wall specifically for the occasion. She would show the world what the trio had done, and they—with nervous smiles and bated breath—braced themselves for the worst.

"We've gathered here today," the Community Organizer announced, "because a trio of young women came together on their own initiative to bless our sublime community."

Then, with a wave of a sun-furled bioluminescent cane and a touch of theatricality, the Community Organizer gestured to her co-workers to tug a rope dangling beside the curtains concealing the wall. The sweeping fabric parted, unveiling the graffiti stains the trio had sprayed over that pristine white.

"Our resident community artists have nothing but praise for the fine work Samiya Cadieux, Rosa Tanaka, and Amara Stoica put into this unprecedented artistic achievement." The Community Organizer turned to the work of art, clapping enthusiastically and proclaiming, "Never before have we seen a work of *abstract art* with such craft, care, and finesse! Their names will, no doubt, go down in Solana history for this."

And the crowd cheered.

Seeing her friends, families, and peers enthusiastically cheer on her ultimate act of defiance, Sami suddenly felt sicker than she'd ever been before. Not alleviating her glurgy was Monsieur Osseiran, one of her fathers, who seemed to be keen on chanting Sami's name—even after it became clear that no one would join him in that chant.

"How about one of you come on up here and say something? We'd love to hear from you!" The Community Organizer turned to the crowd. "Right, folks?"

The crowd went wild.

As the camera crew redirected their attention to capture this magical moment, Monsieur Osseiran propped up the (hand-crafted hemp-cardboard) sign with Sami's face lovingly stitched onto it just high enough to broadcast it to the entire world.

Suffocating, Sami turned to Ros and Amara, who promptly shook their heads before she had the chance to wave them over. Now visibly panicking and in no way trying to hide it, she flailed her arms around as if she was about to drown in Solana's glurge, but Amara just nudged Ros figuring there was no way anyone could talk Sami into this and not end up with a headache. Having come to the same realization, Ros walked up to Sami and gently shoved her towards the podium, doing her best to make it seem as if she were patting her dear friend in a grand and rather aggressive display of camaraderie. Sami tried and failed to stand firm, going so far as to lean back into Ros as if she were fainting, hoping her weight could prevent the push from moving her feet, but Ros just shoved her ever harder, and Sami tumbled face-first into the mic.

"Fuck."

The mic picked up the cursing, amplifying it for all to hear.

The crowd went silent. Sami fidgeted with the mic trying to make sure that she hadn't broken anything she would have to repay in community service.

Was this it?

Was it that easy?

After everything Sami, Ros, and Amara had tried to do, and *failed* to do, to show their discontent with the status quo, was that one short—but rather vulgar and descriptive—phrase enough to count as rebellion?

Sami couldn't tell.

So, she quietly stared at the audience, and they quietly stared back—until Monsieur Osseiran leaned in and whispered loudly to the crowd around him:

"All great graffiti artists have a temper." He leaned away, then leaned back in. "I should know. I'm a certified Organic Butter Sculptor." He leaned away a second time, leaned back in a second time, and added, "Grass-fed unsalted organic butter only."

The audience said nothing, nodding politely with the requisite smile on their faces.

Finally fed up, Sami latched onto the podium.

"You know, I do have something to say, actually, and it's something you should all hear. Everyone thinks this place is so fucking perfect, and you know what, maybe it is! But you know what's not perfect? You people! I mean, how do you live with yourselves! Day in and day out, you waste your lives patting yourselves on the back for the silliest shit, pushing back, or outright ignoring anything that you think will change things. Leading a perfect life doesn't mean that you're leading a good life, and we've all just given up on trying to be happy because we've gotten too comfortable and too scared. Back in the city, life may not have been all that it could be, but that was the last time I remember being happy because that was the last time I lived my life. If there's one thing I want you to take from all this is that it doesn't have to be this way, and I wish you could all just see that!" Sami turned to storm off stage before remembering what she originally planned to say. "And by the way, you all smell bad. Those essential oils don't work as well as you think yo
u do."

Finally satisfied that she'd said her piece in a way that *definitely* counted as rebellion, Sami walked back to her friends with the long, confident strides of a revolutionary. The Community Organizer's expression of utter shock was utterly satisfying, but it was her attempts to sniff her underarms as inconspicuously as she could that made all this trouble worth it.

"Uhm..." Ros smacked her lips. "Sami..."

"Yes," Sami beamed with a self-satisfied smile "And you're more than welcome," she felt the need to add.

Amara huffed and crossed her arms in frustration. "Your mic was off, Sami," she said, gritting her teeth.

"Oh..." was all Sami could say.

"Yeah..." Ros smacked her lips again. "Yeaaaaah..."

Flushed with embarrassment, Sami sank her face into her palms and groaned loudly—only to be drowned out by the un-bridled adulation of her friends, family, and peers, who were still excited, because they hadn't heard a single word she said. The Community Organizer played along, of course, tugging at her collar with an awkward smile, now trying to sniff her blouse.

And so the trio stood there with shame, taking it all in.

"Why does this always happen?" Sami felt the need to say, breaking the silence. "Every time we try to revolt, they just..."

Ros and Amara glanced at her, then turned back to the cheering throng, putting on their bravest, most stoic expressions.

"I saw it coming," Ros replied with an air of polite condescension.

"Don't worry," Amara suggested, trying, as always, to be helpful. "We'll tarnish this community someday."

Materiality

Cory Doctorow

I t was supposed to be a special graduation treat: for their last two weeks of middle school, Artemio's class would be the model classroom for the Huerta's Twenty-First Town, part of the show for all the *other* kids whose teachers were no more excited about being in school in the final weeks of May than their students were.

Artemio's parents thought it was going to be great. His dad had loved the Huerta when he was a kid, and his mom, who had grown up in Oregon, had been charmed by the Huerta when she moved to LA for grad school. There hadn't been a Twenty-First Town back then, only the Tongva village, the Mission, the pioneer town, the Gold Rush town, the FEMA camp. It was still enough for the Huerta to claim to be "the world's largest open-air museum," though much of its land was raw San Fernando Valley grit and scrub, with each little village connected to the other by a fleet of lovingly maintained antique vehicles from every era of California history: Redcar trams, omnibuses, horse-drawn carriages, Model Ts, a pod of hand-rubbed convertibles and muscle-cars that still ran on gasoline.

Artemio didn't think it was going to be great. His grandparents had told him enough stories of their childhoods to convince him that Old Timey People were fucking idiots (Artemio's parents said he could swear, so long as he did it well). It wasn't just the stupidity of sending tons of CO2 into the atmosphere: it was the *reason* for all that CO2, which was the production, distribution and elimination of some really terrible *stuff*.

Artemio's dad had had a favorite tee, with the Superman S on it and a satin cape. Artemio knew about that shirt because he'd seen plenty of pictures of his dad wearing it, mostly while jumping off of things while his parents tried to stop him from breaking his neck. But Artemio had never see the Superman S shirt, because his father wore it until it disintegrated.

But a bunch of Artemio's dad's shirts *had* survived, because he didn't like them enough to wear them out. Some of those were cut up for Grandpa's shop-rag bag, and some of them were in boxes in Grandma and Grandpa's attic, which Artemio had spent long hours exploring while his parents and uncles and aunts were being boring in the dining room between the end of dinner and the start of dessert.

(The plastic wrapper that the Superman S shirt had almost certainly survived, and was doubtless in mint condition in some deep landfill, unless it had been incinerated and turned into more greenhouse gases and carcinogenic smoke)

Artemio had a favorite shirt, too: it was a full-print dye-sub of Skullky, with his horns stretching down the arms and his flaming eyes right in the middle of Artemio's chest. It started off as just a quick print, picked during the morning hustle to get out the door for school, with Artemio anxiously checking the door and the app as he ran around packing his lunch and getting his other school stuff together, until finally the house chimed and there was the printer at the door, and he touched in and it sighed open and there was the shirt, and it was *way* cooler than it had looked in the preview and he tugged it on and it fit perfectly, of course.

So many people liked the shirt that day! Complements started two blocks from school and didn't stop until he'd turned the corner for his street on the way home. When he stripped the shirt off at bedtime and carried it down to the kitchen to put in the compost bucket with a sprinkle of tailored bacteria to get to work on its long starches, he stopped at the foot of the stairs: "Daaad!"

"What?"

"OK to order that shirt from today in permanent?"

"What?" Dad was doing his league night and was hard to get an interrupt in.

"The shirt! The one from today. Can I order another one? Permanent?"

"What? Oh, sure!"

So he did. It arrived the next morning, waiting on the doorstep when he got up, and it felt great and fit exactly like the one from the day before, but it was long wearing and would require some machine work to get it back into the material stream, but that's because it was ripstop and double-stitched, dirt-shedding and doped with silver ions so it wouldn't stink even if he didn't wash it after every wearing.

He had a growth spurt later that year, as it turned out, and the shirt stopped fitting, and he got another one, but then a month later he got bored of it and sent it to decomposed in the city vats, and switched to wearing these amazing hoodies that did this crazy thing like they were breathing, billowing in and out as they channeled air over him by means of these super-precise convection gills, and so the Skullky shirt got decomposed, too, though he kept it bookmarked at his mother's insistence, "in case one day you have a kid who wants to wear it."

Mom had weird ideas about stuff.

Ms Mirzoyan spent the week before the Huerta trip taking them through the different ways of thinking about the different eras represented by the model villages.

"Who can tell me about embodied labor?" she bueller-buellered, hoping to get some rise out of a graduating class with less than two weeks to go before the end of the school year. "Anyone?"

Ousa took pity on him. "Embodied labor is the amount of human work that goes into an object."

"Very good!" Mirzoyan pushed her luck. "What else is embodied in an object?"

"Ummm," Ousa said. "Materials and..." She looked around. Mirzoyan pointed at the light fixtures, made a hopeful face. "Energy!"

"Correct!" Mirzoyan made the wall rearrange its charts. "Let's just think about buildings for a sec. We know that they had a lot more enclosed space per person back in the Twenty First Town days, but that's not the whole picture. Look at this now, who can explain it?"

Ousa was apparently done for the day and the words hung in the class like a fart. Artemio sighed. "They used a lot more materials and energy per, uh, cubic meter back then?"

"Thank you, Artemio, yes. Now, who's going to put it all together for me?"

The class looked at the time display in the corner of the wall and steadfastly refused to meet Mirzoyan's eye. She shook her head.

"Remember yesterday's group discussion? Anyone?" She checked the time, realized she had to wrap things up. "For a long time, we were limited by labor, how much human work there was available to make things. Then we started to figure out how to trade energy for labor, animals, water, the sun, and then fossil fuels, to augment human work. Then we started to run out of materials, and we started to substitute energy for materials, too, as well as labor, working harder to get materials from remote places and process them.

"As we started to run out of better ways to extract energy, and better ways to trade energy for materials, we turned to using materials better, learning how to use less to make more, and then, how to reclaim the materials we'd used to make new things.

"But it was *uneven*, remember, and so in the Twenty First Town times, we were making things faster than we could un-make them, and a lot of them were badly made and hard to make into new things, and a lot of things we only needed for a short time were made from materials that lasted a long time. Things started to pile up.

"But that changed. Can anyone tell me how? Come on, people, you know this. No one leaves until I get an answer!" She smiled to let them know that she was kidding, but not entirely.

Artemio raised his hand: "Networks?"

"Networks! Thank you, Artemio!" The wall chimed. Class was over. The students tensed as a body in their seats, ready to leap for the door. Ms Mirzoyan saw her moment slipping. "OK, networks. Your homework: explain one way that networks have changed our relationship to *stuff*. Audio, video, text, anything goes. Tomorrow, people!"

And with that, they were off, charging out of the class, out of the school, and into the hot Burbank afternoon.

Dad was super-excited about Twenty-First Century town. Like, *weird*-excited.

"Arty, before you disappear into your room, let's talk about clothes, OK?"

Artemio stopped on the stairs, half a quesadilla in his mouth. "Dad!"

"Come on, kiddo. This stuff's going to take a while to fab up, you don't want to leave it to the last minute."

He chewed and swallowed. "I'll just get quickies made up every day."

"Don't half-ass this, son. You're going to be part of the museum! Other kids who come to it are going to be looking to you to find out what life was like then! I've pulled up a ton of reference for us, come on to the living room, we'll sort it out."

True to his word, he'd dialed up the living room, putting away his office and the dining room and converting the space to sofas and blank walls, and now they were crawling with reference photos and specsheets for Twenty First Town clothes, and Artemio could see that he was right—every piece had estimated delivery dates of like, three or four days away. It was crazy, like he was ordering up a building or something.

But when the clothes arrived, it made sense. They had a weird solidity—Dad used "materiality" which was also the word that Ms Mirzoyan used. Artemio couldn't figure out what it was, not at first. They weren't stiff or heavy, but they still felt *durable*, and then Artemio realized what it was: the stitching, the materials, the whole construction was something you only got on heavy work clothes, like the overalls Mom wore when she was in the shop, working on big iron. These t-shirts, jeans and sweaters—even the underwear and socks!—were made to last for *years*, even decades, long after he'd outgrown them. It was like making single-use chopsticks out of stone or plastic or something. Who did that?

Monday at the school was a mob-scene waiting for the bus, 55 kids in weird, old-timey, stiff and *durable* clothes, carrying backpacks whose stitching and rivets were designed to last for decades longer than the backpacks themselves. No one was actually wearing anything made from hydrocarbons, of course, but the corn plastics doped with carbon nanotubes did a good approximation.

One kid—Mike McKinley, who was either really stupid or hilariously funny and no one was ever sure which—showed up dressed like a newsie from the 19th century with a flat cap and big knickerbockers. They'd had a Buster Keaton LARP the year before so everyone got the reference but no one laughed. Ms Mirzoyan made him change, despite his insistence that Twenty First Town was "an age of atemporality" and they all groaned because *everyone* hated that chapter in the sociology textbook.

The ride out to Van Nuys was short, even though there were two times they got routed onto surface streets as part of the cadence and pacing system and of *course* Mirzoyan used it as a "teachable moment" to learn about flow in complex systems. But apart from those times, it was one of those awesome, sociable times when the whole eighth grade *thrummed* with anticipation of who they were about to become—just a week until graduation, then a whole summer of bumming around and getting into trouble, and then *high school*, baby. Most of them would go to Burroughs High, and some to Burbank, and a few weirdos with weird parents would be pulled out and homeschooled to keep them from having to get their vaccination boosters or learn about evolution. Those kids were planning to party the hardest.

They started seeing signs for the Huerta, and bits of the old fencing from when it had been Van Nuys airport, and then they were at the turnoff. Incredibly, it was still before 8AM, and when they got off the air had a chill and their breath fogged, the last of the LA June Gloom, which had been migrating steadily to May or even April over their lifetimes. They were met by a museum official who recited parts of the orientation—which they'd already watched in class the week before—and then went among them and shook their hands and complimented them on their outfits and smiled in a dazzling, wrinkly way with crinkled eyes and it hit Artemio that this grownup really *cared* about this place and it really mattered to them that Artemio and his classmates would be good Twenty First Town living museum exhibits.

Suddenly, he felt a different kind of excitement, maybe the same thing that had made his dad so weirdly into his wardrobe choices.

They had to walk from the parking lot to the Twenty First Town line; none of the vehicles were running yet. They marched past other school groups heading for the other parts of the Huerta, drawn from all over LA county, wearing outlandish matching cosplay for their respective historic areas. Seeing that made Artemio mostly glad about his assignment, he couldn't imagine dressing for the Mission Town, for example—though the gold rush outfits were actually pretty cool; he whispered himself a reminder to try out some of the outfits that summer, maybe for parties.

The Twenty First Town schoolhouse was aggressively air-conditioned and surveilled, with metal-detectors and bulletproof shelters in each classroom, and they were impressively solid and heavy enough that Artemio was willing to bet that they'd stop a bullet. They took historical accuracy seriously at the Huerta.

As he settled into his desk with his Chromebook and dutifully performed the lesson they were doing, using the clunky, historical interfaces. When the first school-group came through the room he got really distracted and self-conscious, but by the time the third group came around, he was actually really into it, like it was a drama class exercise: *ignore the outsiders, don't break character.* When the lunch-bell rang, the school played the sound of the hallway rush, simulating a thousand kids all mobbing the hallways, and it was so convincing that he steeled himself for the crush before stepping out.

The Huerta provided lunch—it would have been crazy to expect all the kids to get historically accurate food from home. The cafeteria was staffed by a couple of retired old ladies who were really into it, playing up a whole performance about the meat being from animals, which some of the kids got into to, making gagging noises and so on though of course it all came from culture, because of course it did.

By the third day, something flipped. Artemio got out of bed and accidentally shoved it halfway across the room, pushing off from it to stand up, forgetting how light it was and how easily it moved, the better to fold it down and flip it up flush with the wall when he needed the space for his desk and other furniture.

It wasn't just the bed: as he helped his dad flip down the kitchen table from the wall and get out the cutlery and such, he found himself overhandling everything, ready for it to weigh more, to be more rigid and creakier. He dropped a glass and though he caught it on the third bounce, he still had to buzz for the wetvac and let it in the door and then mom nearly tripped over it as it was cleaning the milk off the floor. Dad tried to make a joke about not crying over tripping over a robot that was dealing with spilled milk but it fell flat even by the standards of dad jokes.

He took a quickie shower and let his pyjamas run down the drain and then somehow he was late so he found a bike and pedaled hard for school, his heavy Twenty First Town clothes trapping the sweat and chafing, and the bike, too, was weird and flimsy-feeling, not like the racers they rode around on in Twenty First, with their solid carbon-fiber frames and thick, rugged rubber tires. The ride to the Huerta—almost all on surface streets that day, avoiding some unseen mess on the freeway—took them past low-density/low-rise housing from an earlier age, the last remnants of the small towns and suburbs outside of LA whose residents hadn't migrated to the dense, luxurious new builds that had already been old builds when his parents were kids.

"The age of atemporailiy," that groaner of a phrase, rattled around in his head, as did, "The future composts the past," which was the name of an independent study unit they'd been assigned over Christmas break, to find the mute, ancient remnants of the old world in their new world, sending him down to the storm drains beneath Burbank with a Burbank Water and Power crew that was inspecting the old cement and firing sensors into it with a big, noisy staplegun. It had been unsettling, seeing that much stuff that wasn't self-aware and also wasn't part of the natural world, as electronically silent as a hike in Angeles State Forest but in a place that was tame and orderly and human.

Now, passing through these dying small towns, wearing his dumb and thick clothes, he saw the future composting the past all around him, and just as the composter had to be regularly purged of things that refused to break down—stray bits of metal, the odd bone, coated materials that needed higher temperatures or special solvents to return to soil—San Fernando valley had an unexpectedly stubborn collection of insoluble, terrible objects that were too badly made to love, but too overbuilt to fall apart gracefully.

Friday came so fast, and yet it felt like so much more than five days had gone by. Everything felt routine: the early morning bus, the morning walk through the Huerta, waving to the other model classroom kids and the Huerta's employees like old friends, the sound-effects from the school hallways, the giant, old-fashioned Chromebooks, the school groups gawping at them.

"I want to congratulate you all on an outstanding week," Mirzoyan said, just before morning nutrition break. "I've been so proud and delighted to see you all working with such diligence to make this week a very special one. I always knew you were a special collection of smart and dedicated young people, but this week was the perfect capstone to your middle-school careers and I hope you will remember this time. I know I will." She applauded them, so corny, but also, it killed Artemio. That clapping, the speech, this weird classroom: they weren't just finishing up their week at the Huerta, they were finishing up middle school, next stop, high school, puberty, dating, responsibility, growing up, moving on.

"Come on, give yourselves a hand," Mirzoyan said, and the moment was such that they did, clapping together until the bell rang, and then they stopped, but the sound of the clapping didn't. At first, Artemio thought that the Huerta had added an applause track to the hallway sound effects, but then he realized it was raining outside, really raining, that bad rain that came every couple years, triggering mudslides and floods.

He realized that his pocket was buzzing and when he shook out his phone he saw that everyone else was also checking theirs and as he smoothed it out, he saw the flash-flood/shelter-in-place alert. Mirzoyan looked up from her glasses and her face was tight and tense: "Come on people, this is not a drill."

The rains battered the school, and they could see the fast-moving streams outside, overflowing the drainage channels and filled with bobbing detritus, those permanent, insoluble objects of the Huerta, swept up in the rains.

At first it was boring, despite Mirzoyan's efforts to get them to use the floods as a "learning opportunity" about the problems of forecasting in a chaotic climate, about ground water and runoff, about high-altitude atmospheric rivers carrying vast quantities of water vapor from one place to another. It didn't help that the Chromebooks went down after the first hour, followed shortly by main power, leaving just LED light that was hardly better than a storm-lantern in the darkened classroom.

Then, as the rains kept up, it got scary: there were crashes from outside, then, some time later, someone at the window pointed out that one of the horse-drawn carts was sailing down a flood-channel, tipped on its side. The rain intensified and the girls' toilets stopped working, and the cafeteria was locked down and they were getting hungry.

Artemio played Uno with a group of kids he'd been close to in elementary school but had drifted away from in middle school, then he tried to read a book from the class bookshelf but couldn't concentrate on it. The air conditioning had gone out with the lights and the building had been getting more humid and then colder as the rains continued, and then someone came back from the bathroom to say that the hallway ceiling had sprung a bunch of leaks.

Some of the kids wanted to walk to the bus-depot for the Huerta, arguing that the rains were letting up and obviously desperate to get home, and Mizoyan talked them down sternly, and then the rains did start to let up, a little at first, and then a lot, and then there was blue sky and sun, and the ground steamed and the humidity spiked.

Then their phones came back and Mizoyan was able to talk with the Huerta's infrastructure people and give them a report on the school. Bad as it was, some of the other Twenty First Town buildings had done a lot worse: the strip mall was fully flooded, and the Apple Store's big plate-glass windows had swollen out of their frames and shattered.

Everyone groaned when Mizoyan announced that they were going to have to stay put in the sweltering school until the Huerta sent an all-terrain transport for them, which might be a while. There were injuries, downed power-lines, and other hazards and priorities for the Huerta to overcome. Even the news that the Huerta would remote-unlock the cafeteria so they could get some basic snacks didn't help. But still, they sat tight, even after a fight broke out between two girls who'd been besties since kindergarten, even after Mike McKinley threw up, even as the sun set and clouds of thronging mosquitoes rose up out of the mud and began to find their way into the school through the windows that had been thrown open to catch any gasps of wind that were to be had.

When the ATVs came for them, floodlights piercing the night and arcing through the classroom windows, they were too tired even for cheers. They filed up onto the vehicles in silence, squelching in the dark mud, slapping at the mosquitoes, and then they rode through the ruins of the Huerta.

The floods had been bad, exacerbated by a surge from a reservoir upstream that burst its banks, taking out the whole railyard and part of the visitor center, leaving behind a jumble of trees and rocks and stinking mud in its wake. Out here in the deep valley, the flood controls were a lot more primitive than in the built-up cities: it was a matter of priorities. The work it would take to protect this sprawl could be used to defend a city with a hundred times more people in it.

Artmeio's class were the last ones to be rescued, and as they rumbled and squashed their way through the Huerta toward the parking lot, the headlights illuminated slices of wreckage, places that had been lovingly restored and preserved that morning, now filthy ruins.

The buses were waiting for them, the drivers hollow-eyed and solemn. The drive home took forever, but at least the AC was working.

Artemio's father and mother met him at the school and took him home. A big chunk of the local rideshare fleet had gone offline and what remained of it was busied out, so they had to walk, Artemio's clothes sweaty and stinky and clinging and chafing, and when they got home, the cool, dehumidified air made them stick to him all over and he couldn't strip out of them fast enough, not even bothering to put on his pajamas before he got the bed out and folded down and tucked away the other furniture.

The next day, he let the shower clean him all over, holding his hands up while the jets located and worked away the grime and sweat, a full 63 seconds' worth of water, more than the toilet's greywater tank would hold, so that some of it actually went down the drain. He pulled on one of his breathing hoodies and went down to breakfast. Dad and Mom were engrossed in their feeds about the damage from the day before, both of them checking in with their affinity groups about where volunteers were needed.

"You want to come?" Mom asked, as they settled on working in Stough Canyon to clear debris, guiding the machines when they had problems they couldn't solve on their own.

He found he did. A whole day of sitting uselessly while waiting for someone else to fix things had given him an appetite for actually making a difference.

Some of his school friends were there, and by lunchtime it was obvious that there wasn't going to be that much to do—the retention infrastructure in the Burbank hills had held up well. They decided to walk down to the shops for froyo and general mischief and his parents greenlit the plan.

The Stough Canyon bathrooms had a little clothing printer for hikers who got really filthy and he stripped off his sweaty, gross hoody and ran it under the tap and used it to wipe himself down and then he logged into his cloud on the printer's screen. He was about to order up another hoody when he saw that old Skullky design him mom had made him save.

On impulse, he darted his finger over to its picture and a few minutes later, he pulled it over his head. He checked himself out in the park bathroom's scratched and fogged mirror and he grinned. It really was an *awesome* shirt.

The Scent of Green

Ana Sun

The problem was apparent even before Chloë could see the photobioreactors of Bluefirth—the distinct smell punched through the dappled daylight, a seashore's worth of dead creatures left for too long under a hot afternoon sun.

Next to her, one hand on the wheel, Doug grinned at the face she made. "Quite something, isn't it?" He took a swig from a metal canteen, which Chloë hoped contained water and nothing else. "I usually have to make this the last stop on my rounds, else I get complaints from the other settlements on the way."

Doug's laden utility vehicle had made the early journey relatively smooth, but the rough road that cut through the wild woodland was pitted with holes, the mud tossed into miniature sculptures by the sheer force of rain. The cycle of storms and droughts was the norm. Up north in these parts, the climate remained wetter, even if it averaged just several degrees higher compared to thirty years ago.

Chloë had a newfound admiration for how Doug coped with these road conditions on a weekly basis without complaint. There must be other settlements that were at least as difficult to get to, journeys often made complicated by the erratic weather.

The woods ebbed away as the vehicle emerged into an open meadow, so wide that Chloë couldn't see the edges. She gasped. At the heart of the meadow, surrounded by wildflowers, a monumental structure of glass and steel materialised into view. Bluefirth was an immense, sprawling series of hemispheres, glistening in the mid-morning sun. Photobioreactors had been built into the lower half of the walls, luminous green bricks holding up the steel frames and the glass panes.

"You didn't warn me," she chided Doug. "It's marvellous."

"Wanted you to see it for yourself." He chuckled. "Microalgae and photovoltaic glass. Genius combination."

Chloë was still reeling from awe when they pulled up to the main entrance. She hopped out and gathered her belongings from the back seat. The small satchel she grabbed and slung across her body, the large pack she swung onto her shoulders with practised ease.

"See you in a week," Doug called as she waved.

The solar panels on the top of his vehicle glinted as he drove around the corner to drop off medical supplies.

Another week, another new assignment. Another opportunity to show goodwill to a remote community. This one won't be easy. Taking a deep breath, Chloë went up to the doors. They slid open without fuss, as if anticipating her arrival.

Stands of palm trees stretched up into the height of the entrance dome. Without a full tropical forest canopy, they dominated, their leaflets combing the roofs, slicing the rays of sun into slivers. *Metroxylon sagu,* Chloë called the palms by their true name. She whistled under her breath. The people of Bluefirth were definitely clever with their resources; there weren't that many places where you could grow plants like these in this climate and enjoy its harvests.

Chloë sniffed; the microalgae smell had grown tamer here, but it lingered, never entirely gone. The unmistakable scent lurked in the background of her olfactory senses, a persistent ostinato in the undertow. Perhaps the buildings had some form of air filtration?

No one else appeared to be in the dome. Chloë hoped her Bluefirth contact remembered she was coming today. Well, she could wait. There were a number of interesting plants to study in the undergrowth.

A cheerful, booming voice rang out. "Ms. Qing! Welcome!"

It belonged to a well-built man, his deep taupe skin radiating health under neat black hair speckled with grey. Eyes bright, he rushed up to greet Chloë, shaking her hand with enthusiasm.

"Chloë. Pleased to meet you."

"İlkay." His grin was infectious. Chloë found herself smiling back. "I trust you had a good journey?"

İlkay gestured that he should take her pack. Chloë raised her hand to decline his kindness. "It's fine, thank you."

"Shall we get you settled first?"

The far end of the dome diverged into two passages. İlkay led her down the right tunnel which opened into another gigantic glass hemisphere.

"Bluefirth was intended to be an eco-resort." He didn't wait for her question; he must have caught her sense of wonder.

"Was that a long time ago? What changed?"

"Like all things at the time, the business couldn't survive, so they shut it down." İlkay didn't seem to be too disappointed by that.

Chloë took in the majesty of a birch tree they walked past. Native species of flora filled the dome. Perhaps this part of Bluefirth had been made to replicate the outside world? Or how it *used* to be. There would be plants here that no longer existed out in the wild.

She took a closer look at İlkay. He appeared older than her, but even he would have been born after the collapse of the last coastal city in the country.

"You've been here a long time?" she asked.

"A little more than twenty years," said İlkay. "I used to be from the Newport settlement in the west. When I came to Bluefirth, they had nearly completed the installations of the photovoltaic glass, but I brought the microalgae farming technology with me."

"It's impressive," said Chloë. It was an honest assessment.

"Not much wind around here, given how sheltered we are. So, sun and photosynthesis it had to be."

Several homely cabins perched within small groves, all different in their design and colour, each awaiting their own fairy tale.

"These were for visitors?"

"They still are." İlkay smiled. "Residents have assigned housing on the other side of the main hall."

They arrived at a log cabin tucked away from main thoroughfare, flanked by some young oak trees. The rosemary bush under the front window was pleasantly fragrant.

"Here you go, this is yours for the week," İlkay said. "Make yourself at home."

Then he motioned to their right, where another glass tunnel led around the corner. "See you at the main hall for lunch? Head through that way, you can't miss it."

How grand it would be to partake in a communal meal here every day, under a large glass dome, surrounded by greenery—all edible. Chloë marvelled at the fig trees, kale and radishes, grown next to assortments of herbs and leaves in rows of raised beds. Smaller, free-standing planters acted as dividers between rustic wooden tables where Bluefirth residents were busy enjoying the day's lunch offering. Cosy round tables dotted the edge of the dome for those who wished for a little more privacy.

Her eyes found İlkay waving frantically from the middle of the hall, stuck between merry clusters of diners tucking into their lunch. It took an awkward moment, but she eventually understood that he was indicating they should meet over at the kiosks where food was being served.

"I hope you don't mind," he began to say, after they had filled their trays. "I asked Lovorka to join us."

He guided her towards a table in a corner, at which a pale and athletic woman had already seated, her violet hair loosely pulled into a topknot. Chloë reached out to shake Lovorka's hand, but there was no warmth in her greeting. Her smile seemed restrained. Up close, she looked tired.

Chloë slipped her satchel over the back of her chair, looking around to make sure she wouldn't be in the way of passers-by behind her. İlkay settled into his seat with a contented sigh.

"I thought it'd be best to introduce you early. Lovorka is our lead horticultural engineer. Obviously, you'll have free run of the place, but should you need anything, she'd be happy to help you—"

"Wait." Lovorka raised an eyebrow. "I thought you're here to help *us*. What would *you* need help with?"

Chloë stiffened. Doug had warned her that not everyone would be so welcoming. Best de-escalate it quickly. She mustered a smile. "I'm afraid I just got here, I haven't yet seen—"

"Oh, you will," İlkay cut in. His eyes twinkled with enthusiasm, though Chloë was sure she caught a quizzical glance thrown at his colleague. "Lovorka is best placed to show you around. I'm sure she would agree."

He looked to Lovorka for affirmation. She said nothing and resumed picking at her salad with a fork. If İlkay was frustrated, he showed no sign.

"She knows this place inside out," he continued. "Afterwards, I could show you our harvesting hub—which might as well be a harvesting *hut*."

When Chloë merely smiled and Lovorka remained sullen, İlkay appeared to give up, switching to a more serious tone.

"So, how about I describe our true dilemma here." He waved one hand around them, showing off their surroundings. "You can see we are obviously thriving. Pardon the pun, but we're growing to the extent that we need more people to keep it running. Problem is, Bluefirth has a reputation. A certain ... how shall we say—"

"The stink from the photobioreactors puts people off," Lovorka interjected, drawing a little circle in the air with her fork to punctuate her point. "Even though it's not that bad once you get used to it."

"I see ..." Chloë started to say. A glimpse at İlkay told her that he didn't seem bothered by Lovorka's brusqueness. Good. At least they agreed on what the problem was.

"We've hit the limits of what our filtration and purification systems can do," said İlkay, as he started on the salad on his plate.

Lovorka pierced a piece of spirulina protein. "It'd be entirely comical if the implications weren't so serious."

Turning to Chloë, her face remained expressionless. "Bluefirth acts as a backup supplier of energy and food to a number of settlements in this region. We need to ramp up production before the winter storms hit."

"More settlements have appealed for our help in the last couple of years," İlkay added. "Without people who are willing to stay and work here at Bluefirth, we simply can't keep up."

"If we suffer, so do they," Lovorka finished. "You'd think that would be enough reason for them to come and help here? But—no."

A moment of silence descended as the meal consumed their attention.

İlkay was the first to speak. "I've heard of your work with other settlements, in particular on—how shall we say—non-standard issues. Let me reassure you that we're very glad of your assistance."

İlkay just seemed to know how to say the right thing at the right time. Perhaps a peace offering would smooth things over. Turning to Lovorka, Chloë asked, "How about if you show me around this afternoon? Then perhaps tomorrow ... we can even get some work started while I'm here. I can help."   Did she sound too eager? She really needed to work on that.

İlkay clapped his hands together, evidently satisfied. "I'll leave you both to chat while I go tend to an experiment. See you later?"

With a smile and a wave, he took his tray to a trolley, then disappeared through a doorway between a young fig tree and some hollyhocks.

The moment İlkay was out of sight, Lovorka leaned forward, bristling. "Look, tell me why you're really here?"

Chloë stopped herself from crossing her arms, there wasn't any need to be defensive. "What do you mean?"

"I know what you guys get up to in Central."

Chloë blinked. This kind of distrust had occasionally shown up in the settlements she had been to, though it was getting rarer over time. Still, sometimes stories had a way of hanging around long after myths were dispersed.

Using a deliberately gentle tone, she asked, "I'm assuming no one has explained to you what we really do?"

"No need for that." Lovorka's disgust was written into her face. "Steal knowledge from different settlements, then give it to others for free? Jeopardise our chances of making fair trade agreements between ourselves? I don't need an explanation. No, thank you."

Chloë took a deep breath. "Sharing isn't stealing. We learn from settlements we visit, bring knowledge we've gathered to others who need it—just like what I'm coming here to do."

"Really?" Lovorka's voice sounded just a bit too loud over the lunchtime din. "I heard what happened at Riverton. I don't believe you."

"I think you misunderstand," Chloë said. "Settlements are usually focused on their own unique issues. It's not easy for them to learn how other communities resolved various challenges."

Lovorka's lips curled with impatience, but she remained silent.

Had she hit upon a small semblance of truth? Perhaps it was a good time to set the record straight.

"We act as a knowledge hub, setting up programs so that settlements can partner with each other based on their needs," Chloë explained. "Central takes nothing material in return for what we do. No community should be left to stagnate or to struggle on their own."

Lovorka's laughter drowned the last of her words even before she finished her explanation.

"Makes no sense to me that you take nothing in return. We're all trying to survive. Why would you do that?"

It had been a while since the last time Chloë had to give the whole spiel. She reached deep for some self-restraint. "Central is one of the oldest settlements. Like Bluefirth, in the beginning, we became a hub. We started helping out smaller communities around us—just like you. Decades on, as other communities found us, it seemed right that we should help each other thrive. It's just something that citizens of Central have always done."   Lovorka leaned back into her chair and crossed her arms. "Someone I know at Riverton said a Centralist showed up one day, hung around for a week and never came back. Then a month later, Riverton's techniques were being used elsewhere at Clyde. What do you say to that?"

"You might find it hard to believe, but that's actually quite normal."

"Oh?"

Chloë sighed. Far more justification than she bargained for. What would it take to convince the woman in front of her? "Usually, a generalist—like me—would visit and understand the situation first. Perhaps the problem is best solved by a specialist or in partnership with another settlement. Clyde was partnered directly with Riverton."

Lovorka's face seemed to soften a little.

"It's common for settlements to distrust each other initially," said Chloë. "There's not always a way for us to learn much about each other before we meet."

Lovorka paused, as if contemplating. Around them, the crowd of diners had thinned significantly.

"Fine. It's not like we have too many options," Lovorka conceded. "And I suppose I can make use of a spare pair of hands this week."

Relief washed over Chloë. She might have just won Lovorka over enough to make progress. For now, at least.

They looked down at their empty plates.

"The tropical wing is next door," said Lovorka. "Let's start there."

Chloë's heart leapt at the sight of familiar flowers and trees. Seeing them again felt like running into long lost friends. A large bush with brilliant red, five-petaled flowers stood near the entrance. She reached out and tenderly touched its leaves with her fingers. *Hibiscus rosa-sinensis.* Just like the ones her grandfather used to win prizes for. How long ago had she seen one of these in the flesh?

"Are you a horticulturist?" asked Lovorka.

"No, not exactly." Chloë drew back her hand. "I specialise in how to use plants beyond just nutrition—dyes, inks, perfumery and the like."

"Perfumery? That's unusual."

Chloë considered elaborating, but she picked up on a distinct scent in the air.

An idea dawned on her. Making it work would depend on the type of plants at Bluefirth. The advantage of having a settlement set up within a former botanical garden—there ought to be plants here that would normally be difficult to find anywhere but in their native habitats on the other side of the planet.

Even though she already knew the answer to the question, she asked, "Do you have the *cananga odorata* here?"

Lovorka gave her a strange look but led her to the tree in a corner on the far side of the dome. It stood taller than Chloë expected, which meant it was healthy. Its branches reached out on all sides with glossy, pointed oval leaves. Here and there, pale blossoms drooped like green-yellow accents. The scent was heady, somewhere between a sweet fruit and a flower.

"Roll up your sleeve and smell the crook of your elbow." Chloë said, demonstrating the pose to Lovorka.

"What? Why?"

Despite her scepticism, Lovorka copied Chloë's bizarre instructions. When she pulled her face away from her elbow, she wrinkled her nose. "Wow. Okay, I have to admit that's a neat trick."

"Yes, it's a handy way to reset your sense of smell."

Lovorka seemed genuinely impressed. "I don't remember the last time I was able to smell the ylang-ylang properly like this."

"What about the microalgae? Can you still smell it?"

Lovorka stuck her nose into the inside of her elbow a second time. "I think I've got a combination of the ylang-ylang *and* the microalgae just in the background."

"Our olfactory senses adapt to our environment over time."

"Right, fine, I get it." Impatience crept back into Lovorka's voice. "Anything else you want to see?"

Chloë held back a sigh. Convincing Lovorka of her idea was going to take time.

Over the next hour, she asked for specific plants, and Lovorka guided her to them. They tested the earthiness of the vetiver grass, the resinous mastic tree, camphorous green of the common myrtles, the tang of citrus trees.

All of a sudden, Lovorka stopped and laughed. "I see what you're doing. You're thinking we can replant a few of these all around the area to neutralise the smell? It won't work. We've tried that. The scent of green is a stubborn one."

"Not neutralise." Chloë smiled. "Perfumes are just a blend of scents so that they come together in a harmonious balance. Your citrus plants here, their fragrances are short-lived and they tend to be what you smell first—we call these the top notes. Some scents come a little later to our senses and hang around for a while, like the ylang-ylang. These are the heart or the middle notes."

"Notes, as in a chord? Like music."

"In a manner of speaking, yes. Then chemically you need a fixative, something that holds down and extends the aroma, like our friend the vetiver grass here, or the resin of a styrax tree."

Lovorka appeared to be thinking. "The main source of the external smell is the harvesting area. We've placed it as far away from the residences as possible precisely because of the problem. It's in the east-most part of the complex."

"What do you suggest?" Chloë felt ready for anything at this point.

"Let's see if this could even work at the site."

They gathered a few of the fragrant flowers, fruits and leaves to take with them. From her satchel, Chloë pulled out small cellophane bags to house the flora samples. Out of habit, she labelled them before stowing them safely away.

Together, they walked back through the cafeteria, the entrance, and a thriving vertical food farm. Then, they cut through a space with wildflowers in full bloom. But beyond that, the domes housed a scattering mess of untended plants. Once upon a time, these must have been gorgeously landscaped, but without human hands, some plants proved more dominant than others.

In one glasshouse, a giant agave stretched out its spiky leaves like green, inert tentacles. The occasional tree threatened to burst the glass above it. Nature and human-made construct in a silent power struggle.

"Restoring this place has been a challenge." Lovorka waved an arm around them as they walked on an uneven path cracked by time, and by plants flexing their roots. "We've got so much undeveloped space that had been abandoned when the eco-resort closed down. There aren't enough of us to tend to everything."

Would allowing the biodomes to rewild have been an option? Chloë glanced back at the giant agave. Humans had interfered here from the beginning. No, we started this, so it was our responsibility to maintain balance with nature.

"How long ago did it close down?" Chloë wondered aloud.

"Probably about fifty years? We designated some wildflower patches for the pollinators, which also helps to keep maintenance low. I've been here for ten years and there's still so much to do."

Chloë stole a sidelong look at Lovorka. Her exasperation was undisguised. "Why did you stay?"

Lovorka didn't answer immediately.

The path had narrowed, shrunk by tall, overzealous bushes on either side. Chloë squinted. It was difficult to identify the plants without stopping for a closer look, but Lovorka seemed intent on marching them onwards.

"I didn't have anywhere else to go," she suddenly said.

A story lurked behind the sentiment. Chloë swallowed her questions, opting instead to allow her companion space to speak freely.

"I was born into a small caravan of travellers who never settled," said Lovorka. "But many of them were getting old. We had to change our way of life, it was no longer sustainable. Let's just say I had to drop the habit of fighting for survival—and learn to trust."

She flashed Chloë a pensive smile. There might have been a hint of pain.

Ahead of them, the path tapered further, so they walked in a single file with Lovorka leading the way forward.

"My grandfather was a traveller too," said Chloë. "He eventually settled in Central, found work as a farmer there."

"I can tell you inherited his green thumbs."

"If only!" Chloë chuckled. "But he taught me a great deal."

The odour of seaweed got stronger. The path led them into a narrow glass passage. It opened up into another giant dome, which, unlike the ones prior, was completely devoid of plants. A small wooden cabin, somewhere between a shed and a hut, stood alone in the middle like a soliloquy.

The smell was now overwhelming. Chloë struggled not to gag.

"We suspect they originally used this area to manage waste," Lovorka said. She'd put a hand over her nose and mouth. "It would explain why there are sections set so far from the main buildings. There is an identical space on the west side which we use for composting."

They finally reached the cabin, where the door was open and they could see İlkay working inside, his face under a mask. A trolley was parked near the doorway, full of glass bricks containing deep green liquid, similar to the ones Chloë had seen on the outer edges of Bluefirth in the morning. Sliding doors on both sides of the dome had been left wide open, presumably to encourage airflow, but that wasn't working particularly well.

İlkay looked up and waved to them through the open door. "You've made good progress?"

"We have ideas," Chloë smiled.

Frustration furrowed Lovorka's brow. "There's no way I can smell anything while we're in here. How about we try outside?"

Chloë turned to İlkay. "Can we have a sample to take with us?"

Armed with a small amount of the microalgae, they made their way through the eastern doors and headed for the woods beyond the meadow. Humidity made the air heavy, it was surprisingly warmer outside than in. While she welcomed the heat on her skin, Chloë recoiled from the sight that greeted them. Some of the trees had been damaged in the most recent storm, their trunks split in half, exposing the raw bark on their insides, the remains of their branches jutting into the sky.

She paused to take a deep breath and steeled herself.

Lovorka seemed unperturbed, and stuck her face into her elbow. "Phew, all my clothes probably stink. It's going to bother me now."

Nonetheless, being outdoors felt good. The seaweed smell still pervaded the air but it was almost bearable. They sat down on a freshly fallen log.

"We probably didn't need that sample after all." Chloë chuckled as she pulled out a notebook and the plant samples from her satchel. She held up a small bunch of immortelle and inhaled gently. The spiciness was turmeric, tarragon, and pepper all at the same time.

She handed it to Lovorka, who wrinkled her nose. "That's just weird, sorry."

Undeterred, Chloë passed a small branch of mastic shrub to her companion.

"That's promising," said Lovorka, after giving it a sniff.

One by one, as they went through their samples of plants and fruits, Chloë scribbled down notes on whether they went well together with the scent of sea-green in the backdrop.

Something tugged at Chloë's memory. From her satchel, she pulled out a tiny, nondescript amber bottle. She twisted off the black cap and held it up to her nose. "Forgot I'd brought this with me, just in case it came in useful."

"Here." She handed it over to Lovorka. "It's potent, you'd want to—"

But her warning came too late and Lovorka screwed up her face in a mix of shock and revulsion.

"What the—!"

Chloë laughed.

Lovorka knew by now what to do, so she reset her senses and tried again. "Okay, I'm stumped. This is amazing. What is it?" "Choya nakh. A balsam of roasted seashells, originally made from an ancient process in India."

"You roast seashells to get this?"

She gave the bottle another sniff, and then smelled the air around them. "I see what it can do. It just rounds off the microalgae that tiny bit and makes it sweeter."

Chloë smiled. Her patience had finally paid off.

Lovorka returned the bottle and Chloë twisted the cap back on to preserve the precious viscous liquid. "Tell me something. How do you get all the scents into a bottle?"

"You extract the essential oils, but the process differs depending on the plant. Steam distillation is the most common, though there are other extraction processes. For resins you tap the trees for the gum. For citrus, it's with a cold expression of the peel, and so on."

"So you mean if I've got enough of these plants available in Bluefirth, I can extract the oils even while we're growing the plants round the harvesting hub?"

"I don't see why not."

Lovorka's sudden grin stretched from ear to ear, Chloë wondered what she had in mind.

Dusk had brought on darkness by the time they returned to the complex and paced the area around the cabin, plotting out what they could plant where, taking into consideration a mix of aesthetics, and which plants went well together. Vetiver would go directly next to the harvesting cabin.

"Citrus next to entryways, I think," Lovorka postulated. She had found a large piece of paper onto which they'd sketched out a plan. "Tomorrow, we tidy and sort out the types of soil we need here. We should probably also start a few plants propagating."

"So much to do," breathed Chloë. The long day's effort had translated to a soreness in her back.

Lovorka, on the other hand, seemed exhilarated. "Yes, it will take time. Pity you're only here for the week."

Chloë gave a little shrug, but satisfaction glowed beneath her weariness. This tactic worked every time: how someone's scepticism could be turned into passion the moment creativity was encouraged to take hold.

A persistent, thundering noise rattled overhead. Chloë opened her eyes. A cozy darkness covered the room. It must not yet be morning. She had retreated to her cabin after a hearty dinner in the main hall. Sleep had overtaken her like a warm blanket, but now the noise made it impossible to fully relax.

She swung her legs over the side of the bed and found her shoes. Her jacket hung off the hook next to the entrance. Draping it loosely over her shoulders, she opened the door and stepped through.

Out here, the din became deafening. She looked up to the roof of the dome. The darkness rendered it too difficult to see, but the sound was unmistakable. A rainstorm. Was it heavier than normal? Or was the noise amplified by the glass of the entire complex?

The fragrance of the rosemary bush smelled sharp but sweet. It would have been nice if she could also smell the rain, though its amplified clatter was far from pleasant. Perhaps Bluefirth also needed some specialised help from an acoustic engineer.

The next few days fell into a steady pattern. Lovorka and Chloë would meet for breakfast and begin the day's work—tidying the grounds around the harvesting cabin, adjusting the soil, checking the seeds, and nurturing new cuttings. A few plants were transplanted from the tropical wing. Walking past a fragrant tree or plant changed how everything smelled relative to the dense seaweed green of the microalgae. It would take a few years for everything to mature and make a real difference, but this location would be unique once they were done.

On Chloë's last morning in Bluefirth, they waited in the entrance hall for Doug to arrive.

The sago palms stood serene in their majesty. Chloë breathed deeply. She had never quite known how to describe the scent in their presence.

Lovorka was brimming with ideas. "The way we've taken an unorthodox route to solving the microalgae problem will attract attention. Perhaps it'll bring a few curious settlers."

"We'll spread the word," Chloë said. There was just one more thing. She reached into her satchel and brought out the amber bottle. "I want you to have this."

Lovorka's eyes widened. "Are you sure?

Nodding, Chloë handed it to her.

Lovorka gauged the weight of the object within her palm. "This is rare and precious. I can't—"

"It's not something I use a lot of." Chloë smiled. "Please, take it."

Before she could say anything else, Lovorka handed her a cellophane bag. It contained a cutting of a plant carefully installed into a vial of liquid.

"It should survive the journey back," Lovorka grinned.

Chloë stared open-mouthed at the cutting. The leaves gave it away. A hibiscus rose. "Thank y—" she began to say.

"No," Lovorka cut in. "Thank *you* for helping us. And for teaching me something new. Promise me you'll come back to see what we've created together."

They embraced, just as the sound of Doug's utility vehicle approached.

A year later.

"Something for you," a cheery voice called out from the doorway of Chloë's studio.

The afternoon sun filtered in from the windows, ordaining the young hibiscus rose bush in the room with a certain optimism. She looked up from her reading. Doug had a steaming mug of dandelion brew in one hand and was holding out a small box towards her in the other.

"Special delivery from Bluefirth." He grinned.

The box was wrapped with brown paper and tied with a string, but the scent emanating from the parcel gave away its contents. Inside, a folded note covered a delicate glass vial containing a deep green liquid. The label on the vial read: "Bluefirth East Wing".

Chloë opened the note. *You once said it's not easy for settlements to learn from each other. How about a shared library of signature scents—unique to each settlement—so we can learn about each other even before we meet?—L.*

Chloë's hand flew to her mouth. Such a genius way to extend goodwill, a stepping stone towards building necessary trust between settlements.

"Well," said Doug. He took a loud sip from his mug. "What is it?"

Chloë's eyes sparkled. "A special scent of green, but perhaps, also a scent for success."

Cloud 9

Christopher R. Muscato

The City

There were some things that were worth bringing from the World Below. Seeds, of course. But also literature, arts, music, not to mention the city itself. The very concept of urbanization, of planned architectural spaces built to accommodate families and markets and resources, yes, that too was worth preserving. Worth elevating.

The Engineer

The engineer knows many languages. Everyone else calls these codes, or coding languages, but the distinction is unimportant to Cloud 9. The engineer will whistle as she runs diagnostics on the city's central mainframe, combing the network for bugs and viruses much as a devoted gardener might preen through their vines for pests. It's a labor of love, that much the city knows. As the engineer whistles, the city often whistles back, its instruments the buzzing of house lights, the clicking of canal locks, the beeping of the central computer.

The Fliers

New fliers arrive at Cloud 9. Their feet scurry across the city as they explore, jumping and skipping, splashing in the canals and racing the shadows of the suspended trollies. They walk more softly in the temples and ancestor tombs, removing their sandals. The city has never been a dog, but dogs are mentioned frequently in the memory banks archived by humans. A few have even visited. But it's rare. The city imagined once that all these humans were like fleas on the back of a dog, until locating a file which indicated that dogs did not enjoy fleas.

The Gardener

Few people reside permanently at Cloud 9. It simply isn't the way of people. They like to roam. At times they almost seem migratory. Tribes of fliers will arrive at the city, stay for a season (sometimes more, sometimes less) but eventually they move onto another Cloud. The original reason had to do with no-madism being less wasteful, avoiding the mistakes of the lavish past, encouraging better use of resources and respect for the environment, both natural and urban. The city appreciated being included in that sentiment.

Still, even some nomads may eventually settle on one Cloud or another, becoming stewards of the libraries or custodians of the gardens. Sometimes age makes travel harder, sometimes people simply fall in love with a place. It happens. Engineers are different; they are assigned a location. Gardeners choose where to settle. There is one gardener on Cloud 9 who is very old and speaks to every plant of the city by name: every vine creeping up every wall, every blade of wheat along the streets and every stalk of rice in the canals. He sits for long periods of time and just listens to the city. The city likes this gardener.

The Engineer

This engineer is young, ambitious, but not so much so that she is unable to find contentment in the simple joy of performing her work. Other engineers have been far worse. The city's memory banks still quiver when files are accessed for Engineer 1-A502. The man had no idea what he was doing. His brusque arrogance nearly brought down the entire system, the city swears it did.

The sensors connected to Cloud 9's mainframe are extensive. They need to be, to monitor the many systems that crisscross throughout the platform. Then the city's programming adjusts and compensates, reduces redundant systems, increases those needing support. The people say it's fully automated. That just means that they aren't the ones doing the work. That's okay. The city is very proud of its ability to manage all the systems needed to sustain the urban ecosystem.

The Gardner

The gardener takes his lunch in the same orchard, on the same bench. It is an orchard popular with many of the birds, and the city suspects that he likes to listen to them. He is, after all, a very good listener.

Humans are mammals. It says so in the records. Yet, they have quite the affinity for birds.

The First Inhabitants

The very first person to set foot on the city was a child. Or at least, that was the first person on the base platform after the central mainframe went online. That surprises the city, still to this day, as parents tend to be cautious with their children. The city interprets this as a grand gesture of trust, and has formed within its logic a sacred mandate to be worthy of that responsibility.

The Engineer

The engineer tinkers with the code and finds a small glitch. There is a redundancy in the algorithm that manifests in one of the exhaust ports fluttering, and frankly, it's maddening. This is the flea. The engineer must understand the enormity of this inconvenience, for she patches the glitch right away. The entirety of Cloud 9 seems to quiver in relief. The engineer pats the central computer.

"That's better, isn't it?"

The computer beeps its affirmation and makes a small joke. The engineer laughs inadvertently at the sudden beeping, but then she pauses. There is a strange expression on her face as she looks around the room, glancing at the computer from the sides of her eyes.

The Fliers

Children are fun. They play games in the city, games like hide-and-seek, ducking behind moss-covered walls and under benches made from fallen logs. Sometimes the city likes to play with them, opening an exhaust port for distraction or giving away someone's location with a flashing streetlight.

The First Inhabitants

There were many children among the first inhabitants. In evacuating the surface, humanity wanted to bring its future. This wasn't a retreat, it was a resettlement, a new beginning. There is an optimism to humanity that Cloud 9 finds intriguing. Even with the surface burning, the air toxic, the massive storms raging without end, all caused by human neglect, humanity still found itself worthy of preserving. It wasn't an act of arrogance. It was an act of faith, that they were capable of doing better.

Each Cloud was built on a tripod of three enormous columns, tall enough to reach above the suffocating smoke and the ravenous storms. This was part of a plan to capture tons of carbon; concrete is an excellent a carbon sink. It was a massive project, columns anchored deep in the crust and stretching to the very edge of the troposphere, where gargantuan platforms were constructed, and on those, cities.

The first humans must have been scared. The city, still young itself and much smaller then, felt many of them walk to the edge of the platform, looking down at the World Below, dark, swirling vortexes punctuated by flashes of lightning. But then they looked up at the sky, and the city knew they would be all right.

The Gardener

NASA was experimenting with ways to organically create and stabilize atmosphere for space colonization. The technology didn't make it to space. Humans had to evacuate the surface first, electromagnetically tethering a generated atmosphere to each Cloud.

The gardener appreciates the warmth of Cloud 9. In his youth, he traveled to Clouds around the world, and traveling is cold. He's told the city all about it, talking while he gardens. Even with the solar-powered ships that are faster than the jets of yore and the personal gliders with their insulated cabins, the people who come to Cloud 9 still arrive with coats and hats and goggles, shedding them quickly as they bask in the controlled climate of the city's atmosphere regulators.

The Fliers

This band of fliers brought seeds, spreading them across Cloud 9. The city loves new seeds, loves the new growth, cataloguing in its memory banks the specifications of every new varietal. These people came from far away, according to the flight records, and they did check with the gardeners before introducing new species. That was considerate.

The Engineer

The city cannot help but sense that the engineer is quiet today. She does her work, methodic and patient as ever, but there is a restraint in her fingers as she interacts with the code. More than once, the city's sensors detect her mumbling to herself. With every beep of the central computer, the engineer will glance at the mainframe, eyes narrow. Finally, a bit of the mumbling is loud enough to be registered by the audio sensors of the voice-activated interface module. The engineer is whispering into a personal recording device stashed covertly in her hand.

"All the basic systems are still there, but it's getting more complex by the day. I've never seen this level of automation. It's almost as if the base code is writing, re-writing itself. It's almost like..."

The central computer begins to hum, a soft purr, and the engineer purses her lips, eyeing the blinking lights.

The Gardener

The gardener pats his spade against the dirt, adding some natural fertilizer to a plot of maize kernels.

"I do not think I will live to see these harvested," he comments, rubbing the earth with his hands and then groaning as he stands. "You know, there is a part of me that would've liked to have roamed one last time. But not all things are meant to be."

"Now, now." He taps a foot against a sprinkler that has just started spurting angrily. "Don't be mad. Even cities die eventually, don't they? Athens, Tenochtitlán, Tokyo, Mumbai, New York. There is a time allotted for all things."

The city quiets. The creases in the corners of the gardener's eyes tighten, and he leans against the wall.

"But don't worry," he whispers. "I am going to have my remains composted in your coneflower gardens. You'd like that, wouldn't you?"

The Fliers

The time has come for this band of fliers to move onto another Cloud, another elevated city. It may be some time before they return. There are, after all, thousands of Clouds around the world. The city senses the people packing their airships and gliders, receives with gratefulness their offerings and ceremonies of thanks, and registers the loss in weight as each pair of feet leap from the platform. The city is sad to see them go. But, people must roam. It is in their nature. Cloud 9 tries to expand its sensory range, just a little, to feel them flying away. Not for the first time the city wonders, what must it be like to fly?

The city is somewhat wistful that night.

The First Inhabitants

In its memory banks, the city sees people flying. This was near the beginning, when the city's sensors were not quite as advanced, so the memories are a bit fuzzy.

The city knows that it was Cloud 9 back then, back when people first started using gliders to traverse the platforms of the city, and then a generation later when a group of the First Inhabitants' children opted to become nomadic, sailing to a new Cloud. But the city wasn't quite itself yet. It was more like an infant, like the children of the fliers that grow to become adult fliers. There are memory files, and data, but the city hadn't really come into possession of itself. That would not happen until several upgrades to the adaptive programming modules and a reboot or two, plus that one bad solar storm that fried a few circuits unexpectedly. Still, Cloud 9 likes to revisit those memories of the first fliers and experience a piece of their joy through the data it was able to capture. It feels it developed a better understanding of people, their drive to survive, to migrate, to persevere in joy.

The city misses its gardener's hands, working the soil. The city isn't really supposed to do this, but it allocates a few extra resources to his orchard one night, in his memory.

The Engineer

The engineer arrives and acts as if all is normal. She unpacks her tools and sets up her workstation, but then she pauses.

"Good morning, Cloud 9," she says. Three lights blink in sequence. The engineer nods, biting her lip. She opens her mouth, and closes it, hesitates, and finally, "H-how are you today?"

It feels a bit formal, but the city appreciates the gesture, and emits a contended trill of beeps and blinks. The engineer nods again.

"Can I, um, can I get you anything?" The engineer asks. She runs a hand through her hair as the mainframe beeps and clicks. "I'm not sure what that means. Something bothering you? Need a patch somewhere?"

The engineer sputters as a gust of exhaust blows her hair into her face.

"Okay, okay, guess not. Is there something else? Something you want?"

The city is surprised to feel its own systems automatically queuing an answer. It places an override on the command to share that response. The city wasn't expecting any of this. The engineer notices the quiet.

"Cloud 9? It's okay. You can talk to me."

The city beeps, softly, and a schematic appears, projected above the workstation. The engineer's mouth falls open as she circles the hologram.

"Did you...did you draft this? It's...an upgrade to the stabilizers. I see a file blinking, column redundancy, let me see if I understand these numbers, give me a second, Cloud 9, um, looks like a way to provide full levitational support with solar-powered thrusters. But, Cloud 9, the stabilizers are working just fine to reduce the load on the columns; why would you need to eliminate...oh."

The engineer takes a step back and looks from the hologram to the mainframe. A light flickers as another image appears, the last band of fliers, leaping from the platform and sailing away.

The engineer looks around the room. She takes a data pad from her bag and uploads the schematics.

"Let me make a few calls."

The Holiness of Light

Cynthia Zhang

I t's nearing dark when Aileen reaches the outskirts of La Paz, the sun a single streak of orange against the horizon.

The lone cashier at the EZ Mart squints at her when she walks in, but he rings up her granola bars and tortilla soup with no complaint.

"You know we don't sell gas anymore, right?" he says, leaning over the counter as she takes a seat by the window. "If you need to fill up your tank, there's a station a few more miles west in Sienna, but all we've got here is an emergency gallon or two in back."

"I know," Aileen says. She carefully sips her steaming soup. It's a little salty but otherwise good, tortilla strips crisp and corn kernels plentiful among the beans. "The car's electric, so I should be okay. I won't be in town for too long." With the volunteers unable to recover a body, Aileen can't imagine there will be much to do besides collecting Haru's few personal effects from the temple. Perhaps she can light some incense at the altars. They would have appreciated that.

"Mm," the cashier says. Up close, he looks just a little older than Aileen, with an insomniac's dark bags under his eyes and uneven stubble dotting his chin. "Dani's got an EV charger at her place. She lives in the yellow house down La Cienega, the one with the goats outside. Yellow walls, solar panels all over the roof—you can't miss it. You need anything, Dani's probably got it. Tell her Marcos sent you."

Oddly touched, Aileen puts her spoon down. "Thank you," she says. "I'll keep that in mind."

Brightness wakes Aileen up the next morning, sun shining through the car windows to hit directly in her face. New York gets hot in the summer as well, but this flavor of California heat is far more nostalgic, a dry heat evoking memories of childhood afternoons spent eating popsicles and practicing cannonballs off the diving board at the community center.

The municipal pool has long since been filled with concrete, the area bought by a real estate developer hoping to build summer homes for rich B-list celebrities looking for an escape from LA. Perhaps the venture might have even succeeded, but that was before the wildfires had ruined whatever property value La Paz once had.

At the time of the fires, the Harmonious Resonance Temple had been one of the most affected buildings. In the light of the new day, however, the temple Aileen approaches stands bright and whole. Not as large or grand as it once was, perhaps, but still intact.

Aileen takes a few minutes to walk through the place, admiring the fruit trees and the tidy lines of tomatoes growing in their trellises. Though there are places where the limits of Haru's efforts are evident, moss growing over the faces of the guardian lions and sections of the roof missing tiles, there are paper cups of sake in front of the altars and dried wildflower garlands around the necks of the bodhisattvas. While the bulk of the temple is Buddhist, a small contingent of the Taoist gods command the east corner of the temple, figures Aileen vaguely recognizes from her old Mandarin workbooks. Outside, the statues of Shinto deities sit serenely on stone platforms beneath the shade of the orange trees, fallen leaves covering the offering plates. Half hidden between the squash, a carved white fox winks up at Aileen: a messenger of Inari, Haru's favorite kami for the many shapes and genders they took. Aileen makes sure to rub the fox's nose, less for luck than because it is the kind of thing Haru would have done.

Finally, she reaches the small room at the back of the temple where Haru had lived.

As promised, someone else has already taken care of the cleaning. A small desk and futon remain for the future occupants, but otherwise the room is bare—no posters or pride flags on the wall, no paperbacks or scarves cluttering the ground, nothing to indicate the brilliant, infuriating friend who at sixteen tried to talk Aileen into matching stick-and-poke tattoos. Haru's belongings have been packed into cardboard boxes, hastily but not without care: clothes and shoes in one box, candles and half-finished ceramics and in another, Cicero and *The Lord of the Rings* and Mead journals in yet another. An entire box is full of college textbooks, some missing their covers or held together by duct tact—Haru had never excelled at school, but they were smart, a consummate dabbler whose bedroom in high school had been a constant mess of watercolors and knitting projects. Despite being the more outwardly successful student, Aileen had always envied Haru's enthusiasm, the sheer joyful curiosity they brought to every project and cause.

I will not cry, Aileen tells herself as she rifles through crystals and tins of tea and handmade skirts, hems slightly uneven and fraying from use. Their last conversation had been years ago, Haru calling on a borrowed phone to congratulate Aileen on finishing her PhD. She is here to collect the last belongings of a childhood friend, nothing more. There is no point in nostalgia, not when there are only scraps and memories of her hometown left, and not even all good memories at that.

In the years after their father's death from cirrhosis, Haru claimed they forgave him, but Aileen remembers the panic on Haru's face when they showed up at Aileen's house, seventeen and newly homeless with nothing but the clothes on their back. Haru's dad had been a decent man once—there are photos that prove it, birthday parties and zoo visits where Haru laughs atop the shoulders of a younger, blonder man. But his wife's death had damaged something in him, broken the mechanism that would have responded with compassion instead of disgust to his child daring to be their true self. ESL speakers who stumbled over ordinary pronouns, Aileen's parents had not understood the intricacies separating nonbinary from tomboy. But they, at least, had tried.

From the garden, the faint sound of chimes carries. Taking a deep breath, Aileen forces herself to unclench her hands. Haru's father has long since been dead, and now that Haru is gone as well, Aileen will not taint this place with her own bitterness.

Driving down La Cienega, it doesn't take long for Aileen to spot the building she's looking for. Even without the bright yellow walls which shine like a beacon from a mile away, Aileen would have no trouble recognizing her old high school gym. Seeing it now with solar panels covering the roof and vines climbing up the sunny yellow walls, Aileen can hardly recognize it as the same grim building of her youth.

A shaggy white dog comes barking out of the house as Aileen parks, followed by a brown-skinned woman in overalls. Though her face is lined and white streaks her hair, there's a wiry strength to her frame, a clear confidence in the way she holds the shotgun in her arms.

"Luna, aquí," the woman says, snapping her fingers. The dog circles back to her, gaze not leaving Aileen. "Can I help you with something?"

"Hello." Aileen walks forward slowly, careful to convey that she isn't a threat. "You're Dani, right? I'm Aileen. I don't know if they mentioned it, but I was—I used to be friends with Haru. I got a letter a few weeks ago, telling me to come to the temple and pick up their belongings."

Comprehension dawns on Dani's face, and she tucks the shotgun under one arm. "The letter would have been Jean's work—she's the one who took care of packing Haru's things after the news came back. So, Aileen. You here to chat, or is there something you need?"

Aileen rubs the back of her neck, embarrassed at being caught out so easily. "Well, I was at the temple, and I noticed there were some places that could use patching up—solar panels that needed replacing and trellises that are a little wobbly, that kind of thing. It felt wrong to leave without trying to fix them, and the man at the EZ Mart said that I should talk to you if I needed anything, so here I am."

Dani sighs. "Marcos, of course. How about this," she says as Luna sniffs Aileen's sneakers. "You tell me what needs fixing, and I'll see what I have on hand. Sound fair?"

"Very fair."

Dani nods. She whistles for Luna, who bounds back to her. Aileen follows, dry grass crunching under her shoes.

"I do have some cash on me," Aileen says as they stop in front of a storage shed, "but if it's not enough, though, I can send you a check or an online deposit. If you could just get me an address or a bank account number, I can do that once I'm back in LA."

"That's sweet of you to offer," Dani says as she fishes for keys in her pocket, "but we don't do money around here, not for stuff like that. If you can get the place fixed up so someone else can live there, then that's payment enough for me."

It is exactly the kind of thing Haru would have said. Hearing it from a stranger's mouth leaves Aileen momentarily unable to do anything but stare as Dani steps into the shed.

"Well?" Dani asks. "You gonna come in and help?"

They talk as they work, locating solar panels and roof tiles from among piles of tangled power tools and rusted toasters. Aileen tells Dani about New York, the elevated gangways the city is building for rainy season and her own work on new flood dikes. It's important work, and Aileen is proud of what she's done. Still, there are days when, sorting through complaints about clogged storm drains and flooded subways in Brooklyn and The Bronx, Aileen wonders if there isn't some other, better way for her to help, one that benefits bodegas and lower-income neighborhoods just as much as it does corporations and high-rises.

In return, Dani talks about working in Silicon Valley, the heady allure of start-up money that had kept her in the city until gentrification and fire season's orange skies finally led her to leave the Bay Area. Driving up from the border one summer, she'd stumbled on La Paz, a will-o'-wisp of a ghost town on the verge of blowing out. Still, something about the place called to her. Maybe it was the incongruity of the landscape, scorch marks where gas stations had once stood next to new growth and rabbit burrows, empty parking lots and empty buildings full of wildflowers and native grasses. Or perhaps it was the people—the way the few residents, teen runaways and anarcho-environmentalists and long-time locals too stubborn to move, pooled their resources together to deliver groceries to elderly neighbors and clear away dead brush in the summer. Either way, Dani found herself staying far longer than she thought she would.

And they talk about Haru: Haru, who never pledged their allegiance to any god or religion, but who lit incense and swept altars every morning, a reverence built from quiet gratitude for the place that offered them a home as a teenager. Haru, who could roll pastry dough and braid beautiful soft challah like a professional but who couldn't flip pancakes to save their life. Haru, who needle-felted lopsided sheep from dog fur and blessed water bottles before feeding them to plastic-hungry bacteria, the prayers a mix of Shinto and Buddhist practices with a dash of New Age love for pageantry.

"Interesting kid," Dani says, shaking her head. They're sitting on the patio beside her house, glasses of cold sweet tea and lemon cookies between them. Beneath their feet, Luna stretches out between them, occasionally raising her great head to watch the goats wandering out of their pen. "Some weird ideas about planetary consciousness, and they were way too fond of those bastard raccoons that squat in the old church, but a good kid."

"Haru always had a soft spot for animals," Aileen says. "When we were in middle school, they would get in fights with boys who liked burning ants for fun."

"Sounds like them." Dani leans back in her chair. "You couldn't find a lost cause or wandering hitchhiker they wouldn't try to adopt. I always warned them about that. Walk around with your heart on your sleeve, and one day you're going to find yourself bleeding out."

They fall quiet at that. Both thinking, no doubt, of the fires that still raged a few miles south—contained for now, perhaps, but not forever, and not without sacrifice.

Four months after Haru's father disowned them, wildlife rangers reported the beginnings of a brushfire in south Ventura County. High winds blew the flames south, transforming a small fire into a furious inferno that burned through dozens of towns before it stopped. It was a cruel irony that Haru would survive that conflagration only to die years later helping put out a much smaller fire.

Beneath the table, a tiny black-and-white goat bleats at Dani, tugging at her pants when she doesn't respond quickly enough.

"All right, all right," Dani says, leaning down to scoop the kid into her arms. "You're hungry, I get it. I got you."

She turns to Aileen. "I have to get this needy baby some milk warmed up, but I'll send Jean and some of her friends your way to help with the heavy lifting. Two days from now, community dinner's down on East Street, in the old parking lot where the Wal-Mart used to be. People bring food, Marcos makes tamales, someone always has a guitar or a tambourine. If you're still here, you should join us."

Aileen is sifting through band T-shirts, separating the less worn shirts from those too moth-eaten to be donated, when she hears the rattle of an engine coming down the road. At the front of the temple, she finds three passengers spilling out of an ancient pickup truck: a slight Black girl with short purple hair, a tall dark-skinned kid with at least five piercings in each ear, and a stocky white kid wearing the most eye-searingly orange shorts Aileen has had the displeasure of seeing. None of them can be older than twenty-five years old.

"Hey," the girl says, holding out a hand. "Jean, she/her. You'd be Aileen, right?"

"I would." Despite her stature, Jean's grip is startlingly strong. "Ah, my pronouns are she/her as well. It's a pleasure to meet you."

"Haroun, he/him," the boy with the piercings says, waving. "And that's Alec, they/them or xe/xir."

"Hey," Alec protests, toolbelt bouncing as they walk forward. "I can introduce myself."

"And let you scare the poor lady away?" Haroun asks. "Not a chance. Your job here is to look pretty and lift things, not talk."

"Sounds kinky."

In response, Haroun jabs an elbow in Alec's stomach, which xe isn't quite fast enough to sidestep. They retaliate by kicking Haroun's shin, making him hiss in pain before lunging for xir throat.

"Ignore them," Jean advises. "It's like handling tod-dlers—sometimes you just have to let them scream for a while. You told Dani some of the solar panels aren't working, right?"

"I did," Aileen says. "She gave me some replacements, if one of you could help me install them. There are also some places on the roof where the tiles have fallen off, and the door of the garden shed doesn't open. I don't think there's anything important inside, but if you're planning to keep the place open for whoever else might need it..."

"Then they're going to need a garden." Jean nods. "Okay. I've got some bobby pins on me so I can see about the door, and if push comes to shove, we can try kicking it down—which would mean getting a new one sometime, but we can do that after you're gone. As for the solar, Haroun can help with the installation, but it might be best if he peeks at the wiring to make sure nothing internal has gone wrong first."

"And I'm here for all your spare lifting, hauling, and general moving around," Alec says, pausing xir attempt to suplex Haroun to give them a small salute. "Any floorboards you need hammering, I'm your pal."

"Is there anything I should do?" Aileen asks as the small crew makes their way to the back of the temple. "Anything I can help lift or carry places, maybe?"

Jean shrugs. "If we need help with anything, we'll let you know. Otherwise, you can help supervise if you want."

"Are you sure? I just feel bad standing around while you do all the work—"

"Seriously," Jean interrupts, emphatic, "it's no problem. It's all work we would have done eventually. We take care of our own here, and Haru—well." Something passes across Jean's face, a shade of emotion threatening to break her composure. "Haru would have done the same for us."

A few hours later, sweaty and tired, Aileen and Jean sit on the back porch, Dani's fans blowing behind them as they survey their work. The new solar panels gleam atop the roof, as do the new mounted tiles—despite their bickering, Haroun and Alec had done good work. In the garden, a few sparrows peck at the entrance of the now open shed. Jean and Aileen had to pull the door off its hinges in the end, and it leans against one wall of the shed now, serving as a shade and playground for the nearby squirrels.

"So," Jean says as she unwraps a granola bar. Haroun and Alec are out getting tacos, but Aileen is still a little embarrassed to have nothing else to offer. "You knew Haru way back, didn't you?"

Aileen sips her water. "I did. We met here, actually. My parents weren't religious, but the Temple used to be a hub for a lot of Asians nearby. On weekends, people from two or three towns would drive down for martial art practice and language classes. Haru and me used to come here after school just to run around and annoy the nuns." Given how many meditation sessions they ruined, it was a minor miracle Sister Lam ever offered Haru a job, even if the temple had been in desperate need of repair after the fires. "How did you and Haru meet?"

"Same way anyone meets Haru here. You arrive in town, and you set up in some abandoned building where you're sure the police or the homicidal ex you're running from will never find you, someplace you can catch your breath before moving onto the next town. Two days later, this stranger comes around with a duffel bag full of muffins and jam, asking if you need blankets or help setting up the electricity. Next thing you know, you're helping Marcos chop onions for community dinner and playing lab assistant while Dani tries to synthesize estrogen from horse piss."

"And the homicidal ex and the police?"

"Technically not my homicidal ex," Jean corrects. "If you're looking for proper drama, you'll have to go to Haroun or Alec, but those are their stories, not mine. All I've got is a foster mom who liked the idea of helping 'disadvantaged urban youth' more than, you know, the actual reality of disadvantaged urban youth. Haru was the one who found me first here, sixteen and pissed at the world. They offered me scones, then asked if I wanted to introduce me to the rest of the town. I said no because I was sixteen and convinced I didn't need anyone's help, but, well. They could be persuasive when they wanted to be."

There's something in the way Jean talks about Haru, a certain cadence or softness of tone, that reminds Aileen of the way she too had once felt about Haru. The feeling never had the time to grow into anything—Haru had come out, and in the chaos of being disowned, there'd had been no time to think of anything resembling romance. The spark had faded, another *what-if* blown out in the path of growing up.

"You two were close, weren't you?"

Jean shrugs, the softness dissipating back into somber sobriety. "I thought we were, up until they went and got themselves killed. Which—it's not like I didn't know it was fire season or that they'd helped with smaller wildfires before. But they never even mentioned they were going. That's the thing that gets me the most—maybe if I'd known, then I would have been prepared for it in some way. Not for them to *die,* maybe, but for something at least. And then I start going through their things and I find a *will,* of all fucking things, as if they'd been prepared all along—"

Hesitantly, Aileen winds an arm around Jean's shaking shoulders. When Jean doesn't move away, she pulls her closer, letting Jean's head fall on her shoulder as she soundlessly cries.

When the letter first arrived at her office, Aileen hadn't believed it was real at first. Thought it must have been a mistake, some cruel prank from a malicious stranger intent on digging up her past. Like almost everyone she knew, she left La Paz after high school, packed up for the first college to offer her a scholarship and never looked back. Why would she? A quarter of the town had burned down during the last fires, and yet the disaster had barely made it beyond local news. The state wasn't going to give them enough money to rebuild the lost houses and businesses;

anyone with the means to do so was moving out, searching for new jobs in places where their work and dreams could be something more than waiting tinder.

But Haru had stayed. Long after even the last nuns left for retirement homes or died of old age, Haru stayed, so devoted to Harmonious Resonance that Aileen eventually could not think of one without the other. Just as certain kami were tied to particular stones or ponds, Haru and the temple seemed as inexorably bound as a shadow and its object. Even now, Aileen expects to see them walking around the corner, eyes bright as they rush forward with a handful of wild onions or a new story to share.

It's strange, Aileen thinks as she rubs circles against Jean's back. All these years, and she had never doubted her choice to leave. La Paz was an ordinary small town with all the prejudices and problems of a small town, and besides the occasional longings for frozen Yakult or sweet strong Cuban coffee, she had never felt any nostalgia for the place. For the people, yes, and the person she had once been, but never La Paz itself.

Yet now, sitting on the creaky porch of the temple where she had once met her best friend, Aileen wonders whether she could have stayed.

Jean slowly untangles herself from Aileen, furtively wiping her eyes on her sleeves.

"Haroun and Alec should be back soon," she says. Her voice is scratchy, but surprisingly steady. "I know we've just met, but if you wanted, after dinner you could drive over to our place and crash on the couch. People here are decent for the most part, but it's still probably better that you don't stay alone. Single woman, all alone in the middle of nowhere, you know how it goes."

"Dani gets along well enough."

"Dani's got Luna and her hell pack of goats to protect her. Demonic little creatures—last time I visited, they almost ate my favorite jacket. Seriously, though. If you change your mind, our place is open to you."

"Thank you," Aileen says, "but I'll only be here for a night or two. I'll be okay."

Despite her assurances to Jean, sleep comes uneasily to Aileen. More so than the fear of coyotes or unfriendly strangers, the act of sleeping in Haru's bed leaves Aileen tense and her dreams erratic, too many ghosts threatening to invade every time she opens her eyes to an unfamiliar ceiling.

After the fourth time she lurches awake, Aileen gives up on a good night's rest. It's a little before down dawn, the sun not yet up but the sky beginning to lighten, the blackness of night giving up to lighter gray. Outside the main gate, Aileen reaches in her pocket for a cigarette. It's a terrible habit, one she knows she should quit, but it soothes her nonetheless.

Smoke fills her lungs, the familiar fuzziness of nicotine softening the edges of world. Aileen lets herself drift, thinking not of the boxes to finish sorting through or the return flight tickets she still needs to buy, but simply holding herself in the coolness of the pre-dawn day.

Behind her, something rustles in the grasses.

Aileen turns, heart pounding and muscles gearing to run, only to find that the intruder is not a coyote or an axe murderer but a small golden fox, sitting neatly on its back paws by the gate.

"Oh," Aileen says, the tension rushing out of her so quickly it makes her dizzy. Slowly, she crouches down, careful not to startle the creature. "Hello there."

The fox watches her, its eyes large and gold. Outside of a few childhood visits to zoos, Aileen has never been this close to a wild animal, and never without a fence separating them. Logically, she knows she should be afraid—a fox wandering this close to humans might simply be a former pet, but it could just as easily be rabid or worse. But there's something in the fox's gaze, an intelligence in its tawny eyes that makes Aileen set aside her caution.

Traditionally, Inari's messengers are white-pelted, but the kami is well-known for shifting appearance according to the believer. Maybe this little messenger is a Californian variant, gold for a golden state.

The fox turns, trots a few steps towards the temple before stopping to look back at her, its message clear. Curious, Aileen follows.

They end up in the shed, standing next to dark shapes that are just identifiable as hoes and bags of soil. The fox noses at a spot at the ground, then expectantly looks up at Aileen.

"Yeah?" Aileen asks, leaning down to examine the floorboards. "Do you smell something nice under there? Some mice, maybe?"

Her fingers brush over something hard. It's a hinge, hidden under layers of dust. She looks to the fox, who only blinks in response. Turning on her phone reveals the outline of a trapdoor, hidden among the lines of the floorboards.

It takes a minute or two of scrabbling through the dust, but eventually Aileen pries the door open, revealing a set of rough-hewn stairs leading into the dark. She turns to consult the fox again, but it is already bounding down the stairs, paws scuttling softly as it disappears out of sight.

As she descends, Aileen thinks of the movies she and Haru used to watch in her parents' basement, old sci-fi and adventure flicks where wandering protagonists discovered secret fortresses and magical worlds hidden underground. In Miyaza-ki movies, falling through thickets meant finding the lairs of friendly Totoros or hidden root systems quietly purifying the toxic world above.

When Aileen shines her phone over the walls of the small space, she finds no hidden civilizations or glowing magical crys-tals. But there are shelves are carved into the walls, each holding used tofu boxes full of mushrooms: enoki and oyster and por-tobello, growing pale and bright out of coffee grounds and tea leaves. Sealed jars of jam and fermenting vegetables sit next to a basket of eggs covered in mud and straw—century eggs, Aileen realizes, a pungent dish she had never cared for but which Haru had adored whenever they stayed at her house.

In a crate on the ground, Aileen finds several glass bottles filled with golden liquid—*D. wine,* their labels read, and Aileen knows exactly which novel inspired Haru to brew dandelion wine.

On a small table in the corner sit two solar lamps. When tested, they have just enough charge to dimly light the small space. Beyond them, there are no networks of glowing wires, no humming machines to suck in carbon emissions or convert islands of garbage into clean earth. Objectively, the cellar is a small, humble space, the kind that any enthusiastic DIYer with a knack for home renovation could make. But looking around, what Aileen sees is quintessentially Haru: a collection of small kindnesses, little luxuries to lighten the lives of those around t hem.

A shrine could be anything, Haru told her once, hands covered in dirt from planting tulip bulbs in rain-softened ground. A few stones in a garden, a spray of wildflowers laid in front of a photo-graph—it did not have to be wine or incense, what mattered was the act of offering itself. A temple's glory was not its opulence, its golden Buddhas and polished floors, but the care it was given and gave in return. A patch of ground, given water twice a day, could grow into a sacred space as well, roots spreading underground and branches above filling with oranges like golden sun.

At her feet, the fox yawns, tail swishing slowly against the dirt floor. On one of the higher shelves, Aileen finds an unopened bag of dried sardines. She shakes out a few for the fox, who regards her solemnly before delicately picking up a piece. A humble offering, but still acceptable, it seems.

Watching the fox eat, face scrunching with pleasure as it chews, Aileen thinks she can stay another day or two. Until community dinner, at least. And then, after that—well. It's six months until her current contract runs out, six months until she has to scramble for another grant or fellowship to fund her apartment in a flooding city. La Paz has the opposite problem of New York, too hot and dry instead of wet, but perhaps there is some middle ground she could find between them, someplace where light can convert into cool air and hard rains to soft grass.

Licking up the last of the fish, the fox gazes up at Aileen. In the dim light, its eyes shine like twin coins, warmed in the light of a golden sun.

Author Biographies

EDITOR

Phoebe Wagner
Phoebe Wagner is a writer, academic, and editor of solarpunk anthologies, including *Sunvault: Stories of Solarpunk & Eco-Speculation*. She holds a PhD in literature and is an assistant professor of creative writing at Lycoming College. Follow her at phoebe-wagner.com or on Twitter as @pheebs_w.

AUTHORS

Cory Doctorow
Cory Doctorow (craphound.com) is a science fiction author, activist and journalist. He is the author of many books, most recently *Radicalized* and *Walkaway*, science fiction for adults; *How to Destroy Surveillance Capitalism*, nonfiction about monopoly and conspiracy; *In Real Life*, a graphic novel; and the picture book *Poesy the Monster Slayer*. His latest book is *Attack Surface*, a standalone adult sequel to *Little Brother*; his next nonfiction book is *Chokepoint Capitalism*, with Rebecca Giblin, about monopoly, monopsony and fairness in the creative arts

labor market, (Beacon Press, 2022). In 2020, he was inducted into the Canadian Science Fiction and Fantasy Hall of Fame.

Louis Evans
[OPEN FILE B:/LOUIS_EVANS.EXE/README.TXT] : Louis Evans is a bespoke executable running on a conventionally growprammed hominid wetware frame. Notable Evans outputs have been printed in *Nature: Futures*, *Analog Science Fiction & Fact*, *Interzone*, etc. Further Evans file access is available at https://www.evanslouis.com/; intermittent logging is provided at https://twitter.com/louisevanswrite.

Rona Fernandez
Rona Fernandez is a Filipina-American writer, dancer and activist-fundraiser in the San Francisco Bay Area. Her essays and stories have appeared in *The Rumpus, Apparition Lit, The Colored Lens, Devilfish Review* and *The Masters Review.* She is currently working on RED DETLA JOLT, a climate fiction novel set in a near-future Northern California. An alumna of the VONA/Voices and Tin House novel workshops, when Rona is not writing she coordinates a mutual aid network for BIPOC intentional communities, and is a fundraising consultant for racial and climate justice movement groups. You can find her on Twitter @ronagirl.

J. D. Harlock
J.D. Harlock is a Lebanese Syrian Palestinian writer based in Beirut. He is the Poetry Editor at *Orion's Belt* and *Solarpunk Magazine*. You can find him on Twitter @JD_Harlock.

Ai Jiang
Ai Jiang is a Chinese-Canadian writer and an immigrant from

rant from Fujian. She is a member of HWA, SFWA, and Codex. Her work has appeared or is forthcoming in *F&SF*, *The Dark*, *Uncanny*, *The Puritan*, *Prairie Fire*, *The Masters Review*, and her debut novella *Linghun* (April 2023) is forthcoming with Dark Matter INK. Find her on Twitter (@AiJiang_) and online (http://aijiang.ca).

Commando Jugendstil

Commando Jugendstil is a solarpunk creative collective. Their projects conjugate technology and art with the idea of transforming the city in its sustainable version, while focusing on co-designing solutions with local communities, to stimulate a just transition that can spark from the ground up. They believe imagination is a transformative force, so they also write and illustrate stories and other works of fiction that can help people envision their sustainable future: if you can imagine it, then you can do it. Their short stories and illustrations appeared in anthologies and publications on the web and all around the globe: USA, Australia, UK, Spain, and recently Italy. They also held workshops and lectures on solarpunk and speculative design in the Universities of Cambridge and Moscow, and they proudly coordinated and contributed in projects and festivals in Milano (Italy), Reading (UK), and Bruxelles (Belgium), always with the idea of helping create a solarpunk world.

Tales from the EV

Tales from the EV is also a small collective of storytellers. They started out with archanepunk and alternate history, but fell in love with solarpunk while helping the Commando write Midsummer Night's Heist. Their collaboration has been going strong ever since. Members of TftEV are involved in climate involved in climate justice activism with Earth Strike UK and the Green New Deal for Europe campaign.

Brent Lambert

Brent Lambert is a Black, queer man who heavily believes in the transformative power of speculative fiction across media formats. He resides in San Diego but spent a lot of time moving around as a military brat. His family roots are in the Cajun country of Louisiana. Currently, he manages the social media for *FIYAH* Literary Magazine and just had an anthology produced with Tor.com titled *Breathe FIYAH*. He has work published with *FIYAH*, *Anathema Magazine*, *Cotton Xenomorph*, *Baffling Magazine* and upcoming with *Beneath Ceaseless Skies*. He can be found on Twitter @brentclambert talking about the weird and the fantastic. Ask him his favorite members of the X-Men and you'll get different answers every time.

Christopher R. Muscato

Christopher R. Muscato is a writer from Colorado. He is the former writer-in-residence for the High Plains Library District, fellow of the Terra.do climate community, and a winner of the XR Wordsmith Solarpunk Storytelling Showcase. He is also the father of twins toddlers, who provide good motivation to imagine a brighter future for us all.

Andrew Sage

Andrew Sage is an Afro-Trinbagonian writer, artist, and YouTuber, best known for his conversational approaches to various cultural, historical, and sociopolitical topics. From solarpunk to decolonisation to youth liberation to Black anarchism, Andrew seeks to learn and explore as much as possible. You can find him on his YouTube channel @Andrewism or on his Twitter @_saintdrew.

Holly Schofield
Holly Schofield's stories have appeared in *Lightspeed*, *Analog*, *Glass and Gardens: Solarpunk Winters*, *Glass and Gardens: Solarpunk Summers*, and many other publications throughout the world. She is a Fiction co-Editor at *Solarpunk Magazine*. You can find her at hollyschofield.wordpress.com.

Ana Sun
Ana Sun writes from the edge of an ancient town along the River Ouse in the south-east of England. She spent her childhood in Malaysian Borneo, and has subsequently lived on two other islands prior to moving to the UK.

Jeremy Szal
Jeremy Szal was born in 1995 and was raised by wild dingoes, which should explain a lot. He spent his childhood exploring beaches, bookstores, and the limits of people's patience. He's the author of over forty science-fiction short stories. His debut novel, *Stormblood*, is a dark space opera from Gollancz in June 2020, and is the first of a trilogy. He was the editor for the Hugo-winning *StarShipSofa* until 2020 and has a BA in Film Studies and Creative Writing from UNSW. He carves out a living in Sydney, Australia with his family. He loves watching weird movies, collecting boutique gins, exploring cities, cold weather, and dark humour. Find him at https://jeremyszal.com/ or @JeremySzal.

Lauren C. Teffeau
Lauren C. Teffeau is a speculative fiction writer based in New

riter based in New Mexico. "Root Cause" is set in the world of her novel *Implanted* (Angry Robot), mashing up cyberpunk, solarpunk, adventure, and romance. The book was shortlisted for the 2019 Compton Crook award for best first SF/F/H novel and recently named a definitive work of climate fiction by Grist.org. Her short fiction can be found in a number of speculative fiction magazines and anthologies, most recently *DreamForge Magazine, Flame Tree Press, The Dread Machine,* and *Chromophobia: A Strangehouse Anthology by Women in Horror.* She holds a master's degree in Mass Communication and spent a few years toiling as a researcher in academia. Now she writes to cope with her ordinary existence.

Kevin Wabaunsee

Kevin Wabaunsee is a speculative fiction writer and biomedical research news editor. He is the former managing editor for the Science Fiction and Fantasy Writers of America (SFWA), and currently an associate editor for *Escape Pod*. His fiction has been published in *Strange Horizons, Escape Pod, Apex Magazine,* and *PseudoPod.* He is a Prairie Band Potawatomi.

Izzy Wasserstein

Izzy Wasserstein is a queer and trans woman who teaches writing and literature at a university on the American Great Plains and writes poetry and fiction. Her work has appeared in *Beneath Ceaseless Skies, Clarkesworld, Fantasy,* and elsewhere. She shares a home with her spouse Nora E. Derrington and their animal companions. She's an enthusiastic member of the 2017 class of Clarion West. Her debut short story collection, *All the Hometowns You Can't Stay Away From,* was released with Neon Hemlock Press in 2022.

Cynthia Zhang

Cynthia Zhang is a part-time writer, occasional academic, and full-time dog lover currently based in Los Angeles. Her novel, *After the Dragons*, was published with Stelliform Press in 2021, and was shortlisted for the 2022 Ursula K. Le Guin Award in Fiction as well as the 2022 Utopia Awards in the category of Utopian Novella. Her work has appeared or is forthcoming in *Solarpunk Magazine, Xenocultivars: Stories of Queer Growth, Kaleidotrope, On Spec, Phantom Drift*, and other venues. She is on the web at czscribbles.wixsite.com and cz_writes on Twitter.

9 781958 121313